TOUGHSKINS

Visit us at www.boldstrokesbooks.com

TOUGHSKINS

by

William Masswa

A Division of Bold Strokes Books

2012

TOUGHSKINS

ISBN 13: 978-1-60282-591-8

THIS TRADE PAPERBACK ORIGINAL IS PUBLISHED BY
BOLD STROKES BOOKS, INC.
P.O. BOX 249
VALLEY FALLS, NY 12185

FIRST EDITION: JANUARY 2012

CREDITS
EDITOR: GREG HERREN
PRODUCTION DESIGN: STACIA SEAMAN
COVER DESIGN BY SHERI (GRAPHICARTIST2020@HOTMAIL.COM)

Christopher Michael
the Island King himself
who first heard and encouraged this story

and to all who wrestle (or have wrestled) with their past to
love in the present

this is for you.

Author's Note

Toughskins received its title from children's jeans sold by Sears and Roebuck in the early 1970s (and again in the 1990s). Toughskins debuted as a new blend of materials, including Dacron Type 59 polyester, DuPont 420 nylon, and cotton. With reinforced knees, they were marketed as jeans children would grow out of before the pants wore out.

PROLOGUE

He swallows the quiet between them, even though it tastes funny. A working boy turning twenty-two tomorrow, Stu wants more from their night together, but isn't sure why. He drops his already low voice so that it slides across even more deep and heated. "Hey, you, ah…you comfortable under those covers?"

Bryce, who did have the sheet twisted around him in a wrestling match he lost, doesn't know how to answer honestly anymore, especially a question like this. Information is one of those things he either lost or stopped paying attention to altogether.

Stu shoots the same question. "Those covers, you comfortable under them?"

No response follows.

The truth is Bryce doesn't answer because the once handsome thirty-year-old is lost in how to answer. These days some things are just that blurry. Even as far back as a week ago, he'd smile at his own confusion.

Most of his smiles are gone now.

Getting the message, Stu moves from Bryce's sight. The bucket on wheels rolls, followed by the slap of the mop against the tile floor that is never, ever dirty.

Bryce does want to answer the question, but no words fill his mouth. It has been some twenty hours since he's talked.

Stu doesn't move for a moment, and then rolls the bucket again. The mop in his hands slaps another area of floor. "As comfortable as you can be," he says to himself. "Got it."

Bryce turns to see the muscled man's back. Short-sleeved red T-shirt, extra-large. Hint of superhero spandex in the cotton, maybe. It's either that or the hard, defined angles and curves just look *that good*.

Yeah, the shirt fits well, but is by no means tight. And scrub bottoms. When Bryce lifts his head, he can see the man's stiff new blue-shaded standard issue hospital gear gathered around his trim waist.

Bryce lowers his eyelids. He imagines the scrubs as pajama bottoms. The warmth from the quadriceps muscles under them penetrates Bryce's fingers before he even dreams of setting his hands on them. The drawstring sways within easy reach—left, right, center—and then gets pulled. A smile. Two souls together. One bed. One kiss. Then another kiss. And another.

"I want to be comfortable," Bryce says in a raspy whisper, similar to what he sounded like after a fourteen-hour day in his office when he became president of a million-dollar marketing agency at just twenty-seven. Now his situation presents itself a little differently. He pops his vulnerable, soft blue eyes open. "Yeah, I want to be comfortable."

Stu doesn't hear him.

Turning to his side, Bryce tries to be louder. "Come here."

The custodian still doesn't stop his work. "Ah, what did you say?"

Bryce swallows. For a moment, he's a little kid all coddled, prim, and happy. "I know. Please. I didn't say, 'Please come here.'"

Stu sets his big feet where they had been a minute ago. He frowns just a bit. This well-practiced pout enables him to get what he wants, and what he wants is to have the distance between this soft-soul guy and him to melt away.

Stu repositions his hands on the mop handle. "You did say please, twice now."

"I did?" Bryce tilts his head, frowns. "How about that?"

"Yeah," Stu swallows, "how about that?"

What's happening can't be happening. Not here. Not like this. Stu, who is too young to be married for nearly two years and too selfish to be expecting his first daughter with his wife in less than two months, knows this is dangerous. This is wrong.

But what does it matter, really? As he decides to keep this going, Stu reaches for the small gold picture frame on the nearby sill. "This your boy?"

Bryce twists some of the hospital gown over his chest and studies the forearms holding the picture—pronounced, muscled, strong, and able to squeeze away disappointment, if wrapped around you.

The question behind Stu's dark eyes has nothing to do with what he's about to ask again. "Is this little guy yours?"

Bryce does have legal custody over his sister's son and loves that boy. This is the strongest emotion he's felt in his lifetime, and this great joy triggers the worst pain of all because, facts being what they are, it doesn't look like he'll ever see the little one again.

The two in ICU Room 14 spend two stolen minutes talking of how the twenty-four-month-old is a good sport. The little squirt goes to bed easily, eats good food without fuss, and, with ample warning, can catch a tennis ball tossed at a distance of ten feet.

Stu's strong fingers cradle the picture frame as he turns back toward the bed. Lips tight, he doesn't share what he's thinking, which is that he'd just like to climb in bed with the man so near to him now and hold him, hold him close.

Instead, Stu takes a careful look at the blond-haired, blue-eyed tyke and says, "Cute kid."

Bryce watches as his guest sets the picture back down. This man doesn't fit here. Doesn't belong. This is the wrong floor. Wrong profession. Wrong life. Those arms, that swagger. The way he holds Bryce with his sad, heavy eyes as easily as he grips that framed photo makes it clear this isn't the place for him.

Yes, Bryce's company should be somewhere else. This man, this night janitor with big boat-like running shoes and a wide neck that needs to be kissed isn't like the others here.

The others.

That sounds funny to the one gathering the sheet in his hand as he thinks of those who used to date him. In another life. Before Johnny. When he had health, a mountain bike not for show but for use, a full walk-in closet the size of a single-car garage, six brand-new cookbooks he'd open someday, a tiny garden complete with koi pond, and no real clue what a white cell does or that radiation meant sores in his mouth.

When Stu doesn't move, Bryce thinks maybe his midnight guest holds some curiosity about the two-year-old in the picture when all Stu cares about is being close to the once blond, now bald-headed man dying of cancer who stirs something he still can't quite explain.

At the wild, impulsive thought of setting his lips on Bryce's forehead, Stu suddenly freaks. *What, me and this guy? Being nice to a dying dude is one thing, but anything more?*

In a fast reverse, Stu wants out of here. Gain a lot of distance from this. Sure, he's flirted here, whatever, but even to *think* of some wild, weird kiss on the forehead? What? Really? And to a guy, especially *this* guy?

No way.

A cold feeling slides along his spine. This connection is wrong. Off. Tilted. Crazy.

Queer.

The father-to-be finds a line to start his exit. "You're...you're good with gettin' a nurse if you need one, right?"

Setting his head deep into the pillow, Bryce has the answer to Stu's question, but it slips away. The medicine. The medicine. Sometimes it is really hard to be here. When his eyes close, he goes back to thinking about—remembering—his boy.

Baby John's mom made the national news. The fourth of five women killed a year ago down in San Diego by a disbarred attorney with two grown children. Cornered in a convenience store, gun in his shaking hand, he ironically took his own life by a display of candy called Red Hot Bullets.

There was never a dad in Johnny's picture; that wasn't his sister's style. From the start, it was just Johnny and Bryce.

Motherhood wasn't Bryce's sister's style either.

"My cousin." Bryce answers a question Stu didn't ask. "Her name is Brenda. She lives in the east. Johnny will go there."

The morphine takes Bryce away again. When he does come back, some forty-five minutes later, Stu is gone.

In fact, Stu never comes back. Quitting the hospital that morning, he swears he'll never think of the blue-eyed man again. He'll never revisit how he wanted to hold, heat, and comfort this stranger.

But that doesn't happen. Stu does think of Bryce at odd or unexpected times, usually around the time he'll celebrate something big with his daughter, like the first sentence she'll read on her own from her favorite nighttime story, *Waddle, Waddle Duck*, her first missing tooth on the morning of her sixth birthday, or her stellar performance as Betsy Ross in the third-grade classroom production of *Early America in Stitches*.

Each time he remembers the man with the warm soul, Stu comes to this truth: that man loved his nephew, and, with that framed photo there in his hands when he died, he wished the boy a life he himself never had, one free of loneliness and pain.

CHAPTER ONE

H e ignores the slightest notion that this isn't right for him. But it isn't.

Pushing his geometry homework across the acne-scarred kitchen table, John won't see this now. He can't.

Instead, the seventeen-year-old anxiously stands and steps into the laundry area beside the only working exterior door to the twelve- by fifty-two-foot trailer. A pack of angry Dobermans on short chains has nothing on this angry washing machine that bucks, snarls, and curses its contents as they whip and whip around in the final moments of the spin cycle.

A foster kid who has lived here a few months, John stares at the Maytag's rust-splotched front. He tells himself he's used to these sounds. When his fingers reach for a few blond curls over his ear—a nervous gesture he never realizes he does—he's not convinced.

The washing machine's rampage continues against the old trailer's floorboards. As a result, the laundry detergent on the top shelf shimmies to the edge. John, who likes to keep things in place because he's been in too many homes since high school began three years ago, moves the gallon jug back to safety.

To escape himself, John closes his bright blue eyes. He imagines he's in his small bedroom a few feet from where he's standing. Yes, there. On the beat-up twin mattress he now calls his own. With the faintest smile, he remembers the feel of the secondhand sheets sliding over his bare skin. Having not been laundered since he arrived, the bedding, scented with his sleep and sweat, holds what he can't name, and that's a guy his age.

All at once, the banging within the machine subsides. The soft-spoken, clean-cut gym boy who barely needs to shave imagines he's still in bed. It's early morning, an hour or so before the sun even thinks of rising. John pretends that Greg is home early, let go hours before his seven a.m. shift ends. The plant let the muscle guy go because they're ahead of production. This can happen during the third shift, maybe once or twice a quarter.

And so Greg walks through the narrow front door. And he's in a great mood. And he has time.

John imagines the slapping sound of Greg's giant-sized work boots echoing off the cardboard-like walls. Coming close, closer, the heavy footfalls stop outside of John's bedroom.

As he's done before, John imagines Greg entering. No knocking. Rather, there's just need, hunger, want.

Warm under the covers, John enjoys Greg spooning behind him. The young man's stomach is stroked, explored, and appreciated by Greg's big, calloused, attentive hands. There's a squeeze—good, hard, and tight—followed by the long, low, lazy embrace of the working man's forearm against John's slim waist.

The daydream ends when the Maytag suddenly spits, gurgles, and thumps the back wall.

Opening his eyes, John studies the washer and its quiet companion dryer. He does not quite know what he sees in this side-by-side couple, but in his tight belly, something churns, then knots. This feeling is more complicated than his West Virginia public school gives him the tools to communicate. In time, however, he'll come to understand that he is the dryer, warm and calm, and that Greg is the washing machine.

The buzzer sounds. On cue, John steps up to the heat the machine gives off. Never one for school even before he was held back a grade several years ago, he won't think about the fact that the geometry homework on the table has been done haphazardly. Nor will he think about the fact that even if he miraculously turned into a B- range student, no four-year college or associate's degree waits. And a trade school? Forget it. There's just what he has now, and what he has now he wants.

His fingers find the curls over his ear again.

He wants this.

Of course he wants this.

He tells himself this tightness in his belly isn't anything.

The gifted athlete, who would rather shoot hoops on a basketball court than wild turkeys in the surrounding woods, thinks of how he should be more like the other high school boys in the trailer park who, with guns and ammo, shoot defenseless birds that cry when hit. Even though he's successful as a varsity wrestler, and that can bring popularity even to a backward kid who's been at this latest school only four months, he knows there is no one he can talk to about how right this is with Greg, how good this is.

John swallows. He knows he's different in a *big* way from his teammates. He also knows he's the one who started all of this with a man the size of an NFL linebacker. And this is true: John came after Greg; it wasn't the other way around.

Quietly, he raises the lid on the machine, which gurgles and pings. As he reaches into the well of wet laundry, he stops. The thoughts he had before he walked away from his homework are back. Greg doesn't know him, not like he should. The divorced father of two preschool children doesn't know the contours of John's heart.

And this isn't love.

This isn't love.

But he won't think of that.

Busying himself, he gets back to work. The high school jock loads the dryer and empties the hall hamper that now contains just the whites. He glances down at two undershirts in his hand—one his, the other Greg's. Stretched and stained, Greg's is a size larger, and no bleach can return it to its original white.

He remembers the last time Greg slipped into the thin, old shirt he's holding. The working man had it on while shaving. Never quite closing right, the bathroom door had crept open partway, giving John a great view of the man who could be caring and gentle.

It had been an especially physical night at the plant and Greg had stepped out of the shower just a moment earlier. Seeing John stopped in the hall, the deep, dark-eyed man smirked. He knew what John had been staring at and asked, "What?"

John lowered his eyes.

Greg's voice was different this second time, sharper, deeper. "What?"

John reached for his own ear, holding the lobe between his fingers. Still looking down, he shrugged and mumbled, "I like lookin'."

With an annoyed-sounding "hmm," which John knew meant that Greg wanted to play along but act gruff, the larger man went back to work, angling his strong, square jaw in such a way that the bridge of his straight, strong nose shined from the bare bulb over the mirror.

John took in the still-steamy air that carried the combination of soap, shampoo, shaving cream and testosterone in its damp layers. He started watching again, his hand still on his ear. With drops of water pooled at the ends of his short, dark hair, Greg seemed vulnerable now. Tender. His expression softened to one like John's when John thought of sliding under Greg and kissing him.

The man's great muscular butt commanded attention when Greg bent further over the sink. The teen could see through Greg's navy sweatpants that the man wasn't wearing underwear.

"Hey, buddy," he asked, turning to show an inviting, floppy front in his sweats. "You sure you don't want nothin'?"

"Nope," John replied, his face warm, his neck heating. "All good. I mean, I...I'm all good."

"Yeah?"

John's face turned a deeper red as he considered all that rested under those sweatpants. To have Greg like this all to himself, to be able to study him, to be near him during a simple, everyday thing like shaving—this was good, really good. He swallowed a heavy, dry lump in this throat.

Greg stood still for a moment, then swished his razor in the water. "Quiet tonight, ain't ya?"

To answer, John raised one shoulder in a shrug.

"Hey." Greg turned to face him, his expression still gentle and inquisitive. They would be connecting soon, touching, holding, exploring. "What? What's goin' on?"

Numb in his thinking yet strong in his desire to take this man—to have this man—he shared again what he said a moment ago. "Me? I'm all right. I...I'm just watchin'."

"Just watchin'." Greg glanced at himself in the mirror. "Uh-huh."

The blue-collar worker went back to his task. Some thirty minutes later, Greg did hear John's heart beat. He felt the blond's muscles tingle. Then, naked and spent, he was gone, asleep beside John on that twin mattress.

If John thinks about it, he can still hear the softest whir of Greg's snore even now as he stands in the laundry area. He can still see the part of Greg's face not buried in the pillow. He can still feel the heat of when his shoulders were squeezed, when his legs tangled with Greg's, and when he could slide his fingers up and down Greg's sternum without the sleeping man ever moving.

But this is just romantic junk. Foolishness. Fantasy. John won't think of how the affection he wants hasn't happened in a while. Instead, he holds onto a future he intends to work for, by pushing away the realizations of what Greg has been lately.

He lowers the machine's lid and sets its cranky dial. With his want-to-be lover putting in long hours through the night, there is no time for fiction. No, these whites won't wash, dry, and fold themselves before he goes to bed.

Walking toward the kitchen, he doesn't count the foster homes he's been in. He can't. There have been too many. And he doesn't need adoption now. Of course he doesn't. This is his home, and what he has with Greg will work. That he is seventeen and Greg is thirty-five is nothing. Nothing. That Greg is also his foster father for now, well, that's nothing too.

Really, it's nothing.

Returning to his homework, he does his best to ignore how the washing machine whimpers as it fills with water. "It's just a machine," he says.

"It's just a machine," he repeats because a seventeen-year-old can still be seven for half a second, and, as playground rules go, saying it twice will surely make it true.

❖

He steps out of his jeans exactly one hour later.

Standing in front of a dresser that would actually make a fine piece of furniture with a little work, John reaches between his shoulder blades and scratches his bare back. When finished, he picks up one of his six wrestling medals that poke out under a loose pile of baseball cards. He should throw the cards out, but decides for the 210th time this year to hold on to the cards awhile longer.

Tired, John finds his way on the familiar mattress—his left foot here, his elbows there. Wearing only his white briefs, he thinks of the hard and hairy chest on the man he wants to love down at the plant. Running his fingers up and along the deep creases in his abdomen, John pretends he's with the good Greg, the one happy to be where he is, the one who will laugh that deep laugh even when another bad night at work finds him. Greg will be close. His warmth will be a furnace, sure and constant, protective and safe.

He reaches over to turn down the light on three stolen milk crates in front of the room's only window. The sheets sliding over his muscles are Greg's fingers, teasing and caressing, calling him, calling him—here in the moonlight—to warm and warmer places.

CHAPTER TWO

E ven a guy with a few beers in him would bet that Greg's trailer won't be around to see a new U.S. president take office. Hell, by the time this year's fawns get big enough to bag as a six- or an eight-point buck, Greg's nearly broken, two-bedroom rusty dump rolled in on wheels will add a significant heap to landfill material.

Ruggedness runs along the trailer's timeworn edges, but Greg knows deep down this façade only hides rust and rot. Even the recent additional cinder blocks under the center of its bowed frame cannot hide the sad trailer's sagging middle.

He thinks about those blocks now. The ones he didn't use on the house trailer wound up in the bed of his Ford Ranger at the start of the snow and ice season a few months ago. The blocks keep his two-wheel-drive truck weighted but don't help his worn shocks. He curses as he bounces off the township road. As he passes them, Greg also curses those damn freshly painted yellow mailboxes at the end of the trailer park's muddy drive because they're too bright for this time of the year.

His own dented box holds only junk mail. The foster care check is coming, but so are the alimony and childcare payments. In, out—only the out has been greater this month.

Greg tightens his grip on the steering wheel as the song he hasn't been listening to ends. His skin turns a shade closer to the overcast mid-January morning sky when the following radio commercial announces that the Ground Hog wants to help get your lawn ready for spring. With just a little bit more than the width of a driveway on either side of his trailer, Greg has no real lawn. He can bum a lawn mower again this summer or just let the damn weeds grow. Last July, the bluebells by the steps looked nice for a while.

After a sharp right, he clicks off the headlights, cuts the engine. He's home. He checks his bandana over the rearview mirror, grabs his lunch box, his thermos, and yesterday's paper the foreman let him have.

The trailer quivers when he enters. The medicine cabinet mirror over the bathroom sink pops open when he passes. In the waving glass, Greg catches a glimpse of his upper body. Work at the plant keeps him trim; the gym a couple times a week keeps him ripped. Though he's not as lean as he was even ten years ago—he's gained an inch on his now thirty-five-inch waist—he likes how he's filled out.

And a guy this built, a man's man put together like this, hell, he should get it. He should get it whenever he wants.

He just doesn't get it like he knows he should 'cause, shit, that takes too much work—and with women, even those at the bar, there are too damn many strings attached.

But he needs it. Yeah, he needs it.

From the back of his mind, Greg pictures John in a T-shirt and white briefs sleeping soundly on his belly in the smaller of the two back bedrooms. Driven by pure want and the thought of that sweet soul so damn close, Greg puts his oversized hand on the pressed particleboard door separating the two of them. When he slides his heavy fingers over the closed door, it's like he is already stroking John's smooth skin.

The familiar doubt slips in just before he opens the minor's bedroom.

No, Greg thinks in what now has become a routine, a routine that should have never started. He can hear his own voice say, *This is wrong*.

But life is wrong. To make it through with what you have and with what you can get is enough. It is enough. So John is seventeen. So the budding young man arrived through foster care still carrying the one and only possession no social worker or foster parent ever thought to buy for him at a Wal-Mart: a three-dollar compass.

A lump rises in Greg's throat. He knows the compass is on John's dresser behind the boy's baseball cards and the lube. The damn lube.

One of Greg's coworkers saw the lube in Greg's cart when both men were in the Super-Eight a few days after the New Year. "What's that for?" The man smirked. "You gettin' some?"

Greg could lie. He should lie.

"Well?" the man who works in shipping asked. "Are ya?"

In that split second, Greg decided to play dumb. "Am I what?"

The coworker hid most of his mouth as he rubbed the side of his face with his gray thumb. "You know."

Standing in front of the baby powder section, no one could hear them.

"Oh, well—" Greg's throat tickled. "No, I'm a...well, I'll tell ya. I'm just lookin'...waitin' for love."

No man in the plant uses the word *love*, and Greg hopes what he just shared will get him out of this.

The moment his coworker blurted out, "Bullshit!" and burst into a big belly laugh, Greg knew the subject would drop.

Though John did start this, he also knows this isn't right. Ignoring the heat under his belt, he moves off to his own bedroom a few feet away from John's door and sits on his double bed. He spreads his knees and his elbows press against his powerful thighs.

Love. *Love?* His open hands rub his tired face. In his Marine Corps way, the six-foot-three, 250-pounder comes across as both handsome and ugly, but this doesn't matter to him. Never has. While he can still kick ass playing backyard football, he will never be light-footed again, and this does bother him. His blue-collar life bothers him too. The grind of the bills, the child-support payments, and those long hours at the plant drive him to his feet again.

"I need this," he whispers as he paces at the foot of his unmade bed. "And when we're together—damn—it's good."

And John teases. And he knows he does. The boy gets that dance move goin', or comes in all nice and slow, nice and slow, wrapping his arms around Greg after a massage he never asks for. The gruff man's nipples are found, warmed, and pinched. And then, tight against his back, John drops down close to Greg's ear, whispers into it. Says good things, sweet things.

A knife burns through his conscious. *But he's a damn minor!*

Greg closes his eyes and pictures the high school wrestler asleep. Frisky, gentle, tender, kind. That's John. Then Greg imagines that the mound between the blond's legs needs his attention. To reach down into the front of those white briefs and...

His fists close. He should have seen this coming, but how could he? To get in good with the social worker, who does see how Greg wants at least 50/50 custody with his three- and four-year-old, he signed up to be a foster parent. It isn't the cash he wants for taking in somebody else's kid. In fact, he didn't really know what he wanted until John—who's a little dumber than he should be—came along. And they connected, but only because John, in sure and deliberate ways, wanted it.

Tired, Greg runs his fingers over what's left of his own thinning hair. He is not wrong about this.

Driven back to the hall, he rests his forehead against the entrance to John's walk-in-closet-sized bedroom.

Trying to make sense of where he is now, Greg remembers their first meeting at the Center ten months ago. John spotted Greg the moment the totally-out-of-place guy walked through those doors. Anyone who was watching could see that the teen was sizing up Greg's neck, his muscled chest, and those brown eyes that held what only John could see: pain, rejection, loss, and sorrow.

"Yeah, man, I like wrestling," John responded to Greg's question after the eligible foster kid—way too old for other homes—introduced himself at the lame-ass meet and greet.

"You do."

John smirked to show clean, white, perfect teeth. "I can take you, big guy."

The barely six-foot, 175-pounder with like 5 percent body fat mentioned wrestling again the next time Greg stopped by, and the time after that. Shortly thereafter, Greg started coming to John's wrestling meets. Nothing steady, of course; he'd show up when his work schedule allowed. John made sure the caseworkers on staff at the Center knew that the divorced father of two had been an assistant high school wrestling coach a few years back, so this was fine. Even the little kids, the ones who were immediately placed, knew John was happy to have Greg around.

And John always initiated wrestling too. In his living room, a good month after John had officially moved into the trailer park where Greg had spent the last eleven years single, married, and now divorced, it started casually as fun, good, silly horseplay one afternoon. They sat side by side watching a Sunday afternoon NBA game. John's feet were down. Greg's were resting over the coffee table.

"My legs ain't no resting place for you," Greg announced when John stretched his feet over the larger man's shins.

"Sure 'bout that?"

Greg reached for his last can of beer. "Sure," he grumbled. "Move 'em."

John scooted down lower on the couch so his calves rested over Greg's lower legs.

The game rolled into a set of commercials. Greg slowly turned his head and asked, "Since when does my body look like furniture, you shit?"

John smiled but kept his eyes on the screen as the game returned. The Lakers had the Knicks by ten at the start of the second half.

Content, John rested his head further into the couch cushion. "You shouldn't swear like that."

"Uh-huh." Greg took a hit from his beer can.

"Bad example."

Greg didn't continue. Instead, he just widened his knees a bit and sighed at the added weight to his legs.

John wiggled his toes. "Hey, Greg, am I askin' for it?"

Distracted because his eyes were on the clock showing on the TV screen, Greg waited a moment, and his deep voice reverberated three-quarters annoyance, one-quarter invitation. "Yeah, you're asking for it."

"Good." John took one of his feet off Greg, slid it under both of Greg's legs, and then, with both legs acting like scissors, began to squeeze Greg's shins, clamping down hard with his long, strong leg muscles.

Stirred inside, Greg kept his eyes on the players charging up and down the court and tried to keep it cool. "You don't wanna go there."

John, still applying pressure to Greg's legs, leaned forward. Face-to-face a good fun spark ignited. "Yeah, I do. I do wanna go there. I can take you in wrestlin', old man."

"Ya think?"

Playfully, John said, "Think? Nah, I *know*."

"What's this 'old man' bit?"

John laughed.

With his size and weight, Greg muscled his way out of John's first few holds. Their T-shirts rolled up in the action and when Greg came down on John, he pressed most of his weight into John's rippled abdominal muscles. The boy laughed with joy. With bare skin against bare skin, Greg rocked his hips once, just once, but each felt the tension and the swollen muscles of the other male. They loved it.

On the bottom, John forced his arms free, but Greg only trapped him again. Then they both laughed. Their sounds were not silly; instead, they came with the excitement of being *this* close. Both had something neither had ever experienced before, and it was hot and right and perfect.

Though they didn't quite know what it was or where it was heading, they knew it was wonderful, so damn wonderful.

Sweaty and content, Greg settled his broad forehead on John's shoulder. He sighed as John cupped the back of his closely clipped hair. Heat, proximity, togetherness, breath on breath, slippery skin, and deep down, aching want was exposed at last. The younger, less experienced grappler then repositioned himself so that even more contact would connect their bodies, one over the other.

To feel even more of the larger man on top of him, John squirmed to raise both of them off the couch. The new equilibrium caused them to slide between the couch and coffee table.

Greg only groaned. Its sound was magnetic.

On the floor, John swallowed. And there, right there on Greg's strong neck, the teen eyed the spot he wanted to kiss.

Getting into position to set his lips on his target, John freed himself, scurried on top, and straddled him.

"What, what are you—?" Greg didn't finish his question.

Their eyes met. Sparks flew. Adrenaline soared. Anger and want popped. They were just so hard everywhere, so close, primal, charged.

This was necessary.

When their eyes met again, the locking of their lips was combustible. It was also masculine and raw, angry at what had been bad lives apart.

And hungry.

Very hungry.

Thirty minutes later, both naked and entwined, not sure where one body ended and the other's started, they stopped. Rug burns would redden their elbows and knees. Their separate showers afterward made everything they had done seem dirty, but it came back. It always came back—again and again. John would start it. Sometimes all it would take would be a look, but the two would go at it and end minutes, sometimes hours, later. They would be covered in sweat, happy, and intertwined in each other's arms.

Something changed over time, however. Greg couldn't handle a young man who cared for him as John did. During his long and dull hours at work, he doubted, questioned, and wondered, what *is* this, anyway? John made his dumpy life a home? John was falling in love, and Greg didn't expect or know how to handle this. Intimacy scared him, especially from another male. So he shut himself off from John, who took this emotional wall to heart. John no longer initiated. Instead, it was Greg who came after John—and this is what Greg wanted—to hunt rather than be hunted.

The relationship became a game to Greg. He pulled away from John emotionally while at the same time came at him for one thing only: sex.

And so it was this morning, and nearly every morning, as Greg walked into his trailer after his night shift. It was wrong, so damn wrong, but he needed John.

So Greg has to do it. He has to. He opens the teen's bedroom door an inch or two. His low, morning voice is deep and strong. "John."

It is 6:03 a.m. John has to be up for school in twenty-seven minutes. "Yeah."

Greg steps into the room.

❖

When Greg finishes, John, euphoric his man is still so close, takes one of Greg's calloused hands and kisses the open palm.

Greg pulls back. To keep the boy at a distance, to keep the power he's gained where it belongs, Greg lies. It's one he didn't plan on telling, or even think through. "Rent's going up."

"What?" John asks, his voice drunk and warm. "I thought you owned this trailer."

"The trailer, yes. Not the site. That bastard Bob's upping this trailer park's rent. Maybe it would be cheaper to move. Git a one bedroom closer to work."

John thinks on this. "That would be all right."

Greg rolls off to sit on the edge of the mattress. "And where'd you sleep?"

"With you." John doesn't hesitate to answer.

Greg stands. "That's not how this is workin' out, junior."

John's heart falls in his chest as he sits up. "Greg, I'll work more hours, then. I still got Sunday mornings open. That's one of the busiest times at the gym. Sometimes guys get tips when it's really crowded. I could see if the manager could get me on the schedule."

"You and them muscles."

"But I can help out with money. You know that."

Leaving his clothes on the floor, Greg turns and holds John's chin for a moment. He feels what the happy boy wants and almost believes can happen—or maybe can happen—then he shuts the door behind him. Satisfied, he sets off to sleep alone in his own bed.

Fifteen minutes later, as John sits with his eggs at the kitchen table, the high school junior plans. If he can work harder and earn more money, then things will be better between them. He won't graduate from high school till he's nineteen, but he'll be eighteen in just four months.

There ain't no free rides.

Yeah, his plan will work. He knows just the person at the gym to ask about making more money.

Instead of washing the frying pan he used to cook the eggs, he thinks again about his plan to earn cash. It will work. It will have to.

Checking the clock, he has to hurry. After a quick shower, he decides he'll wear to school today the shirt Greg left on his bedroom floor.

CHAPTER THREE

Sixty bucks an hour is *a lot* of money. What did he know about being a personal trainer, anyway? With three crisp twenty-dollar bills about to come into in his pocket, what does it matter? He knows his way around the gym. This will be easy.

Or it should be easy.

Nervous, he steps on the welcome mat and rings the bell.

Wearing biker shorts and a black sports bra, Louise Amsterdam answers her door. The single, pampered forty-seven-year-old has her own idea of physical training and John, his heart set on making extra money, does just as she asks. They never kiss—on the lips, that is—and exactly sixty minutes later, John stands where he did just before ringing her bell. He holds another twenty in his hand. It's crinkled.

"Ma'am?"

"For excellent service." She's surprised he's *this* stupid. "Your tip."

"My tip?"

"Next week, then, big boy?" She sets one of her heavy auburn curls behind her ear. "Yes?"

He didn't know. He didn't know anything. What had happened? This glossy, highly professional woman could have practically anything she wanted, and if she really wanted a physical trainer, she'd have found one of the few pros who worked in the area instead of asking him to come over to her oversized condo for workout tips.

"John," she purrs, drawing one leg closer to the other. "Next week? Same time?"

He shakes his head. This isn't what he wanted, although, deep down, he knows now that she was clear when they discussed this in the gym.

But he won't continue.

Louise Amsterdam drops her voice an octave. "I'll give you

eighty bucks next time, up front. But I'll expect just as much from you, deal?"

John doesn't respond.

Annoyed and certainly not used to waiting, she taps her industrial-strength nails against the doorframe. "Well, muscles?"

For the past two months, he's been working Sunday mornings now, just as he had planned the morning he learned from Greg that the rent at the trailer park was going up. To add eighty bucks a week? West Virginia is not an expensive state to live in, so, that would do it, wouldn't it?

John lowers his eyes in a moment of defeat. "You'll get just as much, ma'am."

"Business adjourned."

His steps down her sidewalk are numb. Although she let him shower alone, his skin still smells a bit like her perfume here in the breeze. He doesn't like that.

He also doesn't like that he can't seem to lift his chin from his chest.

❖

A book John didn't read in English class talks about a man who drowns because he couldn't let go of what he wanted. He forgets the name of the book he just carried around for two weeks at the beginning of the new marking period. Now that he thinks about it, he isn't sure if the guy did actually drown, or if his teacher, in yapping on and on and on, just made it seem like he did.

His thoughts circle back to the money, not to what he did to get it.

Eighty dollars a week. To do what he did again. Eighty bucks. He isn't so sure. Not at all.

He is a prostitute now. A whore boy.

How did this happen? And did it matter?

He knew he wasn't the sharpest tool in the toolbox, a phrase he'd overheard a foster parent say of him about a year after his aunt Brenda left him in the system. He also knew he'd have to do something so that it would continue to work out with Greg.

Whore boy.

His stomach ached.

What was the big deal though, really, and who would know?

Yeah, he'll do this deal with Amsterdam. He figures it's just cash. With it, he and Greg will be able to stay where they are. Easy.

Maybe someday they can get a bigger house trailer, one that doesn't tremble when you walk across the kitchen. Or they can move closer to the plant. Maybe get a house. A little one.

You're squishing him, John, he tells himself as he walks through town toward the trailer park.

But a house with a basement, one where they could set up wrestling mats. That would be great! He knows Greg would like it. Really, how awesome would that be?

❖

John waits until the day he turns eighteen to surprise Greg with the extra money. Between the extra hours at the gym and his time with Louise, John has stashed just over seventeen hundred dollars. Since Greg hasn't mentioned the rent hike again, John thinks that maybe it hasn't happened yet, or, hopefully, wouldn't happen. Either way, he believes his birthday is a good day to give Greg the gift he's been working toward for over four months.

Anxious, he can't stop fidgeting in the trailer's kitchen. He has long decided to give the money to Greg today, but, of all the lame things, he doesn't know if he should make his own birthday cake. He'd never made a cake before, least of all one for himself, and can't decide if it is in good or bad taste to do such a thing. The directions on the box cannot be simpler, but that doesn't mean a disaster in the oven doesn't wait. Greg has been so distant now, even more so than on the morning he said there'd be a rent hike. Would a cake make things worse, or better?

He can't decide. He just can't decide.

John drops down into one of the three mismatched chairs at the kitchen table. He glances at the clock. 1:33 p.m. He has to be to work at the gym by five. On Saturday nights, he and a coworker close the place at midnight. John loves work on Saturdays, especially in the evening. No one comes to the gym after seven, which means he can work out, ignore his damn geometry homework, *and* get paid.

Last week, one of his coworkers called him on this. "What, John, it's Saturday night, and you work here all the time. Hello? What about a social life?"

Social life? John is still shy around anyone in school—even Daphne, a girl he meets regularly for ice cream—because he doesn't want anyone to know that, since he's moved so often, he's on a fifth-grade reading level. Too embarrassed to speak up or ask for help, he remains quiet, a trait he's never had to force himself to learn. It just came easily.

And, yeah, the half dozen girls at school who show interest are indeed fine, and the junior/senior prom is set next month, but John knows he's different.

Now, the guys on the wrestling team, or the guys he's wrestled from other schools this past season…and some of those guys are *hot*… still…that didn't work, either. John convinces himself again and again that he's found and enjoys something deeper.

He can't stop thinking about that something deeper now, even as his hands find familiar curls over his ear. He stands. He checks the refrigerator again. There's enough Busch beer there. And he bought a lemon tarragon chicken, baked beans, and a cucumber salad at the grocery store. All Greg's favorites.

Moving toward the counter, John grabs both sides of the boxed cake mix. He stares into space.

Greg's getting a new muffler put on his truck. Earlier today, John thought Greg used the muffler as an excuse to pick up some birthday present, but noticed on the calendar that Greg did have an appointment for his truck this afternoon at one.

Still holding the boxed cake in his hands, he waits in the kitchen until 4:30 and then gets ready for work at the gym.

❖

It's half past midnight—still close enough to call it his birthday.

He hurries toward the trailer. The light in the living room is on, which is not surprising. Sometimes Greg watches a hunting show at this hour. The reading lamp beside his twin bed glows, however, and always conscious of bills, including the one from the electric company, he turned it off before he left for work at the gym.

John ignores this odd detail, and runs up the trailer's three temporary steps. "Greg!" he calls out excitedly. "You're still awake!"

Greg's voice holds venom. "Oh, I'm awake."

He's been drinking. Not just beer. John guesses the red around

Greg's eyes means trouble. This has only happened once, in a foster home he lived in years ago. That time left John with a cut just inside his elbow that John tells himself he deserved.

"I'm definitely awake," Greg says from the corner kitchen chair.

"Then good." John walks through tension and sets his gym bag down near the cabinet that holds the cake mix he set aside. "Maybe we can watch some TV for a while." Some animal will be in season soon. "How about that huntin' show?"

Greg covers his face with his hands.

He shouldn't be like this, John thinks. *He shouldn't be this tanked, this far gone. It's just his ex-wife, the child support payments, the long hours at his job. But I'll take care of him. I'll get him to come to bed with me tonight and sleep this off. Yeah, side by side under the covers, I'll hold him.*

Angry, Greg has no idea what John is thinking. The drunken man stands. "But this is interesting. Your *friend* stopped by." Greg holds out a small, flat box that, now opened, had been wrapped in happy birthday paper. "She left you this."

My friend Daphne, from high school? She doesn't know where I live.

Not knowing of anyone to leave him a gift, John frowns.

"A lady. Amsterdam, yeah. That is her name."

"Amsterdam?" *God, Louise.*

Greg staggers. "You're her whore. You're her male gigolo whore boy. She pays to have sex with you."

"No."

He waves the gift box again. "And she, she brought you this." Greg takes a step forward and lets the box drop. In his enormous hand, he holds a bright red pair of high-cut skimpy men's underwear. "And I want you to wear this now, you bastard whore. I want you to put this whore gear on, and wear it, you whore."

John blushes. "This is not…this isn't what…"

Greg holds the gift between his fingers. His expression says he enjoys the feel of the slippery fabric, but his voice burns with the bourbon down his throat. "Put it on now."

John shakes. "Hey, funny thing. Tonight at the gym, while—"

"What is this with you? *Now!*"

John moves toward the bathroom.

"No, here." Greg watches John's fear grow. *"Put it on right here!"*

Every move is slow and painful, like flesh in frozen water. He pulls off his T-shirt, unbuttons his shorts. He pauses in his white briefs.

Their eyes meet. Greg silently lets John know that he is not finished.

With the hot red underwear on, John stands still. His face is down.

Greg moves in closer. "And I know about the money. The seventeen hundred bucks."

"Th-that's for you," John stutters. "That's f-for you! I wanted to give that to you tonight! Today!"

"Pretty boy," Greg counters, "you're stockpiling some serious cash."

"No! I wanted to give it to you today!" John starts to cry. "I waited for you to come home after the muffler."

"You are a whore in a red thong and you lie!"

John drops to his knees as if he's been hit.

"And stop that cryin'. Christ! Stop!"

There is no energy to move.

Greg leans over him. "Now get this, John. Get this good. You sell yourself and no longer have a home here. That money is mine, for sure. For all that I had put up with. For that woman comin' here." He bends down closer to John's face. "How did that feel to me, to have her here?"

"No," John pleads. "No."

"You started this. This us bein' together deal. You wave your muscles around, you dance in front of me, nice and slow. You tease. You wanted to be my toy. No one else's. And now that's gone."

"No, Greg, no."

"Tonight you leave."

John chokes on his tears. He just wants to get to bed with Greg. Have it be one of those good times when he rides Greg, not the other way around. "No, no. Please. No."

Greg strokes John's blond hair and draws the eighteen-year-old closer to his warm lap. He softens his voice. "What, you wanna stay? You wanna stay here with me?"

John nods.

Greg rocks his hips and forces John's face down. "Then you have work to do."

❖

It's 4:15 a.m. People at this hour are still dreaming good, long dreams. Maybe some who have to wake at this time are hitting the snooze button on their alarm clocks for the first time. Others simply find the one they love under their covers, say a word or two in their sleep, and nuzzle in closer.

Abandoned now, John holds his arms.

There's no way he could have ever wanted what happened between them to happen. What Greg did to John both in and out of that red thing wasn't sex.

At first, John didn't go far. Numb and broken, he silently leaned against the temporary steps to the trailer and waited. Greg would cool down. The alcohol would go with the anger. In the morning, it would be fine. Everything would be fine, forgotten.

But an hour after John had been tossed out, Greg saw him there. Realizing he wouldn't leave the steps, Greg shoved the sex boy in his truck and drove him some thirty miles from the trailer park.

After strong-arming John into the pickup, he said, "This is the story. You ran away from home. No matter what you say, if you git to talkin', everything was fine in my place, but you...whore...*you* ran away from home."

"Greg—"

"You're a whore. After what you did, think some social worker bitch is gonna let *you* come back with me? I got proof you're a whore. That's why you ran away. And that's what the agency will hear, if you *think* you're comin' back."

John whimpers. "Greg, no."

Greg thinks. "No, I'll tell 'em now. 'Yeah, ma'am, hello. I'm sorry to say this, but Johnny left me when I caught on to him.' She and I will call the cops together. Yeah. And Bob'll back me. Hell, with the rent money he'll say he saw that lady come swayin' up to my door with that whore gear wrapped up in a pretty bow. A car like that? Hard to miss. So, you got it? I ain't seein' you again."

"Greg! No!"

Kicks and a few punches follow to get John out of the truck. Except for one on his lip, most land unsuccessfully. He doesn't feel them now, anyway. Instead, he's freezing. Though the temperature on the bank clock says it is seventy-four degrees, he shivers.

❖

For the longest time, John doesn't move from where he's been left. He realizes he's been hoping Greg will come back, but that isn't happening.

He looks around for the first time. A Salvation Army. Yeah. Behind a Grand National Bank, just on the other side of this strip mall, he sees an unlit sign for the charity store. He'll head there.

John realizes that recently dropped off and unsorted donations may be in the back alley.

Clothes!

He walks without thinking, without remembering the last five hours. Around the back he finds his way. Crossing a junkyard arsenal of broken shopping carts from a super-sized grocery store and the confetti of cheap, thin, shopping bags, he finds assorted cardboard boxes stacked near the Salvation Army's back door. Inside the first box, one shirt smells like moth balls. He smiles. People with real closets use moth balls.

It's too small. He's a big boy.

Another shirt. This one has the insignia of a high school where he's wrestled more than once. He lost his last match there to a guy who took an extra-long moment to shake his hand in the hall after the meet. John remembers the young wrestler's deep blue eyes, his square jaw, his smile, and the swollen angles of muscle over his broad shoulders. A quality in this seventeen-year-old made John both uneasy and comfortable at the same time. Even after his girlfriend said hello and introduced herself a moment later—and she'd been standing with them the whole time—something sweet and good connected them.

Back to the task at hand. He's shopping now. Another shirt, another box. Plaid. Wool. Too heavy for June. Below it, there's another. Long-sleeved. Wow, a brand-new light blue dress shirt!

Good.

Finding pants takes more time, but he's successful.

Now to move on. He'd been left nearly naked, and now dressed, he needs to get back.

But how?

Though slowly at first, the sun wakes after a while. A twenty-something-year-old leaving his night shift at the mega grocery store nearby agrees to take John back to the trailer park because he knows all too well about fraternity hazing at the University of West Virginia.

"They left you here?" the helpful guy asks as he starts his well-crumpled, twelve-year-old Honda Civic. "Your bros just left you in a *parking lot*? Frat guys. With me, they never took me this far off campus."

The little car needs a muffler and John's thankful the conversation will be less because of the noise. Still, he's glad for the companionship from a guy who has decided he's had enough with high-end college and, just like him, could use a job in the grocery store chain.

When the two leave the parking lot shortly after seven a.m., they notice a dead rabbit near the center of a rural intersection. John ignores the fact that the bright blood is the color of that red slingshot he wore in front of Greg.

The driver says, "Poor little bunny." He reaches over and punches John's shoulder. "Stupid shit—deserved what he got. Prob'ly had it comin'."

John thinks of himself. *Yep. Had it comin'.*

Worried about the cops, he has to be fast, sneaky. There. One of his T-shirts hangs out of the Dumpster behind the trailer park. Seeing this from some distance, he rushes forward and opens the lid. A wad of his clothes fills both arms. He pulls out more. School notebooks, his desk calendar, and the duffel bag he brought to the gym last night make their way to his salvage pile. The 7-Eleven tumbler that held his pens is smashed and coffee grinds stain his undershirts. His underwear and wrestling gear, including all his jocks and his singlets, are missing.

He finds his shoes under rotting cabbage, and has a sudden thought. School. *I'm not that late and my lunch account is good. He couldn't have taken that away. It's paid right through the end of the school year.*

And with what Greg says about the law—especially those friggin' cops—he...he wouldn't have called the police.

But he'd have to tell the agency.

He wouldn't do that, though, not right away. And I'm back now. I never ran. It was just a misunderstanding. All of it. I can talk my way out of this.

His stomach growls fiercely.

I'm hungry, he admits. *And after gym class, I can shower. There's always somebody's half-full shampoo of bottle around. And Greg will be cooled off by the time I get home. And we'll laugh. We will laugh this off. Yeah, this is just going to be funny.*

But at four that afternoon, John rethinks. Maybe this isn't going to just fall back into place. Maybe this needs more time. Like a night or two more. Just let Greg settle down, maybe forget most of it.

With a blank page ripped out of his geometry notebook, John leaves Greg a note on the steps of the trailer. It says he's sorry. He's wrong. He'll change. John scribbles that he'll be back in two days, when Greg isn't working. Hopefully they can talk.

John pretends he isn't worried about where he'll sleep for the next two days. He just sees Greg sober with a smile on his face.

❖

Louise answers her door some twenty minutes after John left the note on Greg's door. Cocking her hip at an angle, she says, "So, what? *This* is my thank you now?"

"Louise."

"I just thought, red. Red for you."

"Louise." He doesn't move.

She doesn't like this pause. "That big bulldog of a guy? That hole? You live *there*?"

John takes a step forward then stops. "Louise, I need money."

"Then come in."

While he needs the money, he needs Greg more. "I've come for my last payment. My last eighty bucks."

She turns from him, thinking this is new play. She smirks. This... this is different. Fun. Easy.

"First of all," she announces, "you *earn* your cash; you don't just stand there and ask for it; and second, I'm the one who says when this arrangement ends, not you."

"It ends, Louise."

Silence follows, but somehow it's on Louise's terms. It lasts a moment before she lacerates John using the vulgar language Greg uses when angry. But John doesn't move. He can't. He needs that money for a cheap hotel and food.

"So, wait." She shakes her head when her battering stops. A cool, curious expression covers her face far better than her highly expensive makeup. "You just think you can come here for money without your service rendered?"

The chin that he can't lift from his chest is back. He doesn't answer.

"You slab of meat."

This isn't John. This isn't who he is. He's not this man, this toy, this sex thing. "Louise."

"Get out."

John's voice carries an edge never before heard. "With money, yeah, I'll leave."

She frowns.

"With money, yeah. Gimme some cash flow. Now."

"What?"

"Money. Now."

He's not convincing, but interesting. A new thought flashes before her murky brown eyes. Generally, she doesn't give a damn about relationships, especially with young, beefy, dumb men who are honestly only good for sex. Still, there's something new, different, harder at play here. She tilts her head and, without looking, lets her fingers find the finest line along her hairline from her first facelift. "Something's happened to you. What is it?"

To answer could trip him up or reveal too much. He shrugs. "Nothin', I'm fine."

"John, you're a baby...a baby in a good way. That innocence. That hope. And yet you've been smacked around. Maybe not so much on the outside, but even there, if I look, I bet I'd find bruises."

John blushes. That red slingshot had been wrapped around his neck to choke him.

"Yeah," she repeats. "Bruises." Eyeing his neck, she's never spoken to him this way before.

"Just the money," John says, trying again.

His words mean nothing. She is gone before they even say good-bye. On the street a few minutes later, he resets his immediate and pressing goal. He needs cash and a place to crash for a couple of nights.

So he walks.

As he heads east, he replays what he calls his Greg Fantasies, which he does whenever his situation is really bad. In his imagination, he daydreams about the two of them camping in a state park. There's a tent for two near a lake. A fire. Starlight. They are both wearing long underwear bottoms, nothing else.

In another, they hit up the local SPCA for a lop-eared pup. In a third, they go to the sporting goods store, A-1 Athletics, and get mats so they can wrestle in the spare bedroom in their new apartment, if not their first house together.

All of a sudden, he happens upon a random thought of the blue-eyed wrestler, the one he remembered when he was getting clothes to wear behind the Salvation Army store. Yeah. That guy. That smile. That warm, fuzzy feeling against John's neck. They shook hands in the hall after their match.

John smiles now, as if they are face-to-face.

They shake hands again, only their eyes lock for a longer time, a much longer time, and there's no girlfriend.

"No." John catches himself. "It will work with Greg."

"It will work," he whispers with a resolve thinner than the still-creased light blue dress shirt over his hard-muscled back.

It has to.

CHAPTER FOUR

The sign above the doors is perfectly clear, though John reads it two more times.

Sandwiched between two small Cape Cod houses with toddler toys littering each narrow driveway, the low, modern building sits right up on the residential street. His eyes focus as he confirms the name on the sign is the same as the name on the glass doors.

He shakes his head in disbelief because he's come across something he's never looked for, let alone hoped to find, especially in a lower-middle-class neighborhood.

Yet here it is.

He looks down.

He doesn't want this.

Not at all.

But he sees the future in one glance when he raises his chin again.

Nerves. Uncertainty. Fear. His left hand finds some curls over his left ear. He tangles his fingers in his hair and hopes what he's thinking isn't true.

With his feet in motion, he sets off walking again. This just can't be. And it definitely shouldn't be, not for him.

Ten, maybe twelve steps later he stops. Money. This could bring big cash. And he'd be back on track with Greg again bringing in serious flow for a house and a dog and camping trips now and again with a tent that isn't quite big enough for the two them.

Did he really see what he thought he saw back there? *A professional wrestling school?*

He thinks of Louise. After a hard swallow of defeat, he turns back.

Plate glass windows line the building's narrow, unassuming front.

He doesn't see anything of himself in the eight- by ten-inch pictures of eccentric or hard-edged pro wrestlers that decorate the lobby, which is little more than a ramp that rises some four feet. The double doors are locked.

Wondering what to do now, John thinks of the compass that he was able to rescue with most of his stuff from the Dumpster. He pats his front pockets to double-check, but knows he doesn't have it with him now to offer direction.

Professional wrestling? Most of the guys who do it are characters, for sure, but some are athletes. Maybe they are all show-offs in one way or another, but he loves wrestling. *Real* wrestling, that is. Always has. It's just plain fun. The physical aspects—the strength it requires, the mental acuity, the skills.

This is different. These moves and lock-ups are much more dangerous, and he's never thought this through. Then again, he's never had to, until now.

The gym doesn't pay enough. Sacking groceries beside the guy who rescued him in the parking lot wouldn't bring in serious cash, either.

Turning back in the direction he was traveling before he saw the wrestling school's sign, he shrugs this off. Wrestling. Pro. Out there for the world to see. And really, what normal person does this, anyway?

A cold sensation caresses his stomach when he reaches the street's corner. Yes, Greg watched wrestling like this on TV. *Faggot* and *fake* were two words he used when watching two brute or big-bellied guys lock up, but he did watch intently, especially when one or both were great looking or muscled up. If there was a hot one on the screen, however, some hunky guy who'd been all stretched out, he came after John soon after the match ended. Yeah. It's a pattern John now realizes happened every time. Both before and in bed, the foreplay and the sex was all the more physical, all the more fun after Greg watched the pros. With strong holds, Greg had more heat, more drive.

There, on the sidewalk facing the intersection, he stands still but wants to run. Taking in the late afternoon sky and the traffic, he doesn't like his options, but he doesn't like where he is now, either.

Coming out from a dry cleaner's parking lot, a group of teenage girls he's never seen before pulls out onto the street and passes with their car windows down. They stare or whistle at him. He hears one say to another, "He's delicious!"

He bites into his lip that's still sore from when Greg hit him. He will do this. He will make this work. Getting Greg back is what matters, and Greg will think this wrestling is hot.

His steps are slow and measured. Heading back up the street, he stops near the wrestling school a third time.

Maybe Greg won't think this is hot. Maybe another idea, another way. He bites his lip again. *Should I go?*

In his question comes his answer. A living Adonis in his late twenties steps out into the lobby. Wearing a fitted black dress shirt that hugs his impressive pecs and tapered waist, he stops on the other side of the glass doors. A drop of water, pooled at the end of a short curl on the side of his head, splatters his hard-muscled shoulder. He doesn't notice. A clean-cut Afro-American with coffee-and-cream skin, he continues to watch John with his serious brown eyes flecked with green.

The man at the door sees another undereducated West Virginia jock looking for what the unfair world hasn't given him, only this one is pretty, and pretty means a pretty good stack of Ben Franklins to be made. Yes, clearly, he sees the dollar sign he can make off this one. Having played this many times before, he uses his warm, gentle voice when he begins his pitch. "You, ah, were looking to get in, right?"

John takes a step back.

The man has to move fast to hook the meat. He knows this. Scanning the blond boy fast, it's easy to see this one's beat up. His gut tells him to play this soft.

"Yeah," the man at the door says apologetically. "The door was locked. Sorry about that."

"No, I wasn't—" John shakes his head. "I mean, I wasn't here to…"

"Gotcha."

John squirms. He should run. Just bolt. But this stranger is handsome, warm. His white, square teeth show perfection when he smiles.

"So," the man asks, wrapping his hands around his black shirt. "How are you doing?"

No words find John's mouth. His heart is in his throat. His fingers tingle. His thoughts blur. His knees shake. And wait, somewhere does he think that this guy here is handsome and warm?

"Hey, buddy." A spark lights in the man's eyes. "I'm just thinking out loud here, but I'm guessing—just a reach here, but I'm guessing—

I'll get some more words out of you. This is not just for kicks because my own voice solo here gets old fast, but hey, yeah, talking? You know, word after word, whole phrases, sentences?" He shrugs his wide shoulders. "It's always a good thing. And you'll need that for the on-air interviews and promos."

Savvy as a military recruiter looking for numbers, he continues his line. "And, of course, there are all the kids after the matches. Hordes of 'em, sometimes. Loud, fun. In your face. They definitely get you going. And the ladies? Man, you'll have one every night." He draws his heavy thumb to his chiseled jaw. "So, talking," he smiles his showman's smile now, "you just might wanna demonstrate that first."

John is impressed. *This guy? Wow!* He tries to find his feet underneath him but they just aren't there. Even worse, his lips are numb. "H-hi."

The pro smiles and waits for more.

Nothing follows.

After a moment, the muscle guy smirks. "And in talking. Yeah, there could be a bit more here now."

John noticeably trembles.

"For example," the bigger guy says, "you might start with your name, or include it pretty near the front end of this conversation." Playfully, he moves his head left and right as if he's a boxer in the ring. "Yeah, that could work. Your name. Me, I'm Russ Gree."

After John botches his own introduction, Russ folds his hands, one over the other. He's not wearing a wedding band. "Nervous. That could sell."

John sinks, though somehow he must still be standing. He lies. "N-nah, not nervous so much."

Russ waits, letting the pause unfold. "Just not so sure, right?"

"This whole thing…" John's voice still locks in his throat. "Showing up here is…"

With his calming presence, the pro repeats and finishes what John just shared. "This whole thing…showing up here is…*new*."

John looks away and swallows hard. *Yeah, new.*

The wrestling pro starts thinking something he's never thought before. He waits a moment to see if the feeling grows. It does. The twenty-something-year-old takes a step back. In traveling the United States as a wrestler, particularly in the Midwest, he's met a few described as corn-fed—strapping, honest, boyishly cute, naïve—but this one here? Sure, he's built like one you wouldn't want to mess with, but there's more. This kid is a farm boy poster child: wholesome, simple, and innocent.

And maybe a little stupid.

Naw, definitely a little stupid.

Russ shakes his head. Yeah, he hasn't felt this way before with anyone he's met like this. Sure, different people bring out different things; he's known that from all his time on the road, but this? No, what's happening to him is new.

It is also clear.

He looks at John, whose eyes are downcast. Knowing from the blond's expression that he's both lost and scared, Russ's instinct is to guard this big boy, just cover this handsome-faced newcomer with warm, protective heat that only another guy can give.

Yeah, he thinks, *I do—shit—I do want this lost soul, this weary kid to know that he'll be all right. Yeah. With me here, he'll be all right.*

Suddenly, he's off script. Russ wants to reach across and, in doing the guy thing, shoot a friendly jab to the corner of John's shoulder. But even the thought of that isn't right. No, this is new. He wants to hold this one, hug him. Cup the back of the boy's head with his hand and just be still for a long, long time.

Russ does not know about foster homes or the sexual abuse John has endured in more than one home. Instead, he only sees the potential of this crowd-pleasing muscle toy. Only that's changed now. Rather than come on strong, his sales pitch sinks. This has never happened before, and he's not sure what the hell this all means, but Russ is certain of this: he wants to make sure John is both cared for and safe.

Scratching his shoulders through his black shirt so that John can get a just a trace of his expensive, sexy scented deodorant, his voice is different now, sincere. "So, how 'bout I show you what we are all about?" Russ reaches for the door he just exited. "Whaddaya say? Let me give you the rundown on the school. Yes?"

The moment for John arrives now. The decision.

Thinking of Greg and how he's come after him after watching TV wrestling, he barely nods. "Yeah, Russ. Yeah. I'd...ah...I'd like that."

❖

The tour moves fast for the potential new recruit, though Russ continues to be professional and assuring. He's also nonassuming. This, the pro decides, is John's call.

The two walk through an office, another office, and a large room that has long tables, a TV on a rolling cart, and two metal desks that face each other. Pictures of wrestlers hang on the walls everywhere. Many are autographed. Two are faces John has seen on television.

In the largest room, two couches flank a very large, framed picture of a ripped, very muscular man in skimpy wrestling attire. The guy in the shot is Russ.

"Yeah, that's me," Russ admits. "From last year. It's a promo shot from the time I was out touring in the Pacific Northwest."

John looks bewildered.

Russ, who is six foot four, nods. "The Sunday shirt-and-tie pic didn't quite give the look they were goin' for." Russ makes a face by protruding his already strong jaw. "That was a joke, bro. You're so serious. Would ya lighten up there, buddy?"

With more of a nod and a mumble, John doesn't quite answer with words.

"Good," Russ says as he leads the recruit into the center of the building where two wrestling rings stand some twelve feet apart.

"This is the classroom," Russ announces. "We spend all our time—well, actually most of it—here. There's more with wrestling, like your ring name and the gear you wear, the look we'll go after and actually create with you—we even put you in front of a camera for practice—but the bulk of our time is here. This is the place where I teach you to be safe, not only in regards to yourself, but also with the colleagues you're working with."

Colleagues? Who even uses that word? John is amazed with all he hears.

Next, they take a look at the small locker room, and the shower area that is even smaller. Once they bump hands. Another time, Russ is so close that John can feel the larger man's body heat.

"Yeah, the changing area is pretty tight," Russ confesses on their way back to the wrestling rings. "We schedule it so you can have some private time and space, so no worries there." He leans back against the ring closest to the two of them. "Some of the places I've wrestled and where I've had to change could make you laugh." He draws his thumb up to his jaw again. John remembers him doing this earlier, when they met.

"I've changed in a high school cafeteria kitchen twice. There's also been a plastic tent with one open end, a tractor trailer, and when really late for a match, in the back of a Toyota Corolla." Russ smiles again and the warmth of it spreads down John's arms. "So, comparatively speaking, that area back there? Well, that's pretty near to paradise."

"Paradise," John repeats to himself.

Russ finishes the tour a few minutes later and crosses his thick forearms over a trim, hard waist. The pro makes sure their eyes meet. Still new to this care for another guy, let alone another potential wrestler, Russ comes in all close and soft. Like before, this is a tack he's never used before.

"So, tell me about you, John. And why is wrestling important to you?"

Interview time. John remembers similar questions when he applied for his first job at the gym last year. He starts talking, leaving out his history of foster homes since the age of eight, or the past three years in four different West Virginia schools.

John intuitively gives answers Russ wants to hear. He says he can be fairly levelheaded with a good sense of direction. Just when he thinks he should stop because he's not all that sure of what he's saying, he mentions he has long-range goals.

He also stretches it a bit when he says he could be a bit of a performer in front of a crowd when he's never even been in front of a crowd save for his high school wrestling meets. But he has had a gymnastics background from his days in one middle school, and knows this will be helpful for moves in the ring.

"This all sounds good," Russ announces when John finishes. "Yeah, good." A mental calendar clicks in the pro's head, especially now that he's recalculated Blondie's intelligence a bit here. "I don't take many new guys on at a time, this really has to be individualized— and I like to mix more experienced wrestlers with newcomers. That said, new enrollment opens up next month. How does this sound?"

Next month, John thinks. *Wow, that's fast!*

"Yeah," Russ says, easily reading the pretty boy's expression. "Time wise, it is just around the corner."

John pulls his lips together and nods.

"Okay, bud." Russ frowns and poorly feigns disappointment. "Again with the talking thing."

John smiles. "This sounds good."

"Great. There's paperwork to be filled out. Let's grab it in the office. Deal?"

The deal means that half of the two-thousand-dollar tuition needs to be paid up front, and that John has to be eighteen. His age is not an issue; but where to get a thousand bucks and then a thousand more? Louise? Greg? He's screwed.

He stops at his destination, his hopeful home for the night. He reaches out in front of him and the pool house lock opens with one firm tug. The thin aluminum double doors whine and wobble on their hinges, but he stops them, aware any sound could give his private motel away.

He slips inside the tool-shed-sized building, thankful to be alone after a long day. The concrete floor is surprisingly cool when he stretches out over it, but warms under his body. He crosses his hands over his stomach. Having not eaten in a while, he feels his abdominal muscles carve even further into him.

He sighs. Though hungry, he is thankful for the machines beside him that clean the pool in Louise Amsterdam's complex. Safe, he knows no one will hear him.

Wait! He jerks upright. If no one hears him, then he can't hear them, either. If someone were to show up, he'd have no way of knowing in advance, no way of hearing over the constant hum of the filters.

To stay or to go…a pool maintenance shed at 9:15 p.m. on a weeknight is not a high-priority spot, but still, anything could happen, and then where would he go?

He's run from foster homes before, but only when necessary. The act, he knew, called for help, and usually this meant relocation, or addressing "the issues" around his living situation. But now he doesn't want to go. Now he has Greg. And he loves Greg.

Sure, he's gruff now, yet with John's help and understanding, Greg will get through this, and when he does, he will be better. In time, their lives will be solid again. Sex will be mutual.

John swallows. He doesn't think about what happened between them last; instead, he laces his fingers behind his head and says he has to grow up, harden up. Yeah, Greg has problems. We all do. When Greg sees John is steadfast, when he comes to realize John is reliable and patient, he will open up again. Of course he will. He'll share. Talk. Lighten up. Laugh.

And under the sheets of Greg's double bed, Greg will wrap his big hand around John and pull him close. With his hard and heavy muscles, he will nestle against John's backside. Wedged between their two bodies, Greg's manhood will be both the symbol and the reminder of what connects them, man to man. With that thick, warm, and hard connection, they will sleep away every bad thing from their past.

Falling asleep to the idea of Greg behind him, John bolts up. His heart rushes. He's not safe, not here. The urge to move keeps his chest pumping. He can't stay here. But where to move?

Tired, he thinks of how it would be to not sleep on concrete, but on the mat of one of the two wrestling rings he saw with Russ.

He settles back on the hard floor and closes his eyes. He tells himself he's fine here, at least for now. Before he heads off to find a safer place for the night, he'll rest here for a few minutes, only a few.

As he usually does before nodding off to sleep, he wants to think of Greg, but tonight, for the first time, his mind carries him somewhere new. At first, his thoughts of the high school wrestler in the hall float along. They say hello again. John feels the warmth not only in their handshake, but also in their shy stares and sideways glances. Forearms. Fingers. Crotch. Thighs.

And then, just like that, he settles on Russ—those eyes, that voice, that warmth.

While the pool filters hum, John drifts along. Russ's pro school's wrestling rings appear behind his closed eyes and he imagines he's about to fall asleep on one of them.

The lights are very dim and soothing. The faint smells from the men who had wrestled over the soft canvas fill his nose, which is nestled against the heavy pad. All the athletic and even playful energy that had been pounded into that ring vibrates, ever so subtly, back up through him. The hard, powerful bodies that had been thrown, slammed, pressed, and folded on the mat make that ring floor that much softer, more comfortable, and, in some sense, even familiar, as if the canvas itself were his own bed.

He dreams now. Russ settles in behind the new recruit, his upper arm a pillow for John's head.

The muscle pro wears the skimpy wrestling trunks he modeled in that big, glossy promo picture. Instead of boots though, his feet are bare. His heavy leg slides over John's. His free arm folds over John's sculpted, bare chest. With his nose pressed into John's cheek, his whispers are low and heated.

"Strip this wrestling gear off me," John hears Russ say. "I don't want this on with you, buddy."

Both are nude. And there's a sheet over them, thick, heavy, and scented like a forest after a rain storm. Instead of Russ's arm, one deep, long soft pillow brings their heads close, closer.

John dreams on, turning to face Russ. Forehead to forehead now, the heat trapped between them tranquilizes John, who settles his free hand over the small of this great man's back, just above the butt. Russ stirs in response. Protectively, he shifts some of his weight over John, groans, and thrusts once, twice.

The pro's fingers twitch every now and then on John's smooth chest. They remind John that he is not—and will not—be alone.

CHAPTER FIVE

John rolls over on the sofa bed. As he turns, he wakes to the soft morning light spilling into the new bedroom, the one with twin dormer windows. Up from the basement two stories below, hot water pushes through the pipes. This creates the now-familiar clicking sounds that run through the baseboard heaters along the three external walls.

Five months have passed since that night in the pool house. After all that time, it is all right now. It is all good.

Of course, Greg is facing John. Even in his sleep, the working man's arms find and squeeze John so that the high school senior has no option but to nestle his forehead against Greg's warm chest.

Minutes pass. John must have dozed off, and Greg takes advantage of this. His heavy fingers settle in and then down the exact, deep ridge of John's spine. Near-silent moments pass when only their hearts beat, only their bare chests rise and fall, rise and fall. Like two rowboats tethered to a wooden dock, they just barely, barely bump in the wake of calm water.

Taking what he needs now, Greg slides over John. His chin glides over John's face. He nudges John's jaw. Gentle kisses land here, there. A shoulder, a curve in the neck. Guided by heat, Greg's lips send warm probes that continue to explore, survey, and collect data.

The bigger guy lets his three-day razor stubble brush the contours of the young man's rib cage. More kisses connect. More holds draw them closer, closer.

In response, John tops and becomes even more intentional, even hungrier. There is work to do. Rubbing his body over the working man, John heats up Greg until they are both on fire.

And then, as it has been for the last five months, the larger man disappears. He is gone when John more fully wakes.

John has been dreaming. He knows it now. It is only a sturdy couch cushion that he has trapped between the mattress and his hard body.

The sting of Greg not being in bed with him diffuses when John spreads his legs. Not willing to let go, John flops onto his carved stomach. Horny, he traps and cradles one corner of the hard-edged cushion. It becomes Greg's shoulder.

With his eyes closed, John repositions himself more fully over the cushion for a second time. *He is here with me*, John wishfully thinks. *And I will tell him I love him. I will show him I love him.*

He reaches back into his last dream and finds Greg. Over the wad of fresh sheets now under him, he rocks. He rocks away all that happened the night he left the pool house maintenance building and showed up at the trailer. He rocks away all that has happened since the court order mandated him into weekly counseling sessions. He rocks away everything—the new foster parents, the new school, the new required therapist, even this new bedroom that he shares with another foster boy who's not here for the weekend. He rocks it all away.

All—except Greg.

Greg would have done something different, if he could. That night, as he stood outside his trailer, Greg would have shouted, "This is his home!" before the police manhandled John into that patrol car. Days later, he would have stopped that caseworker from enslaving John into new custody. But Greg was hurt—too hurt from what he was forced to do, and that was punish John.

As it's been for months now, John tells himself what has become his truth: that he should have been punished for getting the money the way he did, and keeping it until his birthday.

Punished.

John sees that Greg was right.

He drops his arms behind his head. "I'll take what you give, Greg. I was wrong."

With his eyes closed, he imagines Greg is hurt, yet tender and forgiving. The big man gets into bed with John now. It is Greg's hands, not his own, that slide into the boxer shorts the new foster mom buys for all her good boys. It is Greg who peels down the dark plaid shorts and frees John under the covers; it is Greg who squirms; it is Greg who, with knees spread, needs to be shown what John can do between the blankets.

With a quiet and steady momentum, John resumes rocking, faster, faster. Images of Greg play in his mind as he finds and grinds a soft pillow. Greg, the day they met. Greg, shirtless as he sits in the cab of his truck while thumbing through a hunting magazine in the sun. Greg, in just a pair of jeans as he sleeps on the couch in front of the TV. Greg, the first time he wrestled John. Greg, and his methodical expression when he reaches into the front of John's white briefs after coming home from work at the packing plant.

More images fill John's mind. After a successful shoot from a hand job, he remembers Greg on the steps of his trailer. For Greg to stand there as he did, it had to have been real heartache, disappointment, and sorrow. The love of John's life couldn't move his feet beyond those Busch beer bottles by the door. He couldn't stop the cops from dragging John away.

Greg's next-door neighbor…just who was she, anyway? Calling the cops in the first place? Trailer-trash bitch. She didn't know, she didn't know *anything*. She definitely didn't hear anything. She couldn't have.

John remembers how he had left the pool house after about an hour or so of sleep. When he reached the trailer, he and Greg quietly stood outside in the dark. They were just talking, especially at first. About the seventeen hundred bucks. About John's missing underwear, about the jocks and the wrestling gear.

Just words fell between them. Just words. And Greg was angry, of course, as he should have been by what John had done. And the big guy didn't punch; it was a shove. With John's back slapped up against the trailer's siding, nothing else would have happened. Just a few more punches maybe. But nothing else.

That damn neighbor lady. Those cops. With a real struggle, they forced John away. It took four of them—four big, unknowing police officers—to pack him into the backseat of that patrol car.

And now this. This house. This house in a different school district. A senior year in an entirely different place.

A knock comes on the second-story bedroom door. "John? What was that sound? Was that bed squeaking? I thought I heard something."

"Oh." John swallows, embarrassed. "Nothing."

"Don't roughhouse on that mattress, okay?"

He lies perfectly still. "Oh-kay."

He hates this. Seven more months until his high school graduation, then freedom.

❖

After the final senior class picture is taken on the new high school's stadium bleachers the following June, John's rented cap and gown are returned to the main office. Following a cake reception in the gym, he tells his foster family that he's off to a graduation party they knew about in advance, but this trip he'll be making is one he's been waiting for since the cops came.

He's nervous.

It's a hot June day, hotter than it should be. And the butterflies in his stomach? What's up with those? He double-checks his front pocket for his compass.

Phew. It's there.

He sighs and tells himself that this is Greg and this is right. This is going to work out just fine. He no longer has school. While in school, when not working part-time delivering furniture, he's earned his physical trainer's certification. He cheated on the test because he couldn't read all the answers to the questions, but he did know what he was doing when it came to weight training. Of course he did. Now he can instruct clients in a gym and make some good money that will help with expenses. They can get what Greg had talked about, that one-bedroom apartment closer to the packing plant. This will work. This will really work.

The butterflies grow.

He sees what the future holds for them. There's a new queen-sized bed in a big bedroom. A deep comforter covers it. And Greg sleeps under it every night, beside him. No more pretending a couch cushion or a pillow is Greg's shoulder. No more dreams. In what is pure and perfect need, Greg pulls John even closer to him. He covers him, first with his powerful legs, then his well-worked arms. There are no words, not even whispers. In the quiet, he does not ask. He takes. As he presses into John, he just does what he needs to do—what he has to do.

Driven out by heat, John's butterflies flutter away. He's just two streets away from the trailer park now, then one, then into the park itself.

He rounds the final corner.

John doesn't believe this. Can't believe this. No. Greg's trailer isn't there. It isn't there! A bigger, wider, and newer model replaces what Greg had owned.

John wants to fall to his knees but stands perfectly still. *Oh my God.*

Everything uproots. Everything shatters.

John realizes he's been a fool. A damn fool. Greg's left him. He's moved on. And he didn't call or try to contact him. He didn't leave word for John.

A distant lawn mower fires up, sputters, and dies. A dog barks. Potted flowers—marigolds, maybe—wave as the hot, humid breeze leaves him even more alone.

No, John thinks as he stares ahead. *Please, no.* This is all he has. This is all he's hoped for, held on to. All he wants. This one man. This one life.

Then he sees something familiar. Something he's completely forgotten about, until now. The car beside the new trailer has a bandana hanging over the rearview mirror. It's Greg's bandana. His lucky bandana! It's hanging in Greg's new car!

He moves forward, smiling at how awkward his legs now move. As he comes closer to the mobile home, he shakes his head at what a fool he's just been. Yes, Greg is here!

Greg always keeps the blinds down and drawn, just like they are now. Greg drinks Busch beer and an empty six-pack sits outside the door, right where Greg always keeps his empties. There's a front deck now and a small roof over the door. A tub of sidewalk chalk sits beside the empty beer bottles, and a little light blue plastic lunchbox sits on a small table, but this is Greg's place. Greg's new place.

He doesn't need to knock. There's a doorbell and it's lit. It must work.

John presses the glowing circle and it sounds.

This is going to be all right. This is going to be more than all right, it's going to be great. For sure, Greg's going to be surprised, but he'll be that way only for a moment. Face-to-face, he'll realize he loves John. He'll say that we are right and good together. And he'll hold John, just hold him, and kiss him, deep and long.

There is nothing, however, but the sound of a distant lawn mower being fired up again, once, twice. John's heart beats, but does so just barely.

Seconds pass. He turns to go…but to where? Should he wait here on the deck, or just come another day, or…

The door opens. It's Greg, but it's a different Greg, a slightly older Greg. Yes, of course some time has passed, but there's something John can't figure out.

When they meet, their eyes bring them to that place they both knew during those first fleeting times in bed. Time is lost and it is wondeful. Magic. For one moment, it is completely perfect, then they quickly read each other again and neither understands the mysteries that have happened to the other man since they were last together.

Greg's face changes expressions. It is cooler now, more distant. "You look good."

"You do too."

He actually doesn't. Even more age has found itself in the lines over his face. But John, on the other hand, has filled out even more. His face has narrowed. His jaw is stronger. His hair is different. It's been cut better.

John is wearing a muscle shirt that shows the months in the gym and new, good-fitting jeans that show what God has given him. With a lot of work and good, healthy eating, John has gained fifteen pounds of lean muscle since he first met Greg. He is wearing new white briefs bought just for this moment.

Greg approves. "You're even bigger now. Taller. And you have more muscles. You and that gym."

John thinks of telling him that he's a certified trainer now, but his words are frozen. He just wants to hear from Greg that he's home, that he's home this time for good.

In a futile attempt to reach out, Greg raises his hand from his side, brings it to waist level, drops it. His smile turns vague, unsure.

"You've graduated," he says.

"Yeah. Today."

"Well, congratulations."

"Thanks." An awkward, isolating pause steps between them now. Both change their stances more than once but are not aware of their own empty movements.

There should be more words here, John thinks. *Better words, connecting words.* His heart races. He waits. Hopes. Swallows. Breathes. Only more silence presses up against the palms of his hands. The small of his back tightens.

"I'm sure you did a great job in school."

John raises one of his thick shoulders in a shrug. "Eh...okay, I guess."

More silence follows. It's even meaner now.

Both men look down. For John, it's best to get off the subject of school.

"So, what now?" Greg asks.

"I move on." John swallows. "I move on with you."

Greg's top teeth scrape his lower lip. He shakes his head. "That's not going to happen. That's not what's in the cards here, boy."

John *is* taller. The two are almost eye to eye now when Greg steps out onto the deck. He shuts the door behind him.

"This is it," Greg explains, his eyes set on John's hard stomach. "This is what's happened. My ex-wife is gone. Off across this wide and won-da-ful red, white, and blue f'in' country. A new life, she says, without our kids. And about a week before that happens, my dad up an' dies and, damn shit of all things, he leaves me with enough to get this together—to get this life of mine together. So yeah, my kids are here. Both of 'em."

The toddlers in the pictures in Greg's old bedroom come to John's mind now. Candid shots in piles on the kitchen table—candid shots that always remained in the long, white envelopes postmarked Wheeling, West Virginia, sting John as he drops his head.

Greg takes a step to one side. "I don't have a place for you. This is not your home."

John cannot look up. Nothing would have enough power in it to enable John to raise his eyes.

Greg's words are not well-spoken, but articulate isn't who Greg is. His voice scratches like a bird call when he says, "This is for me now, me and the kids. What is for the best. I even work days now, finally. While they're in school. And the little bitch an' bastard are great." Greg considers this. It's as if he tastes something he's not sure he likes. "Well, we are workin' this through."

John stares at one of the planks that make the deck. The grain is like a relief map. He falls through, or wants to fall through, the cracks and be crushed now, quickly and completely.

This isn't right. This isn't supposed to be happening. No. Just no.

Panic rushes in and around John. This can't be.

Greg speaks. "You were a...how do I...what this was, between us? It wasn't right. Wasn't no good. What I did, what I made you do—that wasn't what shoulda happened." Knowing what John is thinking, his voice picks up an edge. "And it wasn't mutual, John. No way."

John moves his eyes to the tub of sidewalk chalk. He trembles.

"I don't love you, John. I never have."

These words create an incision that does not bleed. Arteries implode. Still, no blood spills. Nothing moves, nothing happens.

Silence comes again, but this time it squeezes him from inside. Hard. Mean. Cruel.

Then, in his mind, John hears the words again. *I don't love you, John. I never have.*

Greg turns. He holds the doorknob. "You go now, boy. You go and make your life good."

John quivers. *This is not happening. This isn't real, or right.*

Greg turns the knob.

In his own head, John screams. No sound comes, however; no energy moves in his direction. Then, when the shudders start, he lets go. He cries. He sobs. Greg catches him, but only physically. John breaks away and runs off, his knees soft as gelatin. He runs without seeing anything in front of him. He runs for minutes or miles, he is not sure. There is nothing but the run, the pace.

He wants to stop. But where, and how? How can he stop? Where can he go? Eventually, he trips over a flagpole and rips open his shin on a ceramic frog that shattered in the fall. His heart breaks out of his chest and flops out onto the sidewalk. It keeps beating and beating. The damn thing won't stop. Red and pounding and pounding and pounding, it won't let him die.

He hides his face in his hands and sobs.

A family of four crosses to the other side of the street, and they don't speak as they pass him. Just two doors down, a woman admires her new impatiens as she waters them with a garden hose. A man and his daughter pull, tug, and curse at an end table as it inches out of the trunk of her little car. Two high school seniors, who also graduated that day, drive by quickly on their way to a party at a nearby lake. They sing loudly to an angry CD and soak up all of John's sound.

CHAPTER SIX

Although his foster family offers him the summer rent-free, John sets out on his own three weeks after his graduation. His chiseled body, boyish charm, and good, clean-cut intentions are the reasons one very wise manager places him in charge of developing and maintaining memberships at a new, upscale gym. John also works there as a personal trainer during his off hours. By the end of July, eight clients fatten what has been his thin wallet.

Careful with money, he rents a dirt-cheap room in a run-down three-bedroom apartment with two others. He paints the old gray walls of his new space with a cool blue the day after he moves in, and a pockmarked desk he found roadside still waits for a chair, but it looks good in one corner of his room. While the wall against his bed literally bakes to eighty-four degrees in the afternoon sun, he has his own compact bathroom, complete with a window by the sink. He lies and says "This is perfect" so often that on some levels it's true.

The money starts. Six hundred dollars saved, seven, eight hundred. He keeps his graduation goal in mind, and by mid-October, he revisits the building he's intentionally avoided since first meeting Russ, the professional wrestler who opened the locked lobby door for him fourteen months earlier.

The day he reaches his financial goal, he ignores the sun-bleached toys the little cape houses can no longer hold for lack of room. Not thinking of his own childhood or the uncle from California whose picture he lost some ten years ago, he passes a skateboard, a plastic lawn mower, and a toddler-sized stove on his way to the school.

Held by a thirty-pound weight, the lobby door stands open this time. It's a good omen, he thinks. His tuition, in cash, feels heavy in his front pocket.

"Russ," he calls out near the open door of an empty office. "Russ?"

He turns, refusing to be disappointed. This will work. This *will* work. He will be happy, "found," and cared for, maybe. He pushes his hope deep down—he may even be loved.

Russ isn't there. An older guy named Mike accepts John's four-page application, which he fills out under Russ's promo picture. Mike says that the next class starts in twelve weeks.

Twelve weeks? John's disappointed, but says he understands.

"He'll also need to approve this," Mike says when he holds John's application. "And he'll need to meet with you first. Russ knows what he wants."

"We—we met before, a while back."

Mike doesn't seem to register this, or care. He stares blankly at the white pages in his hand.

"You're nineteen?"

"Yeah."

"Big for nineteen." He's not looking at the application anymore, though his eyes don't rise. "And the tuition? You got that?"

John ignores the sinking feeling in his chest and nods. "Yeah."

"Then you're set, kid. Wait for his call."

❖

Week after week, the fresh memories of that promo picture stay with John. At first they mix with, and then take over, his dreams. Sleeping, John finds Russ under and then over him. Chest to chest, face-to-face, they are so close. Kisses connect them—wild, free, hungry kisses. They taste of where each had been that day: the gym, the ring, the library, the park where one or both went running. Soul to soul, their touches soak through their skin to say, "I love you."

The dreams stir him so his thoughts blur during his waking hours. Daydreams take off. Sneaking in here and there, they are simple, everyday occurrences. When standing in the produce aisle at the grocery store, John drifts off and wonders what they would cook that night for dinner, if Russ were there. Or, tired from a day of lifting weights and helping others lift weights, he catches himself thinking about what Russ wears—or doesn't wear—to bed as he slips under the covers. As he turns down his light, his head spins. His hopes grow. *If Russ was really that kind when we first met, what will he be like when we know each other better?*

A very long forty-two days pass before the phone rings.

"It's Russ," a voice says one night a moment after John steps out of the shower. "Russ Gree, from the Gree School of Wrestling."

John shivers though beads of hot water pool over his very wide, freckled shoulders. Nerves shoot up his throat. "H-hey."

"Mike here says we've met. I don't remember this. Then again, I don't remember last Tuesday all that well, either, 'cept I was in a match in Calgary."

John starts to explain how they met, but is quickly interrupted.

"Hey, yeah, a young guy…blond hair. A real talker. I gotcha now."

They set a time for meeting at the school the following week. As they are about to hang up, John offers something out of context when he says that he didn't have the money the first time around. That's why he didn't go through with it.

Russ laughs.

John pauses. He doesn't know what to say.

Russ laughs again. "No worries, man. We'll have to see if we can get you in with this next class. It's already full now, so we'll have to see."

❖

This is an audition, a tryout. That's why he's here. Why he's standing in the middle of one of the two school rings. Russ was perfectly frank when he called two days ago and said he has one too many wrestlers interested in his school this time. One will have to be let go—with the stipulation that he can always try out again in the future. The up-front tuition, of course, would be reimbursed.

John doesn't want the future. Nor does he want his money back. He wants this now.

He was called into the ring a minute ago. The rope he used to pull himself up is soft, plush.

Russ, his opponent, squares off in the ring. He grabs his T-shirt from the neck but does not take it off.

The moment everything changes is now. John pauses.

"Aww," says one of the guys around the ring. "The pretty boy's shy."

"Not shy, you nimrod," another wrestler counters as he picks up his water bottle from a nearby chair and gets himself ready for the action. "He's intentional. Deliberate."

"Yeah, dramatic effect," adds a third.

Standing in front of John, Russ considers this. "Yeah, that will actually work."

The first voice bites through the air again. "Strip, pretty. Nice and slow."

Cold, John forces his nerves down to the place inside that is broken and painful. He sets the muscles in his jaw and ignores that he hears Greg in his mind the night he was forced to wear the birthday present from Louise Amsterdam. Leaving his jeans and running shoes on, he peels off his tee. He does this slowly, methodically, rolling the thin cotton in one of his hands when finished.

Russ thinks out loud. "Yeah. The slow strip. Methodical. That's a good attention grabber. Like he's here for business, to get the job done."

Mike says, "He can also be the do-gooder. The clean-cut kid. He *is* pretty. We can always go with that."

Russ nods. The young man before him is just too good to be true.

Mike comes across as the perfect high school gym coach: older, barrel-chested, gray at the temple, and completely no-nonsense. "Put him in something skimpy."

Thinking again of the red underwear, John neither moves nor speaks.

To fill the sudden silence, Russ tries to explain. "This is just marketing stuff, kid. How to promote you. That's what Mike is talking about."

John knew about the marketing. He had to have an image. Project a persona. Whether close to his personality or not, he had to be in character.

Stepping through the ropes, Mike slips between John and Russ. "Rarely do we pit good guy against good guy. It's usually jobber against heel."

John doesn't know what a jobber or a heel is. He doesn't ask, either. Instead, he sees a lit exit sign in a far corner. A part of him wants to run.

But I have nowhere to go.

"Jobber against heel," Russ repeats, sensing John doesn't know the word. "A jobber is the clean-cut guy. The rule follower. He's the good guy, the one who gets his ass handed to him by the guy known as the heel. The heel is usually bigger, older, and meaner."

Mike explains this further. "It's classic good guy versus bad guy.

The greater the tension between the two, the greater the story." He walks around John and stops at John's backside. "Yeah," the older man laughs. "I'm checking out your cans."

Russ smiles. "We get pretty chummy here."

"Big, happy family," Mike adds. He joins Russ to stand in front of John. "Trunks, Russ. Definitely. And tight."

John knows a part of Greg is here, somehow.

Russ misunderstands John's lack of reaction. Some guys are just plain shy, especially at first, but that has to change.

Shrugging his shoulder, Russ explains. "Skimpy or sexy is what we do, or really should do here, with you. It will draw your fan base quickly, and, if you want to make it here, you'll need that."

John swallows but nothing happens. Nothing changes.

"Are you okay with that?" Russ asks, aware John is becoming harder and harder to reach. "John, buddy? Are you sure? Do you want this?"

John's face is granite. "Yeah." No more reaction follows.

"Yak, yak," one of the more experienced wrestlers calls out as he stands outside the ring. "Go on about the slingshot you'll squeeze him into later, let's see you wrestle him, Russ."

Another wrestler pipes in. "Yeah, quit talkin' and check out Goldielocks's action."

John squares off. He will fight the love he lost and, in the process, won't care if he hurts himself. Russ and the first row of wrestlers around the ring realize this, but none will speak on this later.

The air actually changes. Mike hops out of the ring. Face-to-face, Russ and John move in closer. They stare at each other. It is not a game. It's neither for show, nor is it casual.

Russ shakes his head. "This isn't going to hurt. This isn't about how much punishment you can dish out or take. That's not it at all, buddy. This is just to see how you move."

Not hearing a word Russ has just said, John nods.

"So then, you're ready?" Russ asks.

John nods again. Russ slips off his collared shirt. He stands in black nylon athletic pants.

Another pause follows. Neither moves. Then they start, fast and strong.

The younger wrestler backs Russ into a turnbuckle. Their hard, smooth bellies touch and rub. They lock up, shoulder to shoulder, and suddenly it is John's back meeting the corner of the ring.

"Act this out, John, or actually, *react*," Russ says in a low voice close and warm against his ear.

For John, who's so focused, it's just the two of them there. No one else is around. He arches his back as if wounded, exposing his vulnerable pecs to Russ's face.

"That's it," the experienced wrestler says. "Now a headlock and I just roll you over my shoulder to the mat. Okay?"

John nods, and is down on the mat. His jeans slide and scrunch between his legs. He wants to take them off.

Russ stands. His athletic pants were also twisted in the action. He makes a face, one of annoyance, drives his hands down into his front and matter-of-factly repositions himself.

John glances away, maybe too quickly, but he cannot look. Not there, not now. Definitely not now. He swallows dry air. Damn, for a bottle of water.

John's fingers tingle. Is this happening? Really happening? Nerves flicker along the inside of his legs. He wants this. He wants this so badly.

Coming at John, Russ slips on a shoulder clamp that immobilizes most of the younger wrestler's upper body. God, Russ smells so good. His scent is like soap from one of those really nice, upscale men's restrooms.

No sooner does Russ say, "Try to get out," than John muscles out and clamps down on Russ. He folds Russ in half, introducing the pro's face to the mat.

"Guess he got out!" Mike laughs.

John scrambles. He traps Russ's lower back between his thick thighs. His jeans slide down an inch, hinting at the white underneath. The button over his fly digs into Russ's skin.

Russ extends his arm. Catching the middle of John's hamstring, he rolls John to his back. John sees skylights. He smiles as he wiggles his way back to his feet.

Minutes pass. At one point, John, without thinking of the guys around him, steps out of his jeans. He stands still in a white swimmer's Speedo he dared himself to buy for this day. But he did it. He did it. *Just wrestling gear*, he told himself when he pulled his wallet out to pay for it. *Just wrestling gear*. It's not anything like what Louise Amsterdam bought for him.

Russ drives his hand between John's thighs, cups the newcomer's package and, with a great show of power, brings the teen down.

"The young muscle boy in white, our stripper here, why, once he warms up he ain't shy," one of the guys says.

Another replies, "Neither is Russ."

With this response, Russ stops. His eyes narrow and freeze. The expression on his face reads, *"This didn't happen."*

Russ slowly moves his hand out between John's thick thighs.

Silence follows. It is weighted and still.

A voice speaks out from the awkward quiet. "Looks like we have ourselves a new classmate."

Later, both John and Russ will carry each other's touches and wrestling holds far into the night, and what they feel and remember will be well and good.

This is not known to either of them now.

On the mat, John doesn't move. He cannot move. Stunned, he feels the heat where Russ's grip had just been, even though his future teacher no longer has his heavy hand between John's legs.

Chapter Seven

John seems odd to the gym members in that he's a stone-cold fox not hung up on himself. He is polite yet shy when spoken to, and he should be this Great Catch, somebody's best bud, or both.

But he's alone.

Both men and women can sense the loneliness in him, read it in his eyes. While many have tried to befriend him, he is unreachable. He keeps that distance.

Since his wrestling tryout five days ago, which no one knows about, he's even more distant.

And distracted.

John's two roommates secretly call him Bor, some fictitious eighteenth-century Nordic warrior. Eating fish at least five times a week, grunting at the sink when it's his turn to "do the domestic" and wash his own dishes, they are convinced he's all muscle on the outside, all boring on the inside.

John, who's doing his damnedest not to think of Russ for the tenth time this hour, heads to the tap to fill the water filtration pitcher.

"You grunt," one of his roommates says while sealing apple slices in a plastic bag for lunch.

"What?"

"When you have to fill the water pitcher, every time, before you head to the kitchen sink you, well, grunt."

Russ grunted once when John topped him. It was when he was in jeans, and Russ, trapped between John's legs, let out this deep, unguarded sound.

"John, did you hear me? The grunt thing?"

John nods. Worn out from his workout and his run, he keeps seeing Russ's face and can almost feel Russ's body under him. There's tension and more tangling.

And it's perfect.

With the water pouring out full blast and now spilling over the clear plastic pitcher, he can't hear that well, but his roommate shoots off something snide before leaving the apartment through the back door.

Shutting off the tap, John stares in front of him. Out the kitchen window, there's nothing but battleship gray siding everywhere from the house right next door. He stands completely still. His heart stops. His thinking stops. Not even a breeze sways the now nearly black clothesline off the rear porch of the third-floor apartment above.

Nothing moves within or around him until he realizes how numb he is, and how alone.

How desperately alone.

❖

When he overhears one of his other roommates talking to a friend on the phone that morning, John knows what both roommates think of him. From an enormous wad of used aluminum foil from a party they both held in the apartment about two weeks ago, someone made a silver helmet that wound up in the chair closest to his bedroom door. Two bull-like horns adorn it. John knows adorn means decorate, but didn't know then that the helmet was intended for him.

"Yeah, we're looking for bearskin now," the roommate says into the phone. "Oh, right, not too much. We still wanna see all that muscle dumb boy has."

Dumb boy.

"What? No, we each have our own bathrooms. So, yeah, Bor wet in a towel? Not so much, but there is good news. We now know something just smarter than a towel."

John steps into his bedroom. He doesn't bother closing his door loud enough for his roommate to hear.

It just doesn't matter.

When he lets the door quietly click shut, he sets his forehead against the door jamb.

It just doesn't matter.

He doesn't matter.

❖

On his way home from the gym that night, he keeps his head low, intent not to see anyone, especially that hand-holding couple just a dozen or so steps in front of him. It's Friday night around nine, and the sight of a happy couple is something he can't face.

As he rounds a corner onto the busiest street he takes on his walk to the apartment, a gust of wind ripples his shirt. Usually crowded, this part of the sidewalk is his alone tonight. He takes advantage of this.

"Dumb boy," he mutters, keeping his eyes low.

Someone passes quickly from behind. The scent he's wearing reminds him of Russ. Is it? He quickly looks up. Russ?

It's a fifty-something year old man with thinning hair.

John sinks his hands into his pockets. The scent lingers, teases, pulls. *Russ. Wrestling. Stripping my jeans like that? And that white Speedo? None of this shoulda happened*, he thinks. *I should be with the man I love, or want to love, not messed up with these games.*

He scuffs an edge of the sidewalk. To the thick dark sky he raises his head and looks for something he can't see.

The wind that still plays with his shirt won't settle around him. It reminds him of what it's like to be touched, teased.

But he ignores this.

Tonight will be another early night.

He realizes the street will be quieter once he turns off the main avenue—and that is what he wants: more solace, deeper silence. His heart wobbles now. Thinking of the sidewalk chalk and the words exchanged on the redwood deck by the door to Greg's new trailer, he needs a place to hide.

And Russ isn't that place.

Sudden laughter spills behind him. Arm in arm, a mid-twenty-something couple comes up on his left side. After they pass, the woman giggles as the man she's with mumbles something that John can almost hear. She whispers and laughs again. This time it's a shrill bite.

They'd been drinking, and the heels of their dress shoes slap on the street after they step off the sidewalk.

Ahead of John by some twenty feet now, the guy turns around, pivoting his girlfriend with him. With dark blond hair and green eyes, he's handsome, expensive, and pampered. "Yeah, buddy," he says to John, "all serious now, okay? You do have a *nice* ass."

John, caught in his stare, looks down as they turn and continue toward their car parked on the street.

John comes up beside them a minute or so later when a line of oncoming traffic prohibits him from crossing the street. The guy fumbles with his keys before he unlocks the passenger door for his girlfriend, yet watches John.

"Hey buddy, hey," he says in an entirely different, sober tone. "I didn't mean any trouble back there."

The young woman who stops playing with her hair long enough to reach for her seat belt snaps, "Don't mess with him!"

Alone now with John, the guy shares a look that is perfectly clear: he is not drunk and would rather be with him than his date.

How 'bout it? the hungry guy's eyes ask. *You wanna?*

John backs away, but the look he receives from the stranger is even clearer, even stronger. Sounding dirty, he says, "Nice ass," again as he taps the roof of a car John couldn't afford to make even a single payment on.

John slips away, twisting like a fish escaping a net. At home some ten minutes later, he takes the hottest shower he can stand and changes for bed, wearing just oversized athletic pants picked up at a bargain basement and a long-sleeved T-shirt he bought at the same Salvation Army store he'd stolen from.

Under the covers, John builds another wall, one that is thicker than the ones before. It is more insulated, isolating. He knows the white Speedo he wore when wrestling Russ is in his closet just three feet away, but it means nothing. It's just gear. What happened with Russ in the ring means nothing either. It was just a move, just a place where Russ's hand went for a moment.

He swallows what feels like an icy stone. A tombstone. He holds his breath and wills a part of himself to die.

It doesn't work.

Alone in the dark, he feels nothing and sees nothing until the guy leaning over the roof of his car comes back in his memory. John is in the ring. Russ is tangled under him. The guy standing over his car, now ringside, just watches dumb boy in that white Speedo.

Whore. You are Louise Amsterdam's whore.

John rolls onto his pillow, punches it, and says, "No."

❖

Another day passes. Another week inches along. John wakes with a tight knot in his chest every morning and scrambles out of bed to pace the tension away. When he showers with cool or cold water in the stall of his little bathroom, he is numb. Russ isn't there to lather his back, or kiss him.

Then something happens at one of the least likely times, in one of the least likely situations. Just after lunch on his busiest day, Tuesday, he meets a client named Barbara. John appreciates the five-foot-two-inch twice-divorced unpretentiously gray-haired woman because he learns more about nutrition from her than she learns about resistance training from him.

Barbara shared with her friends that John completely focuses on her during her workout time, but this isn't quite accurate, especially today. Right at the start of her scheduled time with John, one p.m., Barbara starts her routine. While helping her trainer maneuver weights off the bench press, she accidentally elbows John's privates. It's not a major bump; it's nothing she really notices and clearly has no need to mention or apologize for, but still, minutes later, as John stands behind the bench press and keeps her increased weight safe as she lifts, he becomes both stirred and restless. He remembers. He goes back to the ring, back to the place and time when that handsome man with the dark eyes had his hand between his legs.

What happened in the ring felt right, even natural, like it had to happen. It was the only course, the only logical ending.

John starts to daydream. It's the first he's had in days, but he dismisses it. Minutes later, however, it comes again. To have Russ there, holding him, wrapping up with him, arm over arm, leg over heavy, muscled leg…it's right. The struggle for power. The show of strength. The need for control over his opponent becomes totally hyped-up play—not out of anger or in violence; no, that is not it, not all it.

If anything, it's the opposite—a give and take that is fun. As the weights click with Barbara, John smirks behind his client's back because, in his mind, boyhood antics find a way to be free with the two of them.

And they laugh.

Together, they just laugh.

❖

Three more days go by and John finds himself standing outside the wrestling school. He doesn't quite know how he got there, or what will happen next, but nevertheless, he's there, staring at the glass double doors. No one enters or leaves. While a few cars pass along the street, it is quiet.

Another three days come and go and he still paces on the sidewalk in front of the school for a few minutes. Just over four weeks remain before the new class starts. He still hasn't heard if he's in this upcoming class or not, but he has not called to find out. Connecting by phone is tricky for him because he only wants good news.

He knows he's not making sense. He also knows he isn't the same since he wrestled with Russ.

Almost silently, a vehicle parks across the street. A car door opens and shuts. John doesn't turn, but thinks he should move on. After all, he is just standing there. But where to go? Which direction?

A scratchy voice comes from the middle of the street. "Hey, Blondie. You were locked up with Russ a while back. Sorry I wasn't there to watch, champ. But I heard about it."

John repels from the stranger's voice because the sound of it makes him feel slippery, eerie. He rolls his shoulders forward and locks them, as if preparing to be hit by a wave.

"I'm Dax," the dark chocolate man says with a good bit of attitude. Dax is just as tall as and seemingly half the weight of an on-the-road work truck. With too much muscle, his rich, shining skin reflects some of the afternoon light. He offers John his baseball mitt–sized hand as if the little wrestler boy should be honored to shake it.

The connection between them is skewed, but Dax pays no mind to it. He knows instantly what he wants, and that is John. That John is nearly incapable of moving makes his target all the easier.

Yes, Dax thinks as he repositions the new, clear bifocals he has to wear. *Yes. This is easy.* He will scoop up this lost one and eat him like a lemon meringue dessert, perhaps night after night.

Dax smiles. *Oh, yes. Easy.*

Tucking one of the short dreadlocks framing his narrow face, he says in a voice that seems too soft for his size, "So, the new pro class starts up in what, about two weeks from now, right?"

John doesn't know what to do, or how to answer. He's cornered. The class starts in twice that amount of time, but he lies. "Ye-yeah, it will. It does."

Dax chuckles condescendingly. "'It will? It does?' Can you be a little more sure of yourself?"

John doesn't know how to respond.

The man eyes the trophy in front of him and asks again, "Well, can you be more sure of yourself, bud?"

John remains quiet. He does not like this guy.

At six foot six, it seems that most of Dax's height is located in his chest, which is enormous. Over his rib cage, two curved muscled shields protect an already steel heart. "Come on, then," Dax says with a disappointed sigh. "Let's get inside."

John keeps his feet still.

Dax takes a few steps and calls over his shoulder, "Oh, you're in, by the way. Saw the roster yesterday. Your letter is in the mail today. You're in Russ's next class."

John doesn't respond, at least not in the celebratory way Dax anticipated.

"You'll wrestle me," Dax announces as he holds the door open for his catch. "If I let you, that is."

John's flat voice hides nothing. "Great."

They enter the building. Once inside, Dax puts his fingers in the middle of John's back. Just as this happens, greens turn to gray for John. Blues dull to a murky brown. That this new stranger is here and crowding him is wrong, totally wrong, but somehow it's too late.

They pass Russ's office without John realizing it. Dax says, "He's on the phone, with the missus."

John keeps moving as if he heard nothing.

Dax knows exactly what he's doing. "Yeah, it's Russ. He's talking with his wife."

John does not want to absorb what he's just heard. He tries to flick this away, to not let it settle, but it's too late.

His wife?

The downward spiral doesn't start fast at first, but gains momentum.

He still moves, right down the hall, but a part of him lingers right outside Russ's door. He lowers his face. There is a knife somewhere inside him. He cannot find the sharp, cutting blade, though he closes his eyes and tries.

Dax pokes him in the arm. "And she's a hot one too." He raises his hands to his chest as if holding volleyballs. "An effin' rack out to here."

Russ, married? Russ, who met me that first time with his black shirt and wet hair? Who smiled at me on the sidewalk? And joked?

Russ, the man I've been avoiding in my own head only to realize I want to know him more? Married?

Dax and John pass through the gym.

"So, we gonna wrestle?" Dax asks as they pass one of the rings.

John gives a look so icy that Dax takes a step back. "Yeah. Let's."

Wrestling trunks are on hand. An assortment of brand-new or laundered ones is in one of two boxes on a folding table in a hallway. Dax hunts for just the right look for his new wrestle buddy.

The trunks he finds are suggestive like the white Speedo John wore when he first wrestled Russ, only these have metallic stripes over the hip.

"Wear these," Dax says.

"But—" John starts to say.

"Yeah." Dax laughs deep and low. "That's exactly what I plan to see. Your butt."

John feels even more lost, more vulnerable. In holding something he'd never like to wear, another part of him dies and, worse, another stone in his wall is set.

Numb from thinking about Russ being married, he does this. He just steps into the ring with a man he met today.

John can smell how much Dax wants him, and Dax, true to form and reputation from his years in the Mid-Atlantic circuit, is the most sexual anyone will be in the ring with John for at least the next six months.

Busy or somehow blind, no one nearby seems to notice the holds Dax stretches John into are either foreplay or sexual in application, including John. In fact, the only clear moment the man with the broken heart remembers out of the next hour and a half is when another wrestler asks Russ about his plans for the night.

"After this?" Russ says, scratching his chest, "Evette and I have company. Her folks are in from out of town. The son-in-law thing is up for me. Dinner plans."

Russ, whose eyes are thick and unreadable, stands in front of John.

Keeping his face down, John thinks, *So, her name is Evette.*

"Hey, John," he says, "you should meet her. I've told her about you."

John can't speak.

Dax moves in. "Hey, John, let's grab something to eat. Just the two of us."

❖

They always go at it in Dax's apartment.

Well, Dax goes at it.

In a plush, king-sized bed with sheets and coordinating bedding that costs what Greg would get for his old trailer if he could sell it, John sleeps with a man he does not want to know. Their time together is empty, which is exactly what Dax wants.

Through all of this, John withdraws even further. John doesn't know that his skin—like his soul—is hard and cool like plastic. Dax doesn't notice this at first and wouldn't want to notice this, either. No, John just has to keep giving up himself for a hard man pounding, which is what Dax is all about.

John rarely says a word, and the larger, older man is fine with a quiet guy who does not ask for or initiate anything—even conversation. To Dax this arrangement is perfect. Even the hold he has on John tightens when they sleep together, but John isn't there.

What does it matter, though?

At first, John is not sure how the 240-pound Adonis reminds him of Greg, but it becomes clear when Dax no longer asks John out for dinner. No, when it comes to food, the big, grazing bull is used to feeding on whomever he wants, whenever he wants.

Dax will move on. John can sense it, so he clams up even more, hoping for a faster release. And the release should come before John starts wrestling school in two weeks. While neither talks of it, both know that Dax is traveling to Japan to wrestle for at least six months. His flight leaves in five days. Freedom will again be John's.

Paradoxically, the thought of this freedom also troubles John. He should want freedom, but knows he'll be lost again. There are times when Dax wraps John up in such incredible and imaginative holds that require great strength. Especially at these times, John closes his eyes and pretends he is with Russ because if he didn't have Dax, he wouldn't have anyone.

❖

On Thursday, ten minutes before their second to last date, Dax calls to cancel, saying he really needs to pack.

Alone in his own bedroom, the Bor paces.

He knows of a gay bar and knows he should go. But he has to talk himself into this night on the town alone. More pacing is required.

Fifteen minutes later, with an armful of shirts, he stands bare-chested in front of his bathroom mirror. He holds up two of them, sets them down on the sink, and comes back to his bed, where he sits with his knees spread.

He drops his back down on the mattress, and rather than stare at the ceiling, he closes his eyes and rests his fingers in the center crease of his abdominal muscles. His eyes suddenly open. He can't do any of this. It's too much, too difficult, too new. A gay bar? Man, he's never been! And to go alone?

In an oversized sweatshirt and jeans he does go—out for a walk, at least. He takes his compass with him. It rests in his front pocket.

At an intersection where he can go left toward downtown and the bar, he takes a sharp right and, minutes later, meanders through a lower-middle-class neighborhood. He doesn't fantasize, he doesn't hope, he doesn't even think.

No one stops or sees him. In looking down as often as he now does, he hides the thought that loneliness can not only hold him down, but also make him invisible.

CHAPTER EIGHT

One drives across the country from California. Another drops down from Ottawa, Canada. There are eight total. Before today, it never occurs to John anyone would travel great distances just for this school. It also never occurs to him that they'd all be funny. From oldest to youngest, they range from a thirty-seven-year-old father of three to a diesel mechanic three years older than John. Besides being the most junior in the ragtag group, John is the only one with a muscular build. The rest, at the end of the first day, decide to appropriately call themselves the Tubs—totally ugly blubber slobs.

The Tubs love John and, within days, become the big brothers he never had. And, together, they are the most dysfunctional family a thirty-minute TV series could ever imagine. Jokes of how messed up their lives are come from a script they write themselves. At various times of the day, each wonders, now that they are pro wrestlers in training, when will they get the girls?

John loves this, having never had a real group of friends before. Unquestionably, they are all straight including Peter, the one with the shaved head, who believed, without doubt, that the preservatives in processed foods could—if he ate enough of them—keep him alive indefinitely.

They all assumed Johnny was straight too, and no one would find out, either. Since Russ's wrestling school demands both physical and mental conditioning beyond what any of them had experienced, Peter, who only ate brand-name junk food wrapped in cellophane, dropped out in the middle of the second week.

After Peter left, Lyle Lowell, the largest of the Tubs, counts all that remain, including John. "Great, now we're the Seven Dwarfs."

"Dwarfs, Lyle? Ah," one beside John asks, "ain't we a little *big* for that? I mean, even Chippendale here isn't small."

Lyle holds on to his vision. "Nope. Dwarfs."

While it is early and Lyle is mostly tone deaf, he sings to the non-responsive group. "Heigh-ho, heigh-ho, it's off to work we…" Not knowing the rest of the lyrics, he's about to start again.

This boot camp roll call is part of Lyle's shtick. Each morning, Lyle keeps up this silliness in the hopes of lifting everyone's spirits because, at this point, all seven are significantly bruised. One has three sutures near his right eye from a runaway kick. Another holds a bandaged elbow. The Tub beside John sticks his foot in a bucket of ice.

Russ, who'd been standing behind Lyle during all of this, shakes his head. As their teacher, he's been with them since the start. In the nine days they've been together, he's demonstrated and practiced moves on all of them, with John being the one exception. John's become even cooler now, even more distant. When Russ and John's eyes do barely meet, there is little to suggest what once happened.

The space and place where men can love each other—even platonically—is never easy to find, and even harder to hold. Lyle knows and challenges this. Not willing to have his lame joke fall flat, the biggest Tub resumes his discourse on the Seven Dwarfs. "You know," he says, as they each begin to stretch for the day, "if anything, those seven lived a cloistered, monastic lifestyle."

"Mon ass what?" asks a Tub known for his particular trumpet sounds after lunch.

"I don't like oysters," adds another.

"If we run with this," ponders the Tub with the injured elbow, "I mean, this whole dwarf thing? Then I'm Hunky."

"No," the first Tub counters. "John is handsome. He's Hunky. You're Chunky."

"Callin' me fat?"

"Guys, okay," Russ says, shaking his head. "Let's start the day with a new move."

They gather around their coach to begin a serious day of training. In the center of the ring, the Tub with the elbow injury asks from the complete silence, "Am I fat?"

Russ claps his hands once. "This move is important, so listen up. I'm going to teach you something called the Victory Roll."

"A roll? *Man*, dang! I *am* fat."

"A Victory Roll."

The Tub shakes his stomach. "There's no honor in this, Russ."

"*Victory* roll," Russ repeats, a little annoyed by the obvious lack of focus. He calls one of the Tubs forward and talks through what he's going to do. "This is another way to go for a pin. I'm going to jump onto my opponent's shoulders from behind. With that momentum, I'm going to roll forward. As I flip over, I'll hook my opponent's shoulders with my legs. That brings my opponent over onto his shoulders."

"Like a flying tackle," Lyle says.

"Yeah," Russ replies, "in a way, but from behind."

"And this leads to a pin?" Lyle asks.

Russ continues. "The attacker—in this case, me—then grabs both of my opponent's legs. That holds the opponent in place for the pin. So yeah, Lyle, this is a finishing move."

From a point some two minutes earlier, the Tub with the injured elbow says to no one in particular, "You know, the Dwarfs were gay, living like that."

Lyle, by far the least homophobic guy in the room, works to build a joke. He frowns. "And *how* do you know this?"

Both Russ and John steel their expressions to become vacant.

"Well," the injured wrestler says, "did any of those guys *even want* to bop that Snow White chick?"

Lyle struggles to get in a quip, but comes up with nothing.

"Fags," a wrestler behind John mumbles.

Lyle turns. He wants to say something, but it's Russ who steps in and moves their morning along by clapping his hands again and explaining the victory roll again.

Jumping onto the shoulders of the opponent is something Russ worries about with guys this size, but, using the middle or top turnbuckle, they all give it a try. They fan out into the corners of the two rings and practice, one pair at a time.

Lyle is partnered with John—since John moved to stand next to the biggest guy in the class.

Russ checks this. "John, you're sure? He's going to be jumping onto your shoulders."

"Yeah, I'm sure."

"No hero stuff," Russ says, frowning. "I'm a bit lighter, Lyle. Let me do it to John first."

Russ climbs to the top rope and hops onto John's shoulders. John wavers for a minute, stabilizing Russ's weight with his thick thighs flexed and bulging.

"No, John, no," Russ calls out. "Give into this. Don't catch me, roll forward with the momentum."

John yields, as directed. As both men start to go down, Russ uses his legs to hook John's shoulders. On the mat, Russ grabs John's legs, ensuring the pin.

Russ lets John get to his feet. When the blond stands, Russ uses a voice with an edge when he says, "Don't hurt yourself, John. You catch and hold Lyle like that on your shoulders and you could blow out a knee or pop your back. That's not safe. Got it?"

John responds by getting into position again. Impenetrable pieces of ice, his blue eyes do not wander from his teacher.

Russ is not willing to let this go. He asks again. "Got it?"

No response follows.

"Do you have it?" Russ asks again.

John has never been colder. "I got it."

❖

They learn a lot. If they plan to kick their opponent when they're in the corner of the ring, for example, Russ tells the charger that the receiver's hand takes the blow, not the head. Likewise, when a wrestler is being slammed to the canvas, he actually launches *himself* toward his opponent. He lands squarely on his back only after his head is safely tucked in, avoiding injury.

Punches are practiced again and again. The punch itself, if real, could easily break teeth or someone's jaw, but the class is taught to "hit" very, *very* lightly, and the contact is done with an open fist.

"When you receive a punch," Russ tells them again and again, "you have to sell that punch, just like you do any other move I teach you. You have to make it believable. The more you do so, the more you act hurt, the better you will be."

After lunch one afternoon, Russ offers another example of how this wrestling isn't real. The coach pulls the Tub with the sore foot out to practice what's known as the eye rake. "This is where the opponent looks like he's getting his eye socket drug along the top rope, but he isn't. His fingers are protecting his face."

Even though they've been at this for nearly two weeks now, the class still shakes their heads at some of this. Russ's words, however, echo again and again. "Practice, practice, practice."

❖

The Tubs grow closer. In literally being shoulder to shoulder throughout the day, they get to know—and trust—each other. Bonds build because, unlike their blond boy prince, these regular men with wonderful hearts are seen by too many as too weird looking, too ugly and too heavy. They survive Russ's school because each knows physical pain is nothing like emotional pain. Each wrestler could write a chapter on how physical pain will heal. Emotional pain, on the other hand, never quite mends.

Only Lyle senses that John's emotional pain is greater than any of theirs.

"Oh, Johnny? He's a daredevil," Russ admits to Lyle one night when just the two of them settle into his office.

Lyle barely shakes his head. "A daredevil? You mean to say that your young male model has what it takes to go big?"

"He's pretty and he's damn well built. Hell, on looks alone he can make it, but if he can work the crowd, get them involved, he can really be a success at this." Russ shakes his head. "I mean, man, he caught me from a jump off the top rope. He caught *and* balanced us both."

Lyle centers over a chair opposite Russ's desk and sits. "He's quiet, though, too quiet. Withdrawn. He's definitely focused, but a hard one to crack open. Either heat him up with some brash, in-your-face personality…"

"Or let him stay silent and steely." Russ finishes Lyle's thought. "He's definitely been that in every practice."

"Yeah, keep him succinct or nervy in words and in manners."

"Robotic."

"Or buzz cut that blond hair and make him militant."

Russ laces his fingers behind his head. He raises and extends his long, thick legs, crossing them over an edge of his desk.

"Or keep the hair and maybe grow it out a bit," Russ suggests. "Make him innocent. Completely vulnerable."

Lyle nods. "The jock out of the gym. Skimpy wrestling gear…he's your all-male centerfold."

Russ sighs and draws his elbows together, hiding most of his handsome face. He takes a breath. "There are a couple of ways we can go here."

They fall silent, each looking at different pictures on Russ's desk. One is of Russ's wife, Evette. With silky brown hair, she smiles through the glass frame with an expression that says to her husband, *I'm happy to be in love with you.* When he sees it, Russ smiles back and remembers her that morning, coffee cup in her hand, his T-shirt her nightshirt that covers the tops of her long, well-angled legs.

The other picture on the desk is of Russ's father, who is the reason Russ no longer wrestles often. He opened the school so he could be closer to his ailing dad.

Lyle speaks. "About John and this whole quiet thing, what is that? I really wonder why he's this way."

Russ thinks on this for a moment and remembers John's application. Foster homes. There were foster homes.

"It's abuse," Lyle says flatly, breaking the stillness between them. "That kid's been pounded. Nothing else would add up. I mean, he's a looker. Doors should open."

It's just what happened to John when the doors were closed. Both men think this at slightly different times.

"Well," Lyle says, tucking a loose spiral of his curly hair behind his ear, "let's get him up there, and out. You have promoters coming, don't you?"

Russ smiles a closed-lip smile. Lyle *is* good at this. Maybe he knows too much already. He's good to have for his immense size in the ring. But big guys come and go—prone to too many injuries. His management skills, however, are intuitive. He has a natural feel for characters and character development. To that end, he would be handy to have around when constructing vignettes in the ring, scenarios pitting one wrestler against another.

Lyle leans forward. "You didn't answer my question."

"Yeah, promoters are coming."

"And they already know about him, don't they?"

"Lyle," Russ says as he brings his feet down under him, "you cannot have my job."

❖

Unlike the other Tubs, Lyle thinks too much. He wonders. As more time passes, he senses that John might be gay. He's ultra-masculine, not effeminate. He is also self-sufficient, internal and, for the love of God, just too dang withdrawn. Above all else, the young man is so damn sad sometimes, though he's careful not to share this with anyone. And, finally, there's the obvious. There is no girlfriend—and a guy this hot would have one.

There's also no boyfriend. No one worries or cares about him like a lover should. No one reaches or holds him. And from John's dress and mannerisms, even the words he does and does not use, Lyle can tell that his classmate is not immersed in any gay culture whatsoever.

The kid is just so alone.

Lyle comes closer to understanding that the abuse John has endured falls from the hands of a father figure. Lyle, who is a good twelve to fourteen years older than John, understands that if he were to get too close to John, then John may blur or misunderstand their relationship. Any good connection the two had would skew and then shatter.

Damn the guy who's done this, Lyle thinks.

Russ approaches just as Lyle finds his fists clenched. A few days have passed since both men met in Russ's office.

Russ comes even closer to Lyle, who's been standing near Russ's promo poster. "What," Russ asks. "What are you thinking?"

Lyle shakes his head and lies. "Ring names. We all need ring names."

Russ nods. "Uh-huh. There's more than one face around here that's easy to read."

"What?"

Russ faces the direction that Lyle faces. "My heart goes out to him too."

CHAPTER NINE

Two promoters sit in folding chairs against one wall. They face one of the two rings. Russ's training program for this particular class is three-quarters over, and this pair here tonight is hopefully the first of three sets of business execs to come see if Russ has been working with marketable products.

It's been fourteen days since they've talked about ring names, yet tonight they use them. The Tubs are nervous and anxious about this dry run, of course. They've spent both a lot of money and income away from dead-end jobs to be here.

With three matches slated, each will square off with a classmate. The Seven Dwarfs are now down to six, as one of the Tubs seriously sprained an ankle and will sit this night out. Lyle and John are paired, and are last up on the evening's card.

The promoters don't want to meet the class first. Rather, they'd like to see how they act in front of the small crowd of thirty that Russ has gathered for the night. Mike, Russ's assistant, will interview each wrestler right in front of the promoters before they step into the ring. The wrestlers have been coached in what to say and how to act.

In the fourteen weeks since school has started, John's hair has not been cut. With Mike's input, Russ and John decide that John should go for the pretty boy look. Tonight he'll be the jobber or "PL," a paid loser.

Before the match, John and Lyle go over what moves they'll use. John will have plenty of ring time to show his strength and style. The youngest in this season's class will almost score the win, but Lyle will use unfair moves and wind up the winner. Mike, who will also be the referee tonight, will add any final instructions to the two before the square-off. Also, Mike will let them know when to wrap up the action.

Lyle and John are the last two in the small dressing area.

John has butterflies.

"I'm kinda nervous," Lyle admits.

"Me, I'm all right," John lies, his voice flat and crisp. Those are his last words before he is to walk out ahead of Lyle for his ringside "interview" with Mike. As he waits in the locker room, he stretches.

He swallows. He realizes he wasn't honest with Lyle a moment ago. What he is nervous about is not the interview or the match itself, but what he has to wear. Though it was discussed in front of everyone, he put out of his mind what he will wrestle in tonight until the package arrived in the mail at the school for him earlier that afternoon. Since his classmates are all super-sized guys with very big stomachs, they are all in wrestling gear that covers them. John, in contrast, is wearing more traditional-style trunks. Over white boots and kneepads, the bright yellow wrestling tights are high-cut on the thigh, especially in the front. The Speedo-type trunks sit low across his narrow waist. Fabric stretches and hugs his hard and sculpted bubble butt, providing an inch or so of a wedgie.

"It's just part of the show," Lyle said that morning when John's lightweight yellow gear came out of the box from a company in Michigan.

In the last seconds before he makes his way to the ring, John looks down. What he fears is true: the position of his heavy cock is there for the world to see.

John is to exit the locker area first.

Lyle says, "You'll be fine, John. This routine tonight will work well and you'll get a pro spot."

Russ comes back and says it's time.

John will be twenty years old next month. To all of this—to Lyle, to Russ, to Dax, to the wrestling tights he's wearing, to the thought of *maybe* making his own boxed birthday cake this year—he, a man who lost the warmth in his soul, just nods at the door.

❖

Russ cups his hands in front of his face like a megaphone. "And now, making his way to the ring, we have our own local West Virginia pretty boy. Weighing in at two hundred and twenty-two pounds, Jah-on-ny Cakes!"

When John meets the thirty excited people in the house who've come to watch along with the scouts, he does something he didn't predict he would do, or do so well, and that's become the character. His smile and his confidence shoot into the crowd, who crank up the temperature in the gym when they see his defined muscles. Along the way to Mike, he stops twice, flexing quickly and yet somehow innocently for the fans. He does as he's told and comes across as young and naïve, and yes, very pretty.

Mike holds a cordless microphone that does not work. He extends his arm and motions for John.

With Mike's arm around John's bare back, Mike starts the interview. "Johnny Cakes, your match tonight with Lord Lard will be anything but easy for you. The man has you by over a hundred and twenty pounds. How'd you prepare?"

The smile comes again and the promoters are already hooked.

Mike asks the question again. "How'd you get ready for tonight?"

Remember the script, John. "I work hard, know my moves, and can handle myself in there against any big guy."

"But, Lard, he's the champ and you're just a newcomer."

Setting his hands on his sides, John improvises. "The bigger they are, the harder they fall."

Impressed, the promoters nod at this.

"But *a hundred and twenty* pounds, Johnny."

"What's that?" John asks, thinking of the jokes on the day they learned the Victory Roll. This part of the interview has not been planned. "He's not fat, he's fluffy."

On cue, Russ calls out Lyle, who does weigh one hundred and twenty five pounds more than John.

Mike starts to ask Lyle a question, but Lyle grabs the microphone and shoves Mike away with one powerful thrust. He turns to John, who has stepped into the ring.

Lyle points to his friend and opponent. "You are a twinkie boy, most definitely crème filled, and absolutely vanilla."

"I'd say crème filled is that belly of yours, Lard!"

The juvenile banter continues. "I will manhandle you. Take your muscle meat and tenderize you even more than you already are, pretty."

John charges to the side of the ring where Lyle is. He steps up on the lowest rope and leans forward. With two fingers extended, he motions for Lyle to enter.

Lyle, clearly acting annoyed, drops the microphone and makes his way up the three metal steps to the ring.

As referee, Mike steps in right after Lyle. A man who could pass for John's grandfather, Mike immediately tries to separate the two, but of course is unsuccessful.

When the bell sounds, John starts hammering Lyle with open fists, each blow dramatized and, as taught, packing no more power than a slap. The larger man defends and then retaliates, but John gets the better of this. He puts Lyle's back into one of the turnbuckles. Up on the bottom and then the second rope, John starts hammering away at the man "trapped" in the corner. The crowd starts counting on the fourth hit. Five, six, seven...

Cocky now, John stops. "Pretty boy, huh?" His muscles shine and swell even more under the overhead lights. "Do you like this?"

The small house roars. This is the loudest they've been so far tonight.

Going for more action, John tries to toss Lyle over into the center of the ring. As planned, however, Lyle counters. Still on his feet, the larger man shakes his head at John's fumbled attempt. The momentum turns. Lyle scoops John up, carries him to the center of the ring and belly flops the boy. Once out from under Lyle, John spreads his knees.

For the size of his barely contained bulge, which neither Russ nor Mike fully considered earlier, he should be wearing more.

The hung horse acts lifeless.

Lyle goes to work. He grabs John by the back of his blond hair and brings the handsome kid to his feet, showcasing the blond's ass to three sides of the ring as he does so. The crowd responds negatively, as they side with the muscle hunk in yellow.

Methodically, Lyle drops John again—but only when the fan's anticipation heightens even more. It is clear they want to see their new hero fight his way back, but not until he endures more from this enormous bully.

With the intention of back torture, Lyle drops his knee into John's back three, four, five times. When released from this assault, John arches and slaps his hand against the small of his back. The crowd feels this. They enjoy their beautiful male hurting like they themselves somehow hurt through life—tensions, bills, their own bullies.

Lyle allows no recovery time. An open fist from Lyle squares John to the mat again. The boy is stunned.

Lyle attempts another belly flop but, as planned, John scoots out of the way just in time. With his body prone, Lyle suffers the damage intended for John.

Back on his wobbly feet, John lifts one of Lyle's legs and puts the large man into a figure-four leg lock, a move stressing the knee joints of the opponent.

Lyle pounds the mat with his fists. "Stop!" he yells. "Stop him, ref!"

Mike "checks" the hold to see that it is legal and applied correctly. He nods to John, who raises one of his arms to do a one-arm push-up. The added strain on Lyle's legs is supposedly too much. Lyle yells.

Quick thinking, Lyle reverses the hold and it is John who calls out in seeming pain. In an impressive move of upper-body strength, John slides both himself and Lyle toward the nearest rope. When John reaches it, the referee indicates that the hold needs to be broken.

Now free, John stumbles to his feet and squares off in front of Lyle. Lyle drops John into a front headlock and grabs enough at John's yellow tights to expose even more of John's perfect muscled ass. He then drops John down, face first, onto the mat.

Russ watches this from the second row. Standing behind a group of the wives or girlfriends of his present and former students, Russ glances toward the promoters, but only for a second. Focusing on Lyle and John again, he thinks, *this is your one shot with these scouts. Make it believable, guys.*

Bouncing up and down in reaction to Lyle's force, John's muscles shake. Lyle moves his opponent and slips him into a Boston crab. This hold lasts a minute or two, yet John does not submit.

Feigning anger, Lyle releases the hold and kicks John repeatedly in the small of the back. In an effort to escape the barrage, John scrambles to the ropes but doesn't make it. Lyle traps John's hand under his big boot. The big man appears to stomp on John's fingers. The small crowd responds with a loud "Boo!"

In response, Lyle pummels John and locks the boy's face with his arms. John, to the surprise of the house, powers out. Each of his pronounced pectoral muscles quivers when he does this. Free, he cranks on one of Lyle's hands, turning out and away from the big guy. Without realizing it, John allows the fans to see him fully exposed, from fingers to feet.

Driven by what he's about to do, John picks Lyle up, flips the badass on his head, and pauses a moment before he performs what's called an atomic drop.

John goes for the cover and hooks Lyle's leg. Lyle, as choreographed, kicks out from the pin position.

Acting frustrated, John slaps the mat and tries a new tack. This time he rolls Lyle up, gets the giant to his feet, and then scoots under him. While buckling considerably, he dead-lifts Lyle, then drops both of them onto Lyle's back. Lyle then grabs the front of John's neck in a fake chokehold. This illegal hold lasts for a minute, despite the ref's empty attempts to call off the larger wrestler.

When Lyle does break the hold, he drops his knee over John's throat and applies pressure. John flails and thrashes. John really bounces in that thin yellow wrestling gear. He barely remains contained in that thin, shiny fabric.

Lyle stands. To finish the match, he scoops up a tired, almost lifeless John. He raises and positions the limp hero so that the underdog's lower back rests squarely over Lyle's shoulders. John's arms and legs dangle. His crotch is exposed. As the powerhouse jostles John, the pretty boy's taut muscles go limp. Not only does pain rocket through John's lower back, but also vulnerability and humiliation flash through his mind.

Being displayed like this is what John thinks he deserves. For what he did to stay with Greg, yeah, this is just punishment.

The ref says something John hears but does not understand.

In truth, he is lost out there, unfocused. The name Greg hurts more than his tired muscles.

The rest blurs for John, including the moves Lyle puts him in prior to his being pinned. In the last seconds of the match, just as he's sprawled over the mat, his six-pack abs making fast and short contractions, John acts like a semiconscious heap. Lyle covers his defeated opponent while the ref counts, "One, two, three!"

Three showerheads jet out from the shower room walls, but with these big guys, only one guy can really shower at a time. The other four wrestling students had gone through after their matches. After icing his back, John goes ahead of Lyle, who talks with his girlfriend, Betty, a woman his age that he met while here in West Virginia.

They find John quiet and alone, wearing just jeans, his hair wet and uncombed, in the locker room. He isn't moving. Another part of him has died.

All four men—the two promoters, Russ and Lyle—gather round the narrow bench.

"We bought it," one of the promoters says. "We bought it all. You being the good guy—strong, eager to win. And you take the hits, act out the hurt really well. You're convincing."

The other promoter moves closer. "And you can lift this guy here." He motions toward Lyle. "Now that's something. Really something. All acting aside, that's real."

"We're impressed," the first promoter says. "Let's talk further, but we like you and Lyle here in combo. We're offering you both a contract."

"We're a progressive, pro wrestling business through West Virginia and the surrounding states," the first promoter continues. "And we want you and Lyle here in our organization, the Mid-Atlantic Wrestling League."

His bright blue eyes don't fix on anything, and then he nods, as he knows they are all staring at him.

CHAPTER TEN

L yle thumbs through a magazine. It's the tenth and final one on the expensive, blue-tinted glass coffee table. He knows it's coming. If not this time, it will be the next, or the next.

For the last hour, he's been waiting to see the orthopedic surgeon and it doesn't look good. Both he and John have been in the Mid-Atlantic Wrestling League for five months after completing Russ's school and signing their contracts. In just under half a year, time in the ring has taken a toll on Lyle's knees. All told, he may make eighteen months, maybe two years, but thinking beyond that would be foolish.

A nurse passes. With her silky, deep blond hair held back with one simple clip, she's amazingly beautiful in a manicured, understated way. With a mole on her cheek and skin so smooth and perfect, she should be a movie star.

With a look of genuine care, she smiles at the enormous man in the waiting area. It's the type of smile that's not as engaging as he'd like. He never receives those. After so many years, he doesn't expect *that* kind of a smile, of course, least of all from a woman who looks like that, but his love life couldn't be worse—unless you count those women who want a one-night only. Those ladies migrate around the ring and locker room door after the show. And they are always there, night after night. Different women who always want the same thing: to be with the freakishly big guy. When the final diehard fans leave because they realize that the kids have school tomorrow or early soccer games Saturday morning, these women remain. They are there with him for a while anyway, then slip away before he ever thinks of hanging the Do Not Disturb sign on his hotel room door.

He thinks again of the high-end nurse with the smile, and then remembers Betty, the former short-term girlfriend he met at Russ's school in West Virginia. For a moment his lips curl.

They were together for almost three months. This minor league demands too much time on the road, as much as it does with the big-time pros, but the difference at this lower level is that travel this cheap will burn you out. To save money, guys share rooms in low-budget hotels that offer little or no amenities. Life is cramped, difficult, and not conducive to any notion of comfort or female companionship. Having experienced this with Lyle, Betty didn't move on completely; she's still single. She has just had enough of faulty bath fixtures, beaten mattresses and old, really ugly wallpaper.

Betty. Lyle drops back in his chair. Damn.

The tenth magazine on the glass coffee table is *Good Housekeeping* and he couldn't care less about how to dress your table for the holidays, but he cannot stop thinking about his old girlfriend. He still cares for her and likes the way he felt about himself when they were together on the most ordinary, yet wonderful, dinner dates. He flips through the pages and sees glimpses of Betty here and there. A part of her life is in the articles and the advertisements. A deep kitchen sink, a knit sweater, and the photo of the author of a "How to Become Closer to Your Sister" article remind him of her. A picture of roasted chicken on a festive plate makes him realize that he wants the holiday table decorated and the life this whole magazine sells.

He wants to come home.

He wants Betty.

He extends his bad knees. They click and crack.

"Mr. Lowell?" It's a different nurse, but one just as pretty as the first yet with a totally different look. She stands at the door on her long, slender legs.

Are all the nurses here absolutely gorgeous?

He lumbers to his feet. And right then, thinking of Betty and home and the wrestling nights ahead, it comes to him.

He has a plan. Yes, a plan—and it's a really good one. He'll create an excuse for his knees. A note from the doctor will be the reason why John has to wrestle someone new tonight. That hot and handsome new guy is coming in from the West Coast, after all.

He checks his watch.

The nurse apologizes. "I'm sorry the doctor is running late."

"Oh no, it's not that," Lyle responds, but says no more.

As the nurse clicks the waiting room door shut behind the two of them, she asks, "Well, what is it?"

He studies his watch again. The flight from Seattle lands exactly at the Cincinnati airport three hours from now.

"It's just good news," Lyle answers. "Just good news."

❖

Lyle sees the two little boys first. Who could miss them? Together they make what looks like a crazy-eight figure on the broad sidewalk in front of the airport. Each wearing a Cincinnati Bengals jersey in different shades of orange, their laughter is contagious. The young man behind them clearly catches their giggles and laughs now too. On his haunches, he watches them with green eyes that light up with their silliness.

Lyle takes a quick glance at him. The young man has to be too young to be the father of these two pre-school children. Maybe he's their much older brother? Stepbrother? Uncle?

Checking his watch again, something he's done too many times in the last two hours, Lyle hurries. He's just on time, but wants to arrive early to pick up the new wrestler flying in from the West Coast to wrestle for the first time tonight in the Mid-Atlantic League.

Lyle hasn't been this light on his feet since the day he started wrestling in Russ's school. The new, lightweight knee braces he's wearing offer such great mobility. When he put them on in front of the physical therapist right after his orthopedic surgeon's appointment, he knew he had found gold.

As he walks through the automatic sliding glass entrance doors, he thinks again of what the orthopedic surgeon said when they were in his office. Lyle's recent MRI shows nothing severe. He is fine for now, which surprises him. The recent pain could be attributed to the onslaught of arthritis, which Lyle knew was in his deck of cards before he turned to professional wrestling. His grandfather and dad, who were equally large men, made this fate clear. But still, to hear that he can continue in the ring, at least for a while...and here with these new braces...the big guy has a spring in his step.

Quickly, he makes his way to the television screens.

He knows the time of the arriving flight, 2:12 p.m. There it is. In a bright, bold green. Flight 1919 from Seattle. Gate B3. ARRIVED.

Arrived? He checks his watch yet again. It's 1:53 p.m. The flight is a whole twenty minutes early. This couldn't...couldn't...he checks the information on the screen a second and third time.

Huh, Lyle thinks, *damn. He's here. The new guy. He's already here.*

But where?

Lyle wanted to be at the airport thirty minutes before the plane touched down, and, according to his watch, which held the right time, he still has nineteen minutes before he's to meet the new wrestler.

There in a wide hall where other air travelers are greeted by friends or family, he turns left and right. No one moves into view who looks like a twenty-one-year-old able to bench press an upright piano. Maybe he's at the baggage claim. Maybe he hasn't left the plane yet, or is en route to getting his luggage somewhere in the airport.

For ten minutes, Lyle stands at the baggage claim for flight 1919. A few remaining passengers from that flight were milling about when he arrived. With the exception of a somewhat flat and beat-up cardboard box, the luggage carousel carried no more items.

Okay, where is he?

Of all the stupid things, Lyle doesn't even have the kid's last name with him. It's back in the car. But he does know the new guy is twenty-one, six foot two, two hundred and twenty pounds with soft red hair, and looks like an athlete whose cover story you'd read about in one of those fitness magazines. Yes, Bret is handsome. Definitely handsome. Lyle saw a picture of a man with great smile.

It dawns on Lyle. That was him. *Of course! That was him!*

He hurries back to the doors he entered. Again, he's so thankful for the knee braces and for the doctor's go-ahead to wrestle further.

And, when he reaches the lobby, he stops. The outside area where the little boys had been with him is empty.

Where? He looks around. *Where to now?*

And then he sees everything he needs to see to know that everything he has planned since entering the doctor's exam room is going to work.

Through the glass he sees Bret and instantly remembers reading his last name earlier. It's McCalagrew. Bret McCalagrew. As Irish sounding as you can get. He's the single man standing still while the little boys scurry off with their mother, who is loading the last of her luggage in the car parked along the curb.

Instinctively, Lyle figures out the whole story, from its beginning hours until now. Standing still and watching, he sees how the day must have first unfolded from the airport in Seattle.

They must have met on the flight—this woman, the boys, and Bret. And they connected, of course. Maybe Bret even shared with the little ones that he wrestled, and boys being boys, sure enough, being a wrestler? Well, yeah, that is the coolest thing totally ever, man.

And, long flights being the cost they are, she's traveling with the boys alone, of course. Her husband stayed back here at home in Ohio while she did what needed to be done in Washington state...wedding, reunion, visit with her parents...and, after the plane touched down here in Cincinnati, she had to do something—something as necessary as checking a reservation or waiting for lost luggage. And, especially since they were early and Bret was going to wait anyway, he didn't mind watching her sons, whom he probably called something like squirts or some other silly nickname that made each boy really smile.

And that's when Lyle passed. The boys were making those crazy-eights while Bret, a sudden chaperone, stood guard while laughing with them.

The boys don't want to get in the car. Their mother gestures back to the airport. The boys know what she's offering and before they ask, they run back to Bret for one more good-bye.

Lyle moves closer to the exit door, but does not go through it. Instead, he simply watches the scene unfold. The dad doesn't appreciate this Other Guy who is obviously very built and a natural sport with his kids.

The boys, each with a hand held by their mom, are escorted back to the car. A moment later, the car slides into the light traffic.

Bret is left alone. He stands still, his hand suspended in his own wave good-bye, the sorrow in his green eyes swells. He doesn't want this life, the one he's about to continue with a different league in a different part of the country. No, he wants the life like the one in the car that's driving further and further away.

Bret is giving thought to just turning around here at this airport and heading back to Seattle. Screw this wrestling life and those few guys he can date.

Yes, because his ride isn't here, maybe it's a sign. Maybe it's an indication he should just stop. Maybe he should head back to the West Coast.

But there's nothing there.

Before he started wrestling, *God*, he's dated. Many men would respond to his pictures and profile on an online dating sight. His shirtless pic alone would get hit, on average, twenty times *every* day. These online guys—and there have been many—from soft to just too damn hard—they either didn't measure up when they met, or the fit wasn't just right.

Bret joined two gay interest organizations and casually dated a few guys for a couple of months—a "wait and see" approach—but he's been left empty, which is how he feels now.

Suddenly, a large group of high school girls enters and Bret turns just a bit to watch them, as he's pulled by the chattering noise and the fact that they all wear large, bright yellow name tags and carry identical book bags.

As the girls file into the terminal, Lyle and Bret see each other, but Bret turns back and faces the approaching traffic.

It's Lyle's cue. He joins Bret.

"Bret?"

He turns. There's that smile again, and a deep voice. "Lyle, is it?"

They shake hands. At six-two, Bret comes up to Lyle's shoulder.

Lyle says, "We must have missed each other."

At the same time, Bret raises a shoulder in a shrug. "We landed early."

In the pause that follows, both comprehend what the other said. Feeling a bit like a diplomat, Lyle continues. "Welcome to Cincinnati. We're glad you could join us."

"Glad this all worked out. Glad to be here."

Just then, the sound of a flight taking off roars overhead. Lyle doesn't see Bret's eyes follow the plane, wondering if he should in fact stay here and begin with this new small-time league, or try to find a guy back where he came from.

It's at this time that Bret thinks of Tim, a man from the past who lingers from time to time in the present. The memory of Tim lasts for a moment that, thankfully, passes.

He's so polite, Lyle thinks as they make their way to short-term parking. Bret's the kind of guy mothers wait for their children to bring home to them as future son-in-laws.

When they drive off in Lyle's old, reliable Jeep whose sound system, Lyle says, only plays bands from 1962 to 1974, they fall into an easy conversation about the flight, the airport itself, and the weather here in Ohio versus what Bret's experienced recently in the Pacific Northwest. They even talk about regional wrestling as they head into the downtown area. Neither man talks about the boys in the orange jerseys.

The conversation slows down. Guiding his Jeep into the parking garage across from the arena where the wrestling will happen tonight, Lyle doesn't want their talk to get snagged. "So, you're ready for tonight?"

"All set."

He smiles. "Gonna show 'em your stuff tonight?"

"Yep."

"You have what it takes?"

"Yep."

For the second time since meeting Bret, Lyle thinks of John who would answer the same question the same way with the same inflection.

"Good," Lyle responds from the quiet. "Then let's bring you down to the ring. You got your gear?"

Standing at the open back end of the Jeep, Bret slings his gym bag over his shoulder, steels his nerves, and says, "Yeah, it's in my carry-on. I'm good to go."

❖

They cross the street and make their way to the ring. Like the big leagues, it's a fifteen-foot flexi-beam square with three cabled ropes on each side that connect to four rounded turnbuckles. The elevated ring floor is made of gymnastic padding, and up close, Bret thinks it looks comfortable enough to stretch out and close his eyes for a bit.

He stares off into space. The temperature may be sixty-six degrees here, but it's cold, unfriendly, unforgiving.

Lyle senses the miles Bret has logged in since he joined a league. They are lonely, empty miles. Both know the nomad life of a traveling show. Depending on what the crowd expects to see and experience, it could also be called a traveling circus, complete with the antics of human animals doing very stupid, often dangerous "tricks," like jumping off top ropes to crush a fellow wrestler eight to ten feet below.

As Lyle and Bret stand beside the ring, each knows this is not a destination. Instead, it's a layover to something better, something permanent. Lyle will search for a woman like Betty who, in his mind, will never be far from him, no matter the distance. And Bret, well... Bret will search too...just as he's doing now.

He looks in the corners of the large Cincinnati Community Center toward areas he suspects he and the other wrestlers will come out from before the matches. With Lyle, he's waiting for the pro he'll wrestle in a few hours.

Bret wants to pace but finds he can surprisingly keep still. In the quiet seconds that tick away, he thinks that maybe tonight is the night. Maybe the guy he wrestles will be the one. "So," he asks, "who do I wrestle again? You said his name was…"

Lyle answers matter-of-factly. "Jason Almire."

"Jason Almire."

Lyle continues. "Jason is a thirty-three-year-old heavyweight who has you by twelve years and fifty pounds. And this unfair advantage will be played out in his favor. The dynamic here is a given: against the big guy, the pretty boy will lose."

Pretty boy. He will never get used to hearing that.

Bret knows nothing more of Jason. He's never seen a picture of this champ. What he does know is that here in this league, just like his last, he'll be a jobber—the one to take the fall. But maybe Jason is something or has something that will click, will work, or will make this hidden and quiet life of his come true. Maybe Jason has the look, the drive, the passion, the heat and the ability to do this—to partner with him.

They are to meet here for a practice. As the seconds move to minutes, Jason is becoming later and later.

For the second time today, Bret thinks of Tim and the complicated story around a long-ago love who was first a friend, and then more than a friend. Maybe this Jason guy, this experienced pro, will make memories vanish. Maybe he'll be handsome, have a great smile. Maybe his heart will be warm and his eyes attentive. Maybe this guy will have shoulders strong enough to make a relationship work. Yeah, maybe with Jason, old ghosts will finally move on.

"Good ring," Bret offers to fill the quiet and change the subject from where his thoughts have been. "Expensive."

"Yeah," Lyle agrees. "Not so bad to fall on."

…or to get bruised on, both think.

Lyle lets heavy moments pass between them. The newcomer pauses for a second and then says, "And they're a good color. Yeah. Nice."

Lyle sees what he's guessed to be true: that part of this young man's charm is that Bret is simply polite. Lyle smiles. He sees a good match.

He also sees more. Before he can imagine it further, however, a distant door opens. A glimpse of hope flickers across Bret's green eyes that Lyle, who has been looking, sees.

Jason makes his way to the ring. Wearing just jeans and his custom cowboy boots, Jason struts toward them at a clip that masks his stiff and battered joints. Even from a distance, Bret notices the heavyweight is actually overweight, not muscular. Jason's bloated belly is taut, though expanded in large curves. His upper body muscles were once bigger and better than they are now. Bret thinks the man is too young to be this old.

During their introduction, Lyle notices that nothing other than the necessary exchanges fall between them. It's just as he had thought, and also just as he had hoped.

Jason speaks with a drawl, though he has never lived in the South. "The locker room…it's locked up tight. No damn body has a key nowhere."

Not surprised by this, Jason unfastens his rodeo belt buckle, unzips his jeans, and starts to strip down to the royal blue trunks he has on before kicking off his boots.

Bret turns left and right. *Where to go?* He takes a step or two in one direction, thinks he has more privacy if he stands between the first and second row of seats, and proceeds. He discovers no more privacy here, but at least he's out of the way.

Grabbing his T-shirt by its collar, he slips it off. His eyes tunnel to narrow slits so that he sees little before him. He finds his trunks, a jock, and his black boots buried under street clothes in his gym bag. Off with his jeans, he stands in his underwear.

Indeed, Bret is built. Lyle knows the crowd will enjoy the sight of this beautiful muscle boy, especially as he's flexed and then stretched out for view.

Bret is reluctant to go further. While Jason waits for Bret's colored briefs to slide down those long, strong legs, he thinks of what holds will best showcase that boy's incredible gym build.

Changing into his jock and light blue Speedo, Bret checks himself and turns. His show face is on. He's ready.

With Lyle watching, the two practice for nearly forty minutes. Bret is another John; there's no denying it. The two are similar in style and in build. Jason expertly puts Bret into hold after hold, all designed to get the crowd to cheer for the young wrestler and boo the old, nasty pro. Some escape moves are planned so that Bret can be known as more than a pushover to his future fans. And, like John, he has the power and strength.

❖

It is 6:35 p.m. The ring action starts at 7:30, and the largest arena the Mid-Atlantic League travels to fills with a hungry crowd.

College boys are the surprise tonight. Many crowd the place. From the concession stands under the high bleachers, they have been drinking overpriced beer. The beer accesses their hunger even more. They want to see something raw, something they crave but don't know how to get.

Beefed-up muscle wrestlers wearing revealing wrestling tights will be called "faggot" and "queer" by these guys who sneak peeks at each other's crotches when their buddies aren't looking. Yeah, they want it. Only acting drunk, they lean on each other, enjoying the feel of their bare arms on each other's skin.

Lyle senses this and knows gifts when he sees them. This will make his plan tonight even better.

One of the sound guys motions toward Lyle. "It's the Boss," he says. "She wants a talk with you on the office phone. She's waiting."

Okay, Lyle thinks. *She's right on cue. Just stick to your script.*

Gail Jackson, known behind her back as the Boss, isn't high in management but acts like she is. She is one of the promoters who thinks she manages this show from her apartment in Manhattan. Tonight, she'll have a surprise.

Lyle sees more college boys standing too close in line to one another as he weaves his way to the office. Their eyes are big and hopeful. Many are half-hard and thankful for loose jeans or shirts that are not tucked in. They wait impatiently to see what they want so badly but do not know, or do not know yet, how to have.

"Yes, Gail," he says as he closes the office door. He anticipates her question.

She snaps. "What! I thought your MRI was good and clear. You pull this *now*?"

He remains calm as he carries through with his lie. "The doc says not tonight for me. And they are bad. Both of them. It's really hard now to even walk."

Gail worries, but not for Lyle. She won't go against what a doctor says.

"Well then, what are we going to do? If you don't wrestle John tonight, who will?"

CHAPTER ELEVEN

When twenty-seven-year-old Vaughn Spiller didn't get a wrestling contract after his training with a school outside of Chicago, he decided to stick with wrestling anyway. He became a crewmember with the Mid-Atlantic League when a full-time tech position became available last summer. Along with lights and sound equipment, he is one of two underpaid employees who set up and take down the ring after each night. He doesn't love this work, but he's a dreamer who always thought a night like this would happen.

Lyle finds him in the hall. "Vaughn, you have your wrestling gear around, don't you?"

Vaughn blushes. The bubble-bellied man with a pockmarked face and a learning disability repeats what he just heard. "My own gear?"

"Yeah."

"You shouldn't know about that. How'd you know about that, Lyle?"

"Oh, I don't know really. Since I know you like to wrestle, it was just a guess," Lyle replies.

"You shouldn't know about that."

"I shouldn't, you're right." Lyle pauses. "You have it here, though, right? I mean…just in case."

"You shouldn't know about that." Vaughn crosses his arms over his chest. "You shouldn't, 'cause it's just my own stuff, Lyle. You know, there ain't no law says I can't have my own stuff. It ain't botherin' you, nor nobody."

Lyle agrees. "You're right. I was just thinking—you just never know when you could use it, that's all."

Vaughn looks away for a moment to see heavyweight champ Jason Almire walking toward him. He turns back to Lyle, who doesn't quite nod in the direction of the seasoned pro but gives enough of a clue away in his eyes. The techie carefully adds this together. *Lyle questions if I have my gear. Jason Almire is walking toward me.* He perks. *Is this, is this really happening?*

"I've talked this over with Gail Jackson," Lyle continues, sensing the question Vaughn hasn't asked. "If you're up for it, you're to wrestle Jason here tonight. We've had to do some last-minute rearranging and definitely want to see you take some heat here in Cincinnati."

"But not much heat, bro," Jason admits, drawing out his words when they stand face-to-face. "I ain't up for much tonight."

Jason is glad for this last-minute substitution. He won't be in the ring with Vaughn for long, which wouldn't be the case if he were to wrestle that dime-a-dozen muscle-punk named Brian or Brad or whatever. The nitwit standing right in front of him will be a quick and easy pin, and this is totally fine with the champ, whose knees really are bad from the time spent earlier in the ring with Bret during practice.

"The action is just one or two minutes, Vaughn," Lyle adds. "Really no more than that. No one gets hurt. Jason will do a lot of talk up front and, when he gets around to business, he just pins you fast. You want it?"

"Well…"

If he says no, my plan is sunk, Lyle thinks.

Vaughn hesitates, only because he's not sure which of his bags holds his tights and boots. But, he figures, he has them somewhere, right? They have to be packed because they were never unpacked, right?

"Yeah," Vaughn answers. "Yeah. I'll do it."

Both Lyle and Jason release deep breaths which neither knew they had been holding.

❖

"Bret?"

Having just passed someone he doesn't recognize, Bret turns back around. "Yeah?"

"It's me. Vaughn."

They stand face-to-face.

Uncertain, Bret flashes a small-town *aw shucks, do I know you?* grin before one of his deeper smiles spreads over his handsome face. He wonders when and where he might have met this guy.

Vaughn second-guesses what he's about to do. The pretty ones aren't always easy to talk to. And he doesn't do talking very well, not like this. He swallows. "It is Bret, right? You are Bret? Right?"

"Yep. That's me."

Vaughn smiles and meets those green eyes. "See, I know your name."

Bret nods again. *Maybe the flight today was too long. The night too short. Something. Have I met this guy already today?* He scratches the side of his strong jaw. "Vaughn, did you say?"

"Yes, of course. Vaughn. That's me."

Bret repositions his feet, barely licks his lips. He sets his hand at his waist and squints just a bit. "Do, do I know you from somewhere, buddy?"

"You know me from here." Vaughn smiles. "From here in the hall. We've just met."

"Oh."

"We just met right here *in the hallway*, silly."

Bret cocks his chin just a bit. "Yeah, but you knew my name."

Vaughn laughs and runs his hands through his short, straight, pale-colored hair receding high on his forehead. "Yeah, I did. I did know your name. It *is* Bret, right?"

"Yeah."

"You're from California."

"You're close. Same time zone. But I've been in Washington. Washington state."

There's a second of confusion before Vaughn's expression goes blank.

Bret quickly adds, "Yeah, right, it's pretty quiet out there."

"Quiet."

"Yeah."

Vaughn repositions the awkward, lumpy bag he's had over his shoulder. "Do you have a girlfriend?" Vaughn asks.

"Ah." It's Bret's turn to be uncomfortable. While he's thought about this for the past few days, he doesn't know what to do. He knows how he should answer but chickens out. "Girls? What? Nah, they aren't for me." He frowns. "They're too much trouble."

Vaughn doesn't believe him. "Yeah, right." Vaughn motions with his hand to his left. "The locker room is still locked. But I'd bet you'd be good at love."

Locked locker room in one sentence and love in the next. Okay.

Bret turns toward the door. He waits a second before saying, "Yeah, I guess the door's been like this for a few hours, eh?"

"Eh." Vaughn laughs because he senses that more is wrong than a locked door. "You should have a girlfriend."

Bret swallows, blushes, and looks down at the floor.

"I like you."

Bret's smile now deepens. The sudden warmth in his chest spreads. "I like you too, Vaughn."

"You should have a girlfriend. I see it in your eyes." Looking right into Bret's eyes for a second time, he continues, "You need a girl. You're handsome."

"Ah."

Vaughn widens his stance as if he's about to dance to a song in his head. "A handsome cowboy is what you are."

"Cowboys." Bret barely shakes his chin, interrupting. "I'm thinkin' they come from the Southwest." He folds his lips off to one side and wants to crack a smile, but manages to keep his face somewhat serious. "Yeah, pretty sure there. The Southwest."

"Nope."

"So, a love for me, huh?" Again Bret struggles with telling this new guy just who he is, but decides to take this slowly. "Okay, you be my Cupid, all right? Find me just the right person?"

Vaughn scratches the thin spot of hair at the crown of his head. "No! You're silly. Cupid only works on Valentine's Day!"

Bret's just a few inches taller than Vaughn and looks down at him. "If I get you arrows, real golden ones with just enough magic, you'd shoot them at the right person, right?"

Vaughn's big eyes brighten. He wants to start dancing again. "I'm a terrible shot, cowboy."

"Then," Bret looks left and right very seriously, "we have some trouble on our hands."

"Trouble is my middle name."

Bret laughs.

Vaughn has to get going. He starts to walk away. Double-checking that the cords to the lights are all securely taped down is something he likes to do. "Magic arrows. You're silly."

"Wait. Vaughn, before you go, how did you know my name?"

Vaughn takes a few more steps, turns and stops. "Huh. Maybe I am Cupid."

❖

Bret finds the nearest staircase and starts climbing. Fast. One flight. Two. Three. Four. *I should have told him*, he thinks as he takes two, then three, steps at a time. *Oh, yeah, Vaughn? Girls? Nah. Me, I'm gay.*

Damn. There are no more stairs. No more running away. He turns. Sets his hands on the cold rail.

He stares through one of the tinted plate glass windows to his left lining what has to be the top floor of the sports complex.

Wanting to keep moving from his thoughts, he walks this long hallway once, twice. There's nothing up here, just extra space, like an attic hardly used and rarely cleaned. When he finally stops, he closes his eyes and hears Vaughn. *You need a girl. You're handsome.*

Bret sits on the floor with a view of the flat tar roof below. Vaughn comes to mind again. He says out loud, "I shoulda told him. Yeah, guy, I'm gay. So a girlfriend? Yeah, not so much."

Bret drops the back of his head against the wall behind him. The fake brick is harder than it looks.

Tired, he closes his eyes for a minute. Lets his mind roam. There was that one guy on the plane. Skinny and long, he looked like a musician in an edgy, angry rock band that wasn't any good, but he was sort of cute.

On the flight, band boy hung with a girl who looked like him enough to be his sister. No guy stays that close for that long to his own sister, does he?

Yeah, they were together. But even if they weren't, even if rock star was gay, Bret was six rows away, and their eyes only met twice.

That was Bret's problem. He never approached. He just stayed locked out at a safe distance. The two boys on the plane with their mom were another story. He was right there. Beside them. Laughing. Joking. Talking. And it was easy. Good. Fun.

He smiles at the memory of the kids and leans forward to rub his temples. In his imagination, he pictures a great-looking date sitting beside him. They are on a flight together. Just the two of them.

Warm and attentive, his touch on Bret's skin is good and deep. Whoever this fantasy guy is, they've been together just long enough to really be comfortable with each other.

Now they are side by side on Bret's living room couch, instead of the plane. Home at last, Bret finds himself stretched over the lap of the guy he's just now calling his boyfriend. He rubs Bret's shoulders, his neck, his forehead, his face. His nose nudges Bret behind the ear, and there's a soft kiss. Taking his forearm, Bret's boyfriend comes in under Bret's arm and squeezes Bret's chest just enough.

Just enough.

And there's another kiss. This one just brushes his temple.

Bret realizes he's been daydreaming but allows himself to continue for another minute or two. More squeezes. Deeper kisses. Warmth. Heat.

Hot now himself, he stretches, yawns .He's not good on days like this. Transition is not easy. Worried about the time, he checks his watch. Still on West Coast time. Yeah, he's tired. It's been a long day.

With some thirty minutes to go before he needs to head downstairs to stretch and warm up, Bret decides to stay here a while longer. It's safer, quieter, easier.

He grabs his shins while resting his chin between his kneecaps. Yeah, he thinks again, it has been a long day, a long week, a long year.

The big decisions he's made over the past year filter in, followed by some from years past. Leaving home at eighteen. Starting college right away. Quitting college two years in. Opting to work full-time in that apple orchard until he could figure things out, which he never quite did.

He remembers that apple orchard. The seasons, the smells, the sound of the rain through the leaves, or on the gothic barn's tin roof.

Joe, the farmer with great kids and a wife who worked as hard as—if not harder than—he did, talked to him one day about transplant shock when some recently relocated young saplings looked more dead than alive.

Transplant shock.

Bret swallows.

He has ten more minutes up here in the hallway. It is easier to be alone. This time lets him regroup, reorient. With his chin still on his knees, he knows he's not readjusting up here—he's hiding.

Running his hands through his somewhat long, floppy red hair, he knows he needs to make new friends. His throat tightens.

Just go back down there, he tells himself but doesn't move.

That Lyle, he seems like a great bud. There's something to that big one, something substantive, maybe even heartfelt. He was the kind of man who would not let you down if he had your back.

Bret sighs. Maybe he could trust Lyle. Unlike what he did with Vaughn downstairs, maybe he could let this guy in. Share the truth. "Yeah," Bret says to the empty air in front of him, "Lyle? Me and having a girlfriend? Ah, not so much. See, I'm…I'm…"

He stops. Even to himself alone he cannot say what needs to be said. Cannot share what needs to be shared.

Agitated, frustrated, trapped, he stands and stretches one last time. His reflection in the window in front of him catches his attention. Walking over to the glass, he just stops. Stares. Frowns. Aches.

Love. What a dumbass thing to want.

CHAPTER TWELVE

John stands in front of an open locker. It's hot in here. Summertime in Ohio can be just plain miserable. Even the arena's air condition system can't keep up with the hazy, hot, and humid ninety-four-degree temperature. Despite this, John is completely dressed in street clothes after having just come from a nearby gym where he pumped up before his match tonight with Lyle.

Shirt off, he hangs it on the hook inside the locker and grabs behind his neck to pull off his thin white undershirt.

He hears the guy who has been out of his life and in Japan for the past six months just behind him.

"Just in time for the strip show," Dax says.

John's heart falls.

"Oh, don't stop undressing."

John doesn't respond. He lets his hands drop. His undershirt stays on.

Dax continues. "Pretty, let's see."

John barely frowns.

"What?" Dax croons, "You like it when I call you what you are—pretty."

John pretends to check something in his locker.

Just like he did when they met that night at Russ's wrestling school, the more seasoned pro moves in for the takedown. He lowers his voice and his hard-ass attitude. He opens his eyes very wide. "I just got in, and am here for you."

John knows this is a line and remains silent.

"I've come all this way, Johnny, all this way to Cincinnati."

John tries to consider this, but his thoughts can't stay in one place. His left hand finds some curls over his left ear.

"It was a long flight, John boy. And yes, I was thinking about you. Thinking about how special it was."

"Special—for you."

Dax repositions his feet. Without saying another word, he watches John closely. Without breathing in, he smells a whiff of uncertainty. Senses a flicker of fear.

Take your time, Dax tells himself. *Slow this down.* "Yeah, all this way to Cincinnati, for you."

John's voice is boyish, innocent and vulnerable. He begins to play with the quarter-sized hole in his jeans that, in his being tight with money, won't be replaced anytime soon. "All this way?"

There's that hope again. It's starting.

"Yeah, I've changed flights to come see you, John." Dax pulls on these mushy lines of a lie even more. "And all I could think of, in all that time and during all those miles, is you." Then he gives that smug look that says *I don't go further; this is all you get.* "You can give me a hug now, John."

John sets his jaw. He doesn't move.

Dax drops his heavy and vein-patterned forearm across the locker near the one John is using. He tucks one of his thumbs into a back pocket. He flexes. His size and his proximity do the talking now.

But damned of all things, that doesn't work, so Dax pulls him in. Because they are in a public place, it's the masculine, shoulder-to-shoulder hug, but something warms within John, and it's not the heat of the humid locker room. He wants to break away from Dax. Something in him stays still, though. He can't move. In the heat of Dax's arms, he thinks the worst possible thought: *maybe this time.*

Then he says no. This isn't what he wants. This isn't who he is. He wants to get away.

Dax lets him go, only to grab him quickly once again. This time, his hand cups John's crotch.

"You like this," he says, tugging on John's balls. "You need this from me."

John shakes his head.

"John, honey. You're mine. You don't have it within yourself to stand alone." A new grip, one more loose and gentle, heats John's crotch.

"Baby," Dax continues, "I know you're lonely. I can smell it on you. And I'm the one to fill you." He reaches around for John's hard and sculpted ass. He presses his finger—hard—way too hard—into John, who stumbles forward.

"See? You can't stand alone there, buddy."

Even though it's rough, no one has touched John since Dax left.
"Dax, no."

He continues with his lips close to kissing John's thick, muscular
neck. "Take a look at where you were six months ago. You know that
your pro wrestling coach, super stud Russ, had it for you. He craved
you, even reached for you. You remember that. I know you do. You
remember it again and again. But in the end? No, he's not the man that
I am. He's not the man to take you."

John squints and frowns. "Russ, Russ is married."

Dax exhales. "You need to be taken, controlled. You like that. You
need that."

John won't hear this. "Russ," he says, backing the conversation up
a bit. "Russ, he is a good guy."

Dax starts stroking John's ass. His hands are so big and strong.
John doesn't turn, however. Numb, he cannot turn.

The larger man tilts his head. "Russ? What? He's a good guy? If
he was your hero or your lover, he would have followed through. But
he shut up and left you on your own. Your own teacher didn't look at or
touch you—and it was his school! So, really, how's that good?"

John couldn't answer. He doesn't like this, doesn't know how to
move around this.

"If he cared," Dax says, his voice holding an edge, "if he cared—
he would have taken you like you need to be taken. Don't you see that?
You need to be taken, covered. Sexually you might top now and again;
you're a strong male; but under that muscle that you pump and pump
and pump, you need to be held, Johnny. You need to be held."

This is too much. Too true.

"You need to be held," Dax repeats as he takes the back of his
hand and strokes John's chest, barely rubbing the muscle boy's nipple
through the thin, extra-large undershirt. Dax slides his forearm under
John's arm and reaches up and around John's shoulder. His tone warms
even more. "You...you need to be held."

John is hollow inside. He can't move. He can't go. Dax has him,
from the inside. Dax understands him better than he understands himself.
Under the muscle, John's chest is hollow and hurting. He doesn't want
this man. He never has. Nerves zap his stomach. He wants to get away,
to run.

But can't.

Dax sits on the bench. With a rise of his chin toward the bleacher
area on the other side of the wall, he says, "Think about the guys who

will watch you tonight. How many out there will want you? How many will close their eyes tonight when they are with their girlfriend or their wife and will find you there? How many will have sex with you in their imaginations yet never come up and speak to you 'cause they're too afraid? Huh? How many, Johnny? These faggots can't even say hello to you—either outside the ring or on the street. They're too shy. Too trapped. Some are so stupid or repressed they don't even know they want you. But they do. They do want you. But..." Dax pauses for just a moment, "unlike me, they have nothing. Are nothing."

Dax leans back. In this position, the muscles in his shoulders harden even more. His knees open even further to showcase all he has below the belt. "So, look, it's me, buddy. Me. For you."

"Please, Dax."

"I'm the one for you."

"Please." John barely shakes his head no.

The agile man also shakes his head, mimicking John. "Please, what? Please stop understanding you? Please stop knowing you better than you know yourself?" Dax moves in for the kill. "You forget how much you say when you are so quiet."

"Please, stop."

Dax doesn't. He plays one last card. "It's your foster pop. He's the one. The trailer trash guy. He's the one who still drills into you, even when he's no longer close."

"No."

"Maybe if you spent more time with me in bed you'll see that things can be different, better."

John remembers standing outside Greg's newer and bigger trailer. He pictures Greg's kids and sees their sidewalk chalk. The empty Busch beer bottles. The redwood deck. The door shut so hard on his heart.

"Greg never came after you like I'm doing now, John. Sure, he sought your ass, but that's only because you were there, under his cheap-ass tin roof. Me, I've come for you. I've come for you because you know, in my heart, that I can claim you."

John shakes.

Dax's voice radiates warmth. "You need to be held. You need to cradled, to be loved. Let me do this, John boy."

John raises his eyes to meet Dax's. Without a word spoken, he asks, *really?*

Dax answers. "Really."

Lost, uncertain, and shaken, John lowers his eyes to Dax's shoulders.

"Trust this, bud. I'm the one for you."

And so the young blond man moves into Dax's strong arms.

❖

Sitting on the opposite side of the large, long locker room, Bret doesn't hear anything John and Dax have shared. For that matter, he really hasn't heard anyone here in the locker room. Tonight is his first match in the Mid-Atlantic League and he wants to do well. He's come too far *not* to do well.

He pulls off his Seattle Mariners T-shirt. The chain around his neck catches and rides, stopping at his strong, chiseled jaw. With one hand, he finds the dingy gold and rolls it between his thumb and his index finger. He can't keep this anymore.

He cradles the chain in the palm of his hand. A camp counselor, Tim was older and wore a shirt only when the head counselors were around. Otherwise, he was bare-chested. Tim had given him what was around his neck on their last night together. There, alone in their cabin, he finally hugged Bret—a long and slow, tender embrace.

And then he was gone.

Bret reaches behind him and unclasps the chain. He holds the cheap and tarnished metal in the palm of his cupped hand, and rolls it out into the bottom of the locker. The chain will belong to someone else soon.

The T-shirt, now wadded in his hands, holds a trace of his deodorant. It smells good, clean. He imagines his bare skin over white cotton sheets, his muscles being kneaded by his fantasy lover who, in ways, is just like Tim. There is a kiss at the base of Bret's neck, and Bret rolls over to straddle this dream man beneath him, kisses his soul mate back. Further and further, the kiss goes deep and long, deep and long. It probes. It finds something substantial, something real, something connecting.

Without his knowing, Lyle has been standing behind him.

"Wh-what? Oh, hey, Lyle."

Lyle straddles the bench Bret is sitting on. "Lost in thought?"

"Nah, just focused."

"Good."

"Focused on what I want."

Lyle figures how best to tell him the news. "Bret," Lyle says, "I've got something, something to tell you, and I think you really going to like it."

"Oh?" Bret replies.

"We've rearranged the matches. Who's wrestling whom."

Bret thinks about the time. The first match starts in ten minutes.

Lyle holds a clipboard with nothing on it but printer paper snatched from a recycling bin. "I'm sitting out tonight. Jason's wrestling someone else, and the guy I was paired with tonight is gonna wrestle you."

Annoyed, Bret tosses his T-shirt into his locker. "And who's the guy who was gonna wrestle you?"

"Come on, I'll introduce you. You'll like him," Lyle says. "Follow me."

Oh, great, Bret thinks. *Me, the new guy. And already there are changes.*

❖

As Bret follows Lyle through the long locker room, he thinks about that chain and revisits the thought that he never should have fallen in the first place, but he did. In an instant, he remembers the night he and Tim were at the end of the dock, their bare feet lingering in the warm water.

It was after dinner—another night of hot dogs with the nine-year-old boys—and they were alone. Side by side, the quiet felt good against their sun-touched skin. When Tim pulled out his lip balm—lip balm Tim knew Bret needed—it was there. In the moment Tim touched Bret's sore, sunburned lips, their eyes met, locked. It was better than any kiss.

Any stupid kiss.

Bret will never go back to a place of longing like that again, and when Lyle, just steps ahead of him, suddenly stops, Bret almost walks into him.

The two move to the left because a sleek dark-skinned wrestler with attitude quickly passes. Bret notices that neither Lyle nor the man the size of a bull say hello or even nod to one another.

Bret continues to follow his guide through the locker room and almost runs into Lyle a second time when he stops.

"Hey, John," Lyle says in an introduction, "this is Bret—the guy you'll be wrestling tonight."

Bret and John say nothing. They just stare at each other. Like a cold and warm front, they are two storm systems that don't mingle. Between leaving a chain and the memory of a fantasy lover from camp in the bottom of a locker or falling into the arms of another wrong man, too much has happened too soon to both of them.

"Well," the matchmaker says, "you should at least say hello. Shake hands."

John stares at Bret's tight, bare stomach. Bret focuses on the hole in John's jeans, but neither moves. Each stand as beefier versions of Michelangelo's *David:* muscle as hard as marble, no known heart.

Lyle tries again. "Bret, Bret here's from the west. The Pacific Northwest."

John's voice dries and flattens just beyond his throat. "Oh yeah? Huh."

Lyle tries again. "Right out there around Seattle, right, Bret?"

Silence.

Looking from one to the other, Lyle continues. "And John and I, we've been wrestling pro about as long as you have. What's that, John, about six months?"

More silence.

Their shoulders tense, their chests are puffed and pronounced.

Words are weak.

In the red heat between them, neither one says, "I will lose."

Tonight there will be a match like no other.

CHAPTER THIRTEEN

*J**ust who does he think he is?* Bret wonders, making his way back to his locker. *He's an ass, for sure. Cocky like that. Those icy eyes and the tough guy 'tude? An ass! I'll take that attitude from him, that damn smugness. Just take.*

He stands at his locker now. He's mad. Mad like he hasn't been in years. He catches sight of his white wrestling boots in the bottom of his locker, then stretches his neck to see his own carved abdominal muscles and the gray band of his underwear just hinting out of his jeans.

Bret's never been this stirred before, this damn *primal*. He wants to top John, just roll over and clamp down on him *hard*. Whether John's gay or straight or in between—it doesn't matter. Bret wants to control that lean muscle hunk, just dominate John when they square off.

And yeah, since nothing's been planned, *anything* can happen.

He kicks off his shoes. Oh, he's going to like this.

As Bret slips off his socks, he thinks John probably never had to pick up broken pieces of his soul that shattered in heartbreak. Nah, not this guy. This superficial stone doesn't know pain or isolation. He doesn't slip under cool sheets night after night because someone warms his bed.

Yes, Bret wants to take him, take him down hard.

Bret thinks ahead. Tonight he debuts in this new league. Lyle made it clear when they were talking that Bret is to lose tonight's match. But since they haven't practiced together, since none of tonight's action between them has been rehearsed, there's no saying that Bret can't dominate John or that he won't be the one who *should* win.

Bret hurries to change into his signature trunks, the ones he wore in his Pacific Northwest League. They are a deep green with a small, glittery shamrock on one hip. The Irish Whip has been his ring name. But he pulls the green off. Not tonight. Tonight he reaches back into his flight bag.

Tonight is the night for something new, something risky and raw, something that will match his mood, his anger at the blond boy but more so at himself for being so damn alone. Tonight he will show Cincinnati that he is and has champion quality; that he will rise to the big leagues. And tonight, win or not—whatever—he'll show his strength and his talent by taking out this Malibu Ken Doll, by really showing his muscle twink opponent and the house that Bret McCalagrew has had enough, that it's time for him, finally time for him, to get what he wants.

To get what he wants.

But what he wants—is love.

❖

The challenger enters first. He notices a lot of college guys in the house. They're loud and they're drunk.

"Go get 'em, champ!" someone shouts as Bret makes his way to the ring.

"Faggot," chides another, which is followed by "Nice ass!"

"Nice indeed," comes from yet another. Bret wears a royal blue Speedo with two red swirls on one side that are complemented by three white stars that shoot toward his crotch. The American red, white, and blue fabric is thin, too thin, and skimpy with its high cuts over his muscular legs.

Yeah, he thinks. *This is the look I want. And this is the reaction I want from the crowd.*

He locks his cocky expression on his face as he thinks again of manhandling his opponent.

A stout, blue-collar forty-five-year-old raises her hands to the side of her mouth and shouts, "Red Hot, you're all *that.* You're comin' home with me!"

Kids, oblivious to the adult comments, hold out their hands for Bret to slap. He does. He loves this part. Their faces, their starry eyes, their smiles.

Bret slides under the bottom rope, crosses to the opposite corner, and stands on the second turnbuckle to face the crowd. With arms half-raised, he nods to the cheering crowd, then flexes in a crab pose. He repeats this in each of the corners of the ring. Clasping his hands, he stomps his feet to the rhythm of the cheering crowd. With both hands over his head, he makes the gesture of a champion. The crowd goes wild.

The ring announcer holds his small white cue card at arm's length and uses that booming voice familiar to everyone. "Innnnntroducing in the corner to my right, weeeeeeeighing in at two-hunnnnnnnnndred and twennnnnty-five pounnnnnds, the Irish Whip!"

Bret grabs the microphone. With perfect boyish quality, he flashes a bright smile. He sets his hand on his thick thigh. "Your announcer here has got the Irish in my boilin' blood right; he sure does; but the Irish Whip is no more. No, I'm American. American made. American tough. And I'll show you who's your champ tonight! I am Adam Bomb and I will flatten whatever this league brings out for me!"

The crowd roars, then quiets.

His face set with real anger, John storms toward the ring. In contrast to Bret, he acknowledges no one in the crowd as he moves. He steps through the middle and top rope. A good bit of his butt is exposed as his solid navy trunks have hiked up on one side as he moved to the ring. John channels his anger at Dax through to this new guy. John slides his finger under his tight dark trunks to fix what Dax pulled a moment earlier when they were alone together.

Confidently, he puts both hands on either side of his lean waist.

The announcer has the microphone back.

John keeps his hands on the sides of his narrow trunks. His abs rippling, he takes a breath in and lets it out. Sweat glistens between his pecs.

"Annnnnnd innntroducing in the corner to my left, weeeeeeighing in at two hunnnnnnndred twenty-seven pounds, Jonnnnnnny RRRRRocket!"

John and Bret take steps forward. Tension builds. Along the metal seats, against the highest rafters, and through the ring posts themselves, pressure mounts. The crowd hushes. Everything stops. Everything just *stops*. One male voice, a dozen or so rows back, says to no one in particular, "Wow."

Indeed, the sight of the two of them face-to-face is impressive.

John, gladiator arms loose at his sides, takes another step closer to Bret. John is leaner and seems a hair taller than the man he meets in the center of the ring. John's shoulders are broader, his clavicles are more pronounced. His pecs are wide; his nipples rest at the crest of his naturally smooth and developed chest.

Bret flexes. His lightly hairy chest, in contrast to John's, is more curved. His pecs appear heavier, more substantial. His small nipples, pale like his Irish skin, almost hide from the sharp light above them.

Both men have six-pack abdominal muscles, yet Bret, who is more anxious, breathes more deeply now. This shows his washboard cuts deeper under his slight yet exact trail of reddish hair that, in one crisp line, dives into the front of his wrestling tights.

They each twitch their hands, roll their fingers. For all of their differences above the waist, they have nearly identical legs. Grapefruit-sized calves hold wide, very muscular thighs. Both have hard, perfect, muscular butts. Each man also fills the front of his wrestling trunks. Both are beautiful in the way that is almost ruggedly perfect.

"Okay, guys," the referee says after a moment, "I know you haven't practiced this, so be careful. Nobody gets hurt here. Okay?"

Neither takes his eyes off his opponent. Neither sees the man he met some thirty minutes earlier in the locker room with Lyle. This is a different place, a dangerous place.

John and Bret circle, each twitching their hands from time to time, waiting for the moment to strike.

When they move, the air changes.

They stop circling. Both—for the slightest fraction of a second—show their defenselessness. Yet here, eye to eye, they tell each other without a word spoken that they are tired of rude, in-your-face fans, nights on the road, and cheap hotel mattresses. Yet this is all they have. This, here, face-to-face, is all they know.

Together, this is wild, confusing. They will touch what they want but cannot have.

Their shields rise again. The show is on.

Bret takes the lead by charging at John's legs for a takedown. Once John hits the canvas, Bret wraps his arms around John's strong thighs. He lifts him up and then slams him down. The canvas reverberates back to the third row of seats.

The crowd likes this action. Bret senses the house is on his side. He raises his right leg as a weapon and drops it down to across John's mountainous chest. He does this maneuver two more times, knocking the air out of John's lungs. Several elbow smashes against John's abs follow.

The crowd cheers, but the ref breaks up the action, pantomiming that Bret was using a closed fist—against the rules. The crowd jeers.

John rises.

They lock up again. John throws Bret into the ropes as the crowd boos. Bret boomerangs off the ropes and John clotheslines him, knocking him back to the mat.

John, pressing his black with blue boot down hard on Bret's belly, hears the boos increase. He calls out, "Ah, shut up!"

John finds himself enjoying being the bad guy for a change. He decides to show the league newcomer what true power is all about. Stepping back into the center of the ring, he raises his arms, inviting Bret to join him in a test of strength. Bret obliges. They lock fingers over their heads. Their chests slam together. They slide against each other as they jockey for position.

With Bret's face near John's ear, he whispers as wrestlers often do in the ring, "Take control. Win the match. But first, let me throw you around for a while—the crowd's with me. Then, bad boy, make one final move and pin me."

"Sure."

But it doesn't happen. Instead, they flip each other, over and over to the delight of those who won't forget this night.

❖

Fifty seconds pass…sixty-five. When they whisper again—both at the same time and each with their own new plan—the crowd is too loud, too wild. They don't hear each other.

John plays his part and kicks one of Bret's white boots. To gain even more from the crowd, Bret overreacts on the third and fourth stomps, allowing John to get the upper hand on their deadlock. John uses his elbow as a battering ram on Bret's chest. After a couple of square hits, Bret goes down.

Mat action follows, and both show their skill as they exchange holds, test each other's strength, and battle back and forth.

Soaking wet eight minutes into the match, John clamps a headlock on Bret. This brings the two of them to their feet. Bret tries to power out, but after the last series of strength-demanding holds John's put him through, he has no energy to do this.

John sets his opponent still and snakes his leg over and around Bret's leg. He bends Bret at the waist, trapping his shoulders in a twist. Bret, now on full display to the house, tries to back into John's front, which means forcing his ass against John's crotch.

Bret squirms in the abdominal stretch.

"Ease up, man!" he shouts to his captor not for his sake but for the enjoyment of those in the first few rows who can hear him. "Ease up!"

John responds. "No way!"

John bends him further, further displaying just how hard and muscular Bret's stomach is. Bret starts to quiver as John brings him closer and closer down to the mat.

Bret tries to elbow John, but it is no use. He's trapped.

This stretch requires only one of John's hands. With the other, he starts stroking Bret's taut abdominal muscles.

John's hand probes further to clamp onto one of Bret's pecs. Bret roars.

Bret bucks and moans. John, whose strong square jaw just hovers over Bret's neck, re-grips, squeezing harder.

The assault is an awakening. It's incredible, hot, fun.

Hungry, Bret wants him even closer. Ass first, the new guy to the league backs further into John.

Perfect flexed muscle, tension, desire. The crowd stomps their feet.

Bret wants to play, hold John differently. In time, the newcomer gains enough strength and momentum to quickly drop to his knees. He takes John with him. John, on impact, rolls over Bret, who leg locks him. Bret clamps both of his hands on John's jaw. From behind, he sits on John's hard and sweaty ass and arches John's back away from the mat.

John squirms. To feel Bret's inner thighs on either side of him, to be trapped, to be held with such strength, such masculine control—it's his dream.

Bret growls. "You like that, don't ya?"

John moans his response—deep and guttural. This man-hungry sound, this low cry, this natural want, rises.

Bret's clamp is warmer, tighter, incredible, sure.

John is limp now, tired, unfocused. He just wants to be taken, owned.

Sensing this, Bret reaches for his opponent's hand and, with it, rolls John to his back. Bret stretches over him, pressing his rippled midsection over John's. The two breathe in one fluid motion as Bret covers for the pin.

The referee slaps the canvas once, twice. John squirms and kicks out.

"Not enough, huh?" Bret asks.

But it is enough. They both know it. John is to win this match, as decided some twenty-five minutes ago.

To appease the crowd, which has never seen anything like this from the small-time league, Bret picks John up by the back of the head. Disoriented, John falls into Bret's rock hard chest. He realizes that he longs to smell Bret, to hear his heart, and be held. In Bret's sure and steady arms, John takes in Bret's natural, clean scent. He closes his eyes, nuzzles in, moans. *He wants this.*

Bret wants this too, but remembers where he is. He slips his arms under John's tight stomach and flips them, easily sending both to the canvas.

John focuses, rises, and lifts Bret. They are belly to belly for a moment, crotch to crotch. Bret lets out a cry of ache and desire. Then John drops to one of his knees, spins Bret upside down, and, with great power in his legs, holds Bret upside down and stands again.

The crowd is wild. They scream. John has Bret totally defenseless. Keeping Bret's face between his own knees, John parades the boy in red, white, and blue around the ring, careful to hold him still in a very tight bear hug.

Then he stops.

And he drops.

Bret doesn't roll his head in time. His head hits the canvas with full force. It's a rookie mistake and he's gone. There's a full minute when he cannot speak, when he cannot move.

John turns for the cover and sees that Bret's eyes are not in focus. "Oh, no!" he says loudly, but no one hears, not even Bret.

As the referee counts Bret out, John yells, "He's hurt! He's hurt!"

CHAPTER FOURTEEN

It's Lyle who carries Bret back to the locker room. With a sense of guilt that is so strong he ignores his bad knees, Lyle lays a limp Bret out on the massage table. Wearing only his wrestling gear, Bret remains dangerously quiet. An EMT leans over the table. He too is silent.

John paces nearby. *Oh God, oh God, oh God.*

Lyle stops him. "He's going to be fine, John."

Bret says something no one can understand.

"See?" Lyle says to John. "He is talking. He's good. He's really good."

The EMT leans over the massage table and asks, "Where are we?"

Bret concentrates.

"Where are we?" the EMT asks again.

No response.

The EMT asks his question a third time.

"In the wrestling place," Bret answers, his speech slurred.

The EMT continues. "What wrestling place?"

Bret doesn't answer.

"Okay, Bret. That's fine. We're just looking to see what happened, and how you're doing. How about another question?"

John moves in closer. He wants to be there, has to be there. *I did this*, he thinks. *I did this to him.*

"Now, tell me what year it is?" the EMT asks.

John moves even closer.

Bret swallows. He looks at John. He lowers his eyelids and raises them again to John. There's just a bit of a smile. "We're in Cincinnati."

"That's right," the EMT says. "In Ohio. Can you tell me what month of the year it is?"

Bret smiles again. His teeth are perfect. He's so handsome to John.

"Bret?" The EMT asks.

His green eyes flicker a bit in concentration.

"It's hot," he says. Turning to John, he tries harder. "It's June. June thirteenth."

He starts answering the questions without hesitation. A bag of ice finds the top of his head, and a sheet covers him for a half dozen seconds until Bret slides it down to the top of his red, white, and blue wrestling trunks. "It is hot," he says again.

"A shower soon," Lyle promises. "Just rest a bit first."

Lyle and the EMT conference about whether Bret should go to the ER, and it's decided that he should definitely get medical treatment.

Hearing this, Bret raises himself up on his elbows. Still sweaty, his muscles shine.

Stepping back, John takes all this in from a distance.

"Bret?" Lyle asks.

There aren't enough words in Bret's head to admit that he should go and get checked over.

"He really should go to the hospital," the EMT insists.

"Pack him up," Lyle says to the nearest wrestlers. "We're off."

❖

Lyle quickly makes his way to the parking garage across the street to get his Jeep.

"I'll get Bret's stuff from his locker," Vaughn says as he passes John, who has backed up to the door. "You watch him, John."

John looks down. He can't face what he's feeling, let alone what happened. Alone with Bret, he stares at the floor.

"If you're going to be a doorman, you're going to have to wear one of those corny little hats."

Did I just hear that? John swallows nervously. "What?"

"Yeah, those corny little hats."

John doesn't understand. "Hey, Bret? About…well, with us in the ring? I'm sorry. That shouldn't have happened."

Bret's voice is low and warm. "I'm the one who messed that up. You were fine."

"You were fine too," John echoes. His stomach sinks an inch or two. He wants to run but stays.

Bret squints. He pulls his closed lips into a frown. It's enough to hold John there.

They stare at each other.

"Definitely a little hat," Bret says, "if you're going to go back to the door."

"Uh-huh."

"And maybe one of those little bells."

"That's for a bellhop, Bret."

"Oh." Bret swallows. "Right, right." He wiggles just a bit under the sheet, crosses his feet at his ankles, and, after sighing just the slightest, faintest sigh, says, "Hey, this pinning me deal?"

"Yeah?"

"Don't get too used to that."

❖

He can taste Bret on his lips. They're coated with his sweat and Bret's.

John continues to walk down the alley just outside the sports complex. He didn't shower after Lyle and Thunder, his hotel roommate for the night, loaded Bret into Lyle's Jeep. He couldn't. He just had to get out of there.

Sure, Bret was okay when lying down on that table, but the moment they moved him, he threw up.

And then he shook.

And then he quivered.

And it's my fault, John says to himself now. His fingers find curls over his ears. *I did this.*

His duffel bag, which is over his shoulder, brushes against the small of his back. He didn't pack it well. Lopsided, it kept bumping into him, but it didn't matter. He just had to get out of there. He just had to go.

Guilty, distracted, and numb—a combo he's never experienced before—John walks for three blocks, maybe four. At a downtown street corner in a bad part of town, the breeze shifts. The scent of Bret's sweat whirls around John now. It's intoxicating.

John turns from the breeze, slips his hand into his shirt, pulls it out, and smells.

Bret. Yes. Bret.

And I hurt him.

The intersection where John stops is very accessible to wheelchairs in that the arched curb opens wide. And John did turn. And the driver of the new compact car with fogged-up windows from the humidity did have one too many at the pub. The flashlight he stowed on the dash did hit the floor and roll under his feet and there was no big blond guy. And then there was his midsection in the headlights. And with one deathly *thud*, John crashed onto the edge of the street.

Nothing made sense at first to either the driver or the pedestrian. Maybe it didn't happen.

But it did.

Slowly John turned in the direction the car had been traveling. And there it was, up the street a bit. Maybe some ninety feet away. Bright red. Little. Shining. Engine running. Brake lights on. White license plate.

The driver couldn't stay stopped. What? This much weed in the glove compartment?

The little red car slid back into a travel lane.

Then John's shoulder screamed. It actually screamed.

❖

An hour passes. Walking with his shoulder out of place makes his steps take that much longer.

Finally, back at the hotel lobby where the Mid-Atlantic League blocked a group of rooms for a cheaper rate, the fifty-three-year-old front clerk says, "Can I get you anything? Call someone? This does not look good."

"No, no," John responds, shaking his head. "Just a little sore. You know how a guy is when he hurts something. Just a big baby."

Having sons and nephews that are poles, she is impressed with his size. "I'll give you this, you're big. But, honey, is there something I can help you with?"

John shakes his head and tells her that with his roommate, Thunder, he checked in this afternoon.

The woman working here for extra income to put her kids through college does some quick calculating as she considers John's age, build, and stiff, awkward movements. And he smells like the road.

Everything changes. The dour expression on her face makes her ten years older. Condemnation spills out into her words when she asks, "You're with that wrestling association?"

John foresees what will happen if he answers. He'd rather stay quiet.

She doesn't. "Well, I don't get any of what you do for *entertainment*, if I can be honest."

John stares at the open newspaper on the counter in front of her.

Seeing that this young man really is in pain, she says, "And I wonder what your mother would say about this, if she were here now."

He presses the button for the elevator with his one good arm.

My mom.

Upstairs, he can't find his room. In his head, he repeats his room number as he moves down each corridor but, after checking each door carefully, can't find it. The one and only directional sign indicates rooms 300-315 are left and rooms 316-330 are right.

His room is here. Somewhere.

He recalls something as he walks along the hall a second time. He remembers a time before foster care began. Living with his aunt, he would pretend he had an imaginary mom. As he keeps searching for his room, he thinks of his pretend mom, a woman very unlike the one he just met downstairs.

Yes, he smiles.

Just like when he was just a little kid, his pretend mom would be a beautiful, plain woman with classic style. And spunk. Definite spunk.

She might have even come to Cincinnati tonight.

If she were here, she'd help him now. She'd have recognized this confusion sooner, gone down to the desk and said, "Excuse me, we can't seem to find our room. If you don't mind, would you please help us?"

The elevator dings. John smiles. That would be her. She'll step out of it and help him.

The elevator doesn't stop on the third floor this time, however. He's on his own.

A minute passes. From where he'd been standing, John moves on when all he wants to do is stop. To keep on going—to live in the future tense—has been John's way of life since the day he first entered foster care—and a cute, blond, Caucasian boy without medical handicaps or obvious mental deficiencies received a lot of attention at first. He learned early what he needed to do, and that was to keep running through the years. Without ever saying it, he came to understand that something better would be down the road. Oh yes, glimpses of happiness were sprinkled here and there—the brand-new bright blue bike when he was ten, the season pass to the swimming pool at the Y the summer he turned twelve, the free art classes he took at a Jewish Center as a gift for his thirteenth birthday—these things were great—but even with Greg he knew this truth: there was always the future, and the future would always be better than the here and now.

Right here between rooms 325 and 327, however, he doesn't want to go on. For the first time in his life, he stops. He just completely, truly stops.

Right in front of him, a hotel room door swings open. A young man his age stands in dark dress socks and suit pants. The front tails of his starched dress shirt, which he just pulled out of his waist, ripple like a cummerbund. In a bright blue summertime dress, the young woman behind him holds his stripped tie. She is so pretty. Her face glows.

Unbuttoning more of his shirt, he turns and asks his girlfriend, "So, honey, the ice machine is where?"

"I don't think they have one," she replies.

He looks at John. That exchange is literally a second, but the young man, seeing John's clothes marked up just enough from the accident that it looks like John is a low-end slob, knows the kind of guy John is. The young professional doesn't ask his question about the ice machine to John because John isn't good enough. It's not a slight. It's a fact.

"We'll just forget it," she says as he shuts the door.

Alone again, John leans against the wall with his good shoulder and looks back to the door that just closed.

He slumps down, right there in the quiet of the hall.

The elevator bell rings again. Maybe it is his pretend mother this time.

❖

Whatever the doctors had given John for the pain must be working, maybe a little too well. He's on a gurney in the ER at University Hospital, the same hospital Bret and Lyle left some fifteen minutes earlier. All he knows is that it's quiet and, for the moment, he's alone.

A few of the wrestlers found John folded over in the hall about an hour earlier.

"It happened in the ring," they said to the intake nurses, and made sure John understood that—for insurance reasons.

Like family, they are waiting in a lobby somewhere. Thunder, John's good-hearted and goofball roommate at the hotel, has been with him this whole time but stepped out to where he could make a cell phone call because, at home, one of his little guys has had a high fever since dinnertime.

John checks his watch. It's 11:20 p.m. While he has not been here long, he should get going. But he can't. His eyes are heavy. His face is warm. His thoughts are drunk.

Staring at a sign on how to perform CPR, he can't feel his right shoulder.

He tries to stay awake, but, in a moment is gone again, deep in the place between sleep and drugs. He can feel Bret's stomach rising and falling against his bare back. He knows it's Bret behind him. The newcomer's soft chest hair, the scent of his skin, and the warmth of his even and slow breath takes John to a safe place, a good place where it's just the two of them alone. There is a duvet covering them. Bret burrows his nose into John's hair, clasps John's hand with his own.

"You're all right, John. You're all right."

A nurse passes. He wakes to her sound. He hears her footfalls and part of a conversation she must be having with herself.

He stares at the CPR poster again—trying and trying to keep alert—until, just like that, he can't keep his eyes open.

He drifts. He dreams. But there is no room this time, no duvet cover, no one holding his hand and telling him he'll be fine.

He has to go. Whatever or whoever is looking at him here in the hospital needs to let him go.

Focusing is hard for him, but he needs to stay awake. He needs to be ready for anyone who comes in with something to say about his shoulder.

More minutes pass. He's waiting for his x-rays, isn't he?

His eyes are heavy again. *Dang this!* That stupid red car. That intersection.

He won't drift off again; he can't afford to go where he's been because with Bret—tender, warm and close—it will never happen.

"The doctor will be in to see you shortly," another nurse says to him.

Quiet as usual, he doesn't respond with words.

The nurse continues. "The doctor, she's just down the hall with another patient."

John's eyes flicker with worry.

She comes closer. "What, what is it?"

"How…how does it look?"

She smiles the way only a night nurse can.

"It looks like you hurt yourself," she answers. "That's how it looks."

His eyes come down all tired and low.

She measures him with her steady eyes. While she's seen all types here—ah, hello, she's an ER nurse working nights in a city hospital—there hasn't been one quite like this. Cute. Guarded. Stoic. Alone.

Sure, there's a small herd of guys the size and weight of beef cows not far from here, but she realizes deep within herself that he's alone. Really alone. He's no wimp, for sure—that shoulder *really* is out of place—but he needs love, caressing, and care.

And then, as only a woman like her can do, she realizes what Lyle has come to slowly understand. The lasting love this man in front of her needs can only come from what another male can provide.

"Yes," she peeks down the hall for the doctor, "just a moment or two more. Okay?"

CHAPTER FIFTEEN

A bout the time the nurse is talking to John, Bret steps out of the shower back at the hotel.

"What do you say?" Lyle asks. "Do you feel better?"

Bret, wearing a very thin towel around his waist, isn't about to tell the very large man in front of him that his head feels worse, or that the pain makes it hard for him to think.

"Yeah," the new guy answers. "I'm good."

"Good? Then let's go."

His head really does hurt. Go? They'd just come back from the ER. Did he miss something?

"Yes, muscles. Let's go." Lyle explains more. "To get a late dinner. Gail Jackson, our promoter, is buying you dinner."

Lyle reads the new guy's expression. "No, you haven't met her, but this is Gail's way of saying hello, from afar. She's in New York City now and has heard what happened tonight."

"And about my mushed-in head."

"And about your mushed-in head."

Lyle folds his hand into the front pocket of his jeans. "Come on, towel boy. Let's eat, just the two of us. She's buying and I'm hungry."

❖

As Bret wonders if Gail Jackson will actually be paying for this, Lyle continues to ponder an ample, plastic-coated menu from a chain restaurant.

Their waiter has just left with their drink orders. Even with what could be a bass drummer pounding in his head, Bret can't help thinking about what happened earlier in the ring: lots of muscle, determination, tension, heat, and those eyes, those don't-take-me but I-want-you-to blue eyes of his.

John in his bright blue trunks. How that wrestling gear fit him so well. Lean. Sculpted. Hot.

"Bret?"

The trunks, oh-so form-fitting.

"Ah, Bret?"

And the weight of him. The feel of this new, dangerous, and sensual man over and under him, and over again. His slippery skin, his ability, his power, and his playfulness. And his belly, when expanded by his breath, nestled into Bret.

"Bret." Lyle taps the table. "Bret?"

"Huh?" Bret sees what's in front of him. Their server sets two tall glasses of ice water in front of them.

Lyle laughs, leans forward, and, looking at their server, says of his dining partner, "Ah, yes, the muscle boy, he's back."

Bret starts to order. Halfway through looking into the menu, he has a little difficulty.

Repeating what the server asks Bret, Lyle leans toward his dinner companion to help out. "Hey there, Rabbit, according to the menu, your salad—your wimpy little green salad—comes with a soup: vegetable, bean, or ham and potato."

"Oh, vegetable."

As Lyle hands both menus back to their server, the big guy frowns the two wrinkles around each eye that now never go away. *Salad. Like what guy orders lettuce for food?*

A quiet space fills between the two of them. In it, Lyle wonders if, in fact, Red here is a rabbit because this shy, quiet personality type fits.

Bret folds his fingers together, studies them, and says, "My ears aren't that long."

"Huh?"

"I know what you're thinking."

Lyle takes a hit off his ice water. "Nobody's that good."

❖

With food in front of them, he has to ask. He has to.

But how?

And how does he not make it sound important? While studying the paper placemat in front of him, he tries not to sound all that interested in his question. "So, Lyle, you two started at the same time?"

Lyle's eyes do not flicker. "'You two?' Who do you mean? Me and..."

Bret swallows.

Lyle waits another second before rolling his hand forward. "Me and..."

"You and John."

There. He said it.

"Oh yeah, we did start at the same time from the same school in West Virginia. John...he was just as determined then as he is now. We didn't wrestle together once we got to the Mid-Atlantic League, though, at least at first. It's not smart to put two novices together, but yeah, we trained at the same school. We actually met there."

Bret plays with the greens on his plate. *Two novices together.*

"I know where you're going," Lyle raises his fingers off the table to make a stop sign out of his hand. "You and John, well, it was Gail's idea. She wanted to bring something to John's character, see what we can do to make him more domineering in the ring. And for him to square off with you...it's a bit different, edgy. Not that two young muscle guys haven't gone at it in a ring before, no, that sells; but that's a story line the Mid-Atlantic League hasn't had in a while."

Bret's focus blurs enough now for Lyle to notice.

"It's your head, isn't it? Are you all right?"

"I'm fine."

He is not fine. Maybe a few deep breaths would help. Maybe when the food settles. And there are low lights. And quiet.

Lyle asks for the check as soon as he spies their server again. When the waiter leaves for their bill, Lyle says exactly what Bret is thinking. "For me...wow...it seems like a long day."

Bret cannot throw up again. He wills this.

He just needs a pillow, a bed, and long, deep quiet.

❖

A soft glow through a half-opened curtain from the parking lot lights below illuminates the queen-sized bed in room 323. This is all the light Bret can handle. He carefully clicks the door closed behind him. The dress shirt he wore to dinner now hangs off one elbow and does not make a sound when it lands on the carpet near the bathroom.

His head hurts too much. He hurts too much. He steps out of his shoes and glides to the bed. He doesn't turn down the bedspread; he doesn't care. He closes his eyes. On his back, he takes in the scent of something like the scent of flowers in a spray can.

Ten minutes pass. Twelve. Fifteen. Maybe a pain pill, but it's too soon from what they gave him in the ER. Maybe Lyle should take him back to the hospital.

This pain increases. He tries not to think about his first night wrestling in this new league and how he would rack up an even bigger hospital bill if he went back. Oh, yeah, that would be great, for sure. Another run to a doctor and he could kiss this wrestling life here in the east good-bye.

And maybe that would be all right. Maybe that is what should happen. Get out of this. Go back to school. In two years, he could have his degree.

To avoid the throbbing in his skull, he thinks of those two boys on the flight east for the second time tonight. Roger and Elliot…yeah… those are their names. Beside him on the plane, Roger said when he grew up that he wanted to be a pilot. Elliot, on the other hand, wanted a girlfriend when he grew up, and a dog, and both a cotton candy machine and a soccer field in his backyard.

In a few years, Bret could see them in his classroom…fourth grade, fifth or sixth. He imagines a big teacher's desk, geography maps, shelves stacked with textbooks and materials for earth science projects…a line of reports over the chalkboard on the Iroquois or the Lewis and Clark Expedition, notes to go to the office, excuse cards, a tub of basketballs by the door waiting for recess.

His head still pounds.

To avoid the pain, Bret shields his eyes by hiding them in the bend of his elbow. As he does this, John appears in the locker room where they met. White undershirt, quarter-sized hole in his jeans. And that face, those angles along his cheeks, his jaw, and those thin, pale lips.

And those eyes.

Heated, Bret squirms over the bed. His bare back rolls over the bedcover.

Somehow John is even closer now. His strong, handsome face tilts. His expression lightens, and then moves to curiosity. His mouth moves to say something but there is no sound.

Close. Closer. They are all right.

They are safe.

Inches apart, their jaws angle for a kiss neither plans. Bret imagines that they both close their eyes when their lips touch. At first, the kiss is smooth and flawless, simple and fragile. Another kiss follows a moment later.

With his hand sliding down his chest, Bret gives in to more of this fantasy. With John, he connects with yet another kiss that carries with it both force and drive. Patience, explorations, and the same intense physicality they engaged when they squared off in the ring hours ago heats up between them. Muscle on muscle, muscle over muscle. John's hands cupping, grasping. Skin, drive, want, combustion, fire.

Bret raises and arches his back so that his shoulders press even deeper into the mattress. Spreading his knees over the bed, his crotch heats and begins to swell.

The pounding in his head swells too. He calls out John's name.

He catches himself and stops. *This is crazy*, he thinks, *crazy.*

❖

He's thrown up. It's a good thing, he tells himself, especially since he made it to the toilet in time. Still nauseous, he sits at the edge of the bed. He'll be better.

Bret sits a long time.

His stomach could erupt again, so he holds his gut and rolls to his side. It makes his head much worse, but his stomach better.

Staring at the wall with the window, he faces how alone he is. Sure, he has friends out west, but there aren't a lot of people he can call just to talk with now, though the numbers are in his phone in his suitcase. There's something else, something bigger. There aren't a lot of people who know him, or who know all of him.

Tonight he doesn't want conversation anyway. He wants love.

John. He's stupid for going as far as he did with his imagination.

Closing his eyes, he thinks of a guy who would be right for him. Someone with his act together, at least for the most part. Someone strong inside and out, with heart and soul. Someone hard on the outside with softness within, who gets a kick out of kids and is quirky in some tech way or good in business. Someone who touches, listens, can be tough and strong and silly in one beat and serious in the next.

Someone who dreams.

Bret thinks about where he's been. Along the way, did he play something wrong? Was there some guy who should've had another chance? Was he looking one way when he should have been facing another?

He lets out a long, slow breath, but that helps neither his stomach nor the ache under his chest. He swallows. Thinks about the questions he's just asked himself. In the dates he's had—such as they were—or when wrestling with any number of guys for fun, he wonders if he missed the guy he was meant to partner with.

Careful to keep his head still, he draws his hand to his face. His thumb traces the curves over his forehead. This feels good. Still, the pain in his head tells him he needs to turn. Slowly, he rolls again onto both shoulders and his back.

He maneuvers his legs so the bedding begins covering him. When the sheet and the blanket slide he thinks John is here again, but he knows that's a dream.

What guy is right for him?

Is there such a guy?

While still wearing his pants, he thinks of himself here in his underwear with his muscles deep and pronounced, touchable, traceable, responsive, ready.

To be touched like this. To be enjoyed.

And to touch someone like this. And to enjoy.

One of the green numbers on the nightstand clock changes. Another minute passes, and another. In this time, he thinks what he has thought before, and that is he wants to get married, be married, stay married. Bret knows he'll be signing on for nights like this, when his partner hugs the toilet bowl on his knees and begs to be left alone but is still only a call over the shoulder away. He knows there will be miscommunication, money problems, and more than one date that turns into pizza in a box in the car.

"Yes," he says to the new number on the clock, "that's what I want."

❖

It's worse.

God! He shouldn't have eaten. To avoid throwing up again, he sits up and slides his feet off the mattress carefully, slowly.

Ice.

He needs ice for his head.

Ice…ice…there's a bucket for it in his bathroom.

He finds no ice on either end of the corridor, nor in either stairwell.

And the room numbers are all weird. And there's all these weird bends to the hallway. Where's his room again?

Down in the lobby, the woman at the desk who is his mother's age tells him that a nearby quick/convenient market sells ice by the bag.

"It's just around the corner. Through the side lobby doors, across the parking lot, and it's a left. Can't miss it. A red and white building."

"Thanks, ma'am," he says, walking away from the front desk.

"Uh-huh," comes her flat reply.

CHAPTER SIXTEEN

A University of Cincinnati undergrad standing in the candy aisle of the convenience store sees a square-shouldered guy, muscular *and* delicious?

And then—*Oh my God!*—he recognizes him. *Yes! It's him! In the ring tonight! Man, up close, he's even bigger, taller, broader. And cute!*

Bret approaches this single guy on his way to the coolers along the back wall.

"Hey there," Bret says.

"Hey."

A minute passes. Bret can't find the ice.

Watching Bret complete his third lap along the freezer wall empty-handed, he comes in closer. "What are you lookin' for? Maybe I can help."

"Nah, no thanks. I'm good."

At a safe distance of ten feet from his fellow shopper, Bret stops. Still staring at the ice cream section, he starts to ask, "You don't...you don't happen to know if there is any—"

"Ice?"

Bret smiles. "Yeah. How'd you know?"

"Just a guess."

"Oh."

"If you want ice," the college guy says, "you have to ask for that at the check-out counter. They keep that out back in the storeroom freezer."

Bret's head is getting worse and what he's just heard seems like one or two more steps than he needs. His expression blanks. "Oh."

"Here," the college student says, "let me help you out. My name is Pratt."

Outside the store, Pratt sees that Bret's in pain.

"Oh God, your head!" Pratt sounds like he cares as he eyes Bret's dress. "When that asshole dropped you! That must really be bothering you, man."

Pratt's hazel eyes flash with warmth and attentiveness and Bret is so lonely. He should try here. He should give this a shot.

But something in Bret's mind says no. Definitely no. He senses something isn't quite right here, definitely not. Bret motions toward the parking lot and his hotel behind it. "Nah, I'm okay, Pratt. This is just… this nothing…I mean, this is nothing."

But Pratt is smooth and fast. Before Bret knows what's happening, Pratt has them back in Bret's hotel room. "Let me help you," Prat says, quickly unbuttoning Bret's shirt and slipping it off.

"What?" Bret wonders. "Why did you take off my—"

"You don't need that," Pratt says confidently. "If the ice drips, your good shirt here could get wet. And you look a little flushed, a little too warm. I care about you, buddy. Let's just get you cooled down."

In one seemingly fluid motion, both are on the bed. The lights are low. Pratt is holding the ice over Bret's pounding head.

"You need to relax more," Pratt says.

Bret is sinking. "No, I'm okay."

"You're not okay, Bret. Here, let me help you."

At first, Pratt's exploring hand is, in fact, therapeutic. It slides over Bret's broad shoulders and hard chest, down the valley of his sternum and out to each nipple, where quick, light strokes bring Bret to attention.

Worried, Bret suddenly sits up.

"Shh," Pratt says, his voice so soft and low. "Just rest, big boy."

Bret drops to his elbows, and collapses again. He ignores the hunger in Pratt's strokes as first they linger, then go lower and lower. Bret is thankful not to be alone, but senses something isn't right. But it will be. Of course, it will be. This is fine.

He listens to Pratt say warm and kind words about life on campus and about all the wrestling he and his brothers enjoyed tonight, especially Bret's match. "All those muscles," he says, "you can get hard."

This should stop, Bret thinks. Just as he's about to speak, Pratt's hand slides back up to his shoulder.

It's as if Pratt can read his thoughts. "You must get lonely, yes?"

Bret doesn't answer.

"I mean, you must be on the road a lot. Different places. Do you have a girlfriend?"

"No. Do you?"

"Yeah." Pratt shrugs. He waits a moment and adds, "Well, kinda."

Bret frowns. "Kinda?"

"You know." Pratt taps Bret's chest.

"I don't know."

Pratt stares at the blank wall nearest the bed, then down at the man beneath him. He can tell that Bret didn't catch what he was just trying to say about having a girlfriend and wonders, *do you have to be dumb to be a wrestler?*

"Well," Pratt tries again. As his hand continues to explore, he says, "Guys are just cool to hang out with too. Not so complicated. There's no games and shit."

"You mean it's just what it is. There's nothing more."

"Yeah."

Bret thinks of Tim, the fellow counselor from summer camp all those years ago, the one who gave him the chain he left in that locker tonight.

Pratt senses Bret being quiet. "What is it?"

Bret doesn't say. He wants more, but not with this guy.

"What?"

Bret looks up. "Pratt, you've been really nice to help me out and all, but maybe I should get some sleep. Yeah, it's been a long day."

"You're so strong, Bret. Just perfect, man. You just need to enjoy your body." Pratt bends enough to kiss Bret's chest, but his lips only hover. He slides his hand into Bret's shorts.

"This isn't going, Pratt," Bret says as he turns.

"You just need to enjoy this, Bret. And I'm relaxing you. Getting the tension out for you." Pratt's voice picks up a little edge. He reaches into the waist of Bret's cargo shorts and tugs on Bret's briefs. "Tough-guy wrestler, you need this."

Bret grabs and squeezes Pratt's wrist.

Pratt bounces out of bed intentionally to rattle Bret's head.

"You need to be cared for tonight. You beef cow. You stupid shit, you need to be looked after. *That's* what I was doing."

Bret can't stop the pounding in his skull and all this talking doesn't help.

Pratt is not letting this opportunity go. Again he'll gain the upper hand.

He finds where Bret is vulnerable. "I just want a boyfriend," he says. "I guess I don't go at it the right way."

When Bret doesn't immediately reply, Pratt knows he has his inroad.

Pratt is all sweet for a while, all tender. He knows how to play this. He'll say what he needs to say to get what he needs to get, and that's a guy this big under him.

Everything is right for the college guy. He even goes so far as to leave a false phone number for Brett to call him, because, really, he says, he just wants to touch another guy's soul.

"Not a one-night stand, you mean?" Bret asks.

"Oh, yeah. Absolutely," Pratt lies. "I want one good and lasting thing. I just wanna guy to hold forever, you know?"

❖

It wasn't to be sex. That's what Bret understood. That's what they had talked about.

But it turned raw. Mean. And Bret—especially with the pain meds Pratt encouraged him to double up on—couldn't squirm out. Couldn't fight back.

In fact, in a scramble, Pratt hit the back of Bret's head hard enough that a hard wall of pain numbed Bret.

There were dry heaves from Bret when Pratt mounted and pushed from behind, but busy with a fantasy he *never* thought would come true, the frat boy never knew that there was nothing for Bret to throw up.

❖

It's John who is standing in Bret's open doorway. Coming back from the hospital, he took the wrong turn because, using the stairs instead of the elevator, he went left in this damn confusing hotel rather than right. And here, in a room he thought was his, is Bret. With the door partially open, he figured his roommate for the night was just ahead of him, and hadn't yet turned back to shut the open door.

Bret, turning to see who's there, doesn't make a sound. With the bedding wadded around him, he leans his back against the headboard. He wants to run. He wants to hide. But he can't get out of bed now.

He's naked.

And he has no idea how to find his clothes among the sheets and bedspread.

Bret looks down to make sure he's appropriately covered. He is.

John motions to the door behind him. "It was open," he says. "That's how I got in."

"Oh."

Trying to ignore what he feels in the pit of his own stomach, John stares at the carpet and, having been hurt himself, just wants to be quiet himself.

He turns back to the door he just walked through, takes a step, but doesn't leave. Can't leave. He knows something's up with Bret. "You good?"

Bret doesn't hear him. In fact, he thinks he's alone again since it's so quiet.

Violated, he wonders, *how did this happen? How could I be so stupid? So weak? That weasel, he didn't want anything except sex, hard sex, mean sex, and he used shallow words to get there.*

And it wasn't consensual.

Bret continues to be silent.

Or was it?

John senses something has happened, something bad. But he has no words. There can't be any words now because this, in a way, this has happened to him before. Two victims. Two fools.

John would cry out, he would kneel by Bret's side, but he doesn't move.

Bret notices the sling.

"Nah..." John says before Bret can ask about his injury. "It's nothing."

Bret sits up, covering himself further. "Your shoulder there... tonight...us...in the ring...I didn't..."

"Nah, not you." Not wanting to be read like this, John swallows and holds his bad arm. "You, you gonna be okay?"

The single word, "Yeah," that Bret releases might as well have been no sound at all.

Had they just come at this differently from the start in the locker room all those hours ago, it would be different, so different. More than likely, there would not have been an injury in the ring. Later, John wouldn't have been standing on a curb about to be hit by an out-of-control car that might just weigh a little more than he does.

And there would have been no frat boy, no stripping down, no view of a college boy who looked good naked in front of Bret, no touches that to Bret felt good at first, then turned cold, vile, and raw.

Their eyes don't meet. There's nothing else to say here, nothing else to do. While Bret still wants to hide, John doesn't move. He can't move. He just doesn't want to leave. To walk out of a room he thought was his is not what John wants to do, but he doesn't know another choice.

"Good night," he says as he clicks the door closed behind him.

CHAPTER SEVENTEEN

Two hundred and nineteen guests sleep in the oddly laid-out three-story hotel that night. The sun will turn the haze above from a soft black to a festering pink that even drawn curtains cannot dim. Even so, most will ignore this awesome wake up call. Sleep is too good, especially during these early hours.

At the moment, a family of four from Montana are happy not be cruising over the interstates, even though at different points in the night, each wakes and swears they're still traveling in their overpacked car. Two floors below them, a couple in their late thirties, who applied for a marriage license yesterday, become pregnant overnight. Three doors down from them, twenty-seven-year-old Vaughn Spiller, one of the two roadies who sets up and takes down the Mid-Atlantic Wrestling League's ring and other equipment, is so tired from his first (and probably only) night of wrestling professionally that he doesn't stir. Directly one floor above him, Lyle Lowell, who has completed phase one of his plan, also sleeps the deepest sleep he's had since his girlfriend Betty broke up with him. With his idea of two muscle boys taking each other on in the ring being a success—and the fan response *was* wild—he's closer to phase two, which is managing even more wrestlers. He'd like this for three reasons: his left knee, his right knee, and, most important of all, he'll be able to stay put in a place where he can have a home with the one woman he loves.

Of the 219 guests, however, two do not sleep at all. In room 323, Bret repeatedly relives his time with Pratt. What he should have said. What he should have done. What he let happen. It all replays again, and again. Idiot jock boy.

It is his fault—totally. It's his own stupid, dumb fault. Letting that slime into his room in the first place was his own dimwitted desire to be held, to be loved.

And John, on the opposite wing in room 303, also doesn't sleep.

At first, he blames the fact that his shoulder is in a sling as to why he's so stirred, why he can't get comfortable.

He won't think about who was running through his mind just before he was hit. There'd been enough of that lately, thank you.

Instead, he imagines that little car is pretty well dinged up, though really, the only injury John has is his shoulder. Except for the big bruise on his hamstring, he doesn't have a single brush burn or road rash.

Yet he can't get comfortable with this damn shoulder thing. Tired of being awake, he glances at the clock between his and his roommate's beds.

He often buddies up with another wrestler to cut the cost of a room. Tonight it's Thunder, who came in smelling of beer long after John was already in his own bed.

John turns further to see the forty-four-year-old married father stretched out, sound asleep. Thunder has been his roommate before, many times. He's glad Thunder is sleeping soundly because he knows Thunder and his wife have an afternoon marathon of midget baseball games the next day.

Minutes pass. When John does close his eyes again and tries for more sleep, he can't help but relive what happened at the end of his match last night. Bret in his red, white, and blue wrestling gear. The newcomer sprawled out on his back across the ring floor, his stomach tightening with each intake of needed air.

John's eyes pop open. The smooth feel of Bret's skin under him. How close they were to each other, chest to chest. Holding one of Bret's legs up in the air, John slapped his other hand over one of Bret's pecs and felt the little rise of his challenger's nipple. The feeling wasn't anything then—in front of a crowd on their feet it couldn't have been anything then—but now, alone in this bed, and with Bret here on the same floor in this hotel, his wood rises.

He remembers their very first meeting in the locker room tonight. Bret was wearing just jeans when he came around with Lyle. Just those jeans. He had that smile too, that good-natured way about him.

How little he'd said when standing in Bret's room just a couple hours ago comes to him. He should have opened up more, made sure the new guy was all right.

But he didn't.

He slides out of his bed and finds the alarm clock between the beds. It's 3:47 a.m.

❖

The meds for pain do make John loopy. In the morning, he'll be driving home alone so he won't take more pills. Maybe they have something to do with why he's out in the hallway now, at 3:49 a.m. *Where in the hell am I going?* he wonders as he passes the elevators.

The hall is quiet and hot. He sees three exit signs over the stairwell doors. And then he does know what he's doing. He feels it in his chest. In a few barefoot steps, he stands outside Bret's door. It's nearly four in the morning and he wonders, *Is his light on? Is he all right?*

He stands there for a quarter hour. John can't even come close to touching Bret's door, which is just plain crazy.

❖

John does sleep off and on, though he'd swear he was awake the whole time. There, on the floor near Bret's door, with his lower back against the wall and his sling cradled carefully between his chest and good arm, he does drift in and out of dreams as long and as dull as this quiet hall. No one has walked by. No one has stirred, or he'd know it.

He's guarding the door because, in a way he can't quite explain, something didn't feel right when he was inside the room with Bret. And he's here now, close by, if Bret needs anything through the night.

Looking up and down the hall, he sees no one, and hears nothing.

Of all the places to be, he can't imagine being anywhere other than where he is now, one door away from this guy.

It feels right. It is right.

It's 6:18 a.m. Standing in his room with his door open, Bret isn't sure what he sees in the hall.

He rubs his eyes again.

John stands holding a bag of ice, just like the bag he bought for himself last night.

Ice? Bret thinks.

Neither says anything at first—it is early—then John blushes and stutters. "Bret, I, I th-thought…you know you…I thought maybe you could use more. For your head."

John takes a small step back after he hands the ice to Bret. Embarrassed, he swallows hard and thinks, *I shouldn't have done this. I shouldn't have done this. Bringing ice? Dumb. This is just so dumb!*

"Thanks," Bret says. "That's really—thanks."

John slumps away, moving back into the hall.

"Hey, man," Bret calls, not knowing how to stop him, not knowing how to turn him around and invite him in for a while. "Yeah," Bret repeats. "Thanks."

Another awful pause follows between them. "Your arm there…"

"It's good." John answers fast and he turns back to Bret. His look is stone.

Bret nods.

"Later, then," John says.

"Later."

John shoots a glance back over his good shoulder. In front of his door, Bret looks lost and alone. John thinks someone should come up from behind and wrap their arm around him and hold him, just hold him.

John swallows and stops. Damn. He doesn't know how to do this. He doesn't know how to do this.

He turns and walks back a dozen or so long steps. About ten feet from Bret, he looks down and says, "We, well, Lyle and me…and a couple of others, we, we have breakfast." His words feel like paste in his mouth, and, he knows he sounds stupid. "A couple of us guys. My roommate and me. You met him. His name is Thunder. There's a few others too. We'll get together in the lobby. It's at eight or so, if you wanna."

John doesn't wait to hear Bret. He can't, actually. He can't do or say more, not now. His neck is too flushed and his throat too tight. Turning, he says, "See you."

He walks into his room and sits at the edge of his bed. He leans forward. He stares at the pattern in the carpet and ignores how tight and nervous his stomach is.

❖

"Coffee, six coffees," their waitress says as she stands beside John. "All of yous, right?"

The six all answer affirmatively, and politely, at the same time.

"Good boys."

She sets a coffee cup before each of them. Her name tag reads *Beverly*.

"So this coffee," Lyle says, "it's good, right?"

"Honey," she replies, "this coffee is so good."

"And you ground the beans yourself, right?" It's Thunder who speaks this time. Like Lyle, he isn't shy.

"Well, of course," she replies with a twinkle in her eye.

Both John and Bret remain safe behind their large menus, finding comfort in the easy, ordinary conversation that continues around them. John and Bret sit as far from each other as they can at the two tables joined together. Three sit on each side of the table, but only four of the guys face each other. No one sits directly across from either John or Bret. John is closest to Beverly. As she goes around and takes each man's super-sized breakfast order, he is last.

John remains guarded and shy. He hands her the menu before he speaks. Beverly takes it under her arm with the others, but stops him from placing his order by raising her index finger. "Ah no," she says quietly, "first things first. Tell me now, what happened to your left gun there?"

"Even the muscle boys can break," Thunder says a moment later, but Beverly tilts her head to one side.

Later, when she comes to clear their tables, she hears them talking about Frederick, Maryland. One of them is moving there. An apartment of a friend of a friend along with a construction job is there that wouldn't interfere with whatever they do that brings them together mostly over the weekends. She guesses it's the redhead who's moving because he nods regularly, sometimes pensively.

Beverly asks him as she catches his green eyes, "So what's this, you're moving away from me here in Ohio?"

She realizes the Irish-looking one is just as cute as the blond at the opposite end of the table. *Good bones* is what her ninety-three-year-old mother would say to describe him, *good bones indeed*.

"Yes, ma'am."

She tilts her head. "Yes, ma'am what?"

"I'll be moving."

"Well, it's gonna be some commute to get your breakfast here now, ain't it?"

He gives her a warm, genuine smile. "But I'll come back?"

"You know," she says, "I'd like that." She touches his broad shoulder. "I'd like that."

❖

They'll all be heading back to their different towns after check-out. Some live several hours away, but because of this messed-up job that pays too little and asks too much, most of them meet for matches every weekend or every other weekend. Over these last couple of weekends in June, the Mid-Atlantic League travels to Baltimore, Maryland, and Allentown, Pennsylvania. The six do a mental head count to see who's wrestling when and where.

They had talked about John's prognosis before breakfast arrived. According to the doctor from the ER last night, he'll be out for at least six weeks, if not eight or nine.

"So, it's back to West Virginia, John?" Lyle asks as the two of them head to the elevator to pack up and leave.

John's voice is flat and gives away no emotion. "It looks like it."

When stuffing his duffel bag some five minutes later, John comes across the receipt for the ice he bought that morning. He paid cash. He throws the small white paper away in the bathroom garbage can. Before he shuts the hotel room door, however, he takes the receipt back out of the garbage can and, awkward with his arm in a sling, he places it in his wallet.

CHAPTER EIGHTEEN

A h, no," Lyle declares to Bret as they make their way back to his Jeep parked in the rest area parking lot along the interstate. "I drive. I'm going to trust my life and beloved four wheels to *your* driving after you couldn't even tell the server what kind of soup you wanted last night? Let me see. Thinking about this…thinking about this…um, we're going to go with a 'no' on this one."

Bret frowns. "Hey, he got an answer."

Lyle walks around Bret. "Passenger side, pretty. This chauffeur business is all mine."

Lyle's glad for the companionship, even though this swing to Frederick, Maryland, takes him well out of his way home in south central Pennsylvania. He's driving Bret after a shuffle with cars and drivers took place in the parking lot of the hotel a few hours ago.

From the quiet, Lyle hears Bret say, "Pretty?"

"That's Beverly's word there, muscles, not mine."

With his hands in his front pockets, Bret tries to figure out if he knows someone named Beverly. Then he remembers—their server that morning. *But wait, did she call him pretty?*

Lyle unlocks the doors. "And I think she liked you."

Bret drives his hands in his front pockets. It's nice to be outside on a morning like this. "She likes me? Nah. You're her type, big boy. And she didn't call me pretty, but you—yeah, my memory is kickin' in here—she called you her fella."

Ready to get more miles on the road, Lyle slowly folds himself into the driver's seat. Bret just watches.

Impatient, Lyle closes his fingers around the steering wheel and waves to the two ladies on the sidewalk still staring at Bret and says, "And you're *in* the jeep, *pretty*, or this show leaves without you."

A mile back on the interstate, Bret speaks first. He says, "I do think she likes you."

But she was worried about you, Lyle thinks, but keeps quiet.

Bret leans back. Though he's wanted to throw up a couple of times because his head just won't stop pounding, he spreads his knees and sighs. This is good, being with Lyle.

Lyle sets his cruise control and glances over toward his buddy. "Rest now."

"And dream of pancakes."

"Yeah."

Bret smiles. "A breakfast for two, for you and Beverly. Starched white tablecloth, single red rose, and flapjacks made into the shape of hearts."

Keeping his eyes on a car he wants to pass, Lyle says, "Shut up."

Bret repositions himself so he's totally facing Lyle. "You're in love."

Lyle glances over toward Bret with a look of one who's getting a flu shot.

"Yes, love." With his index fingers, Bret does some dashboard drumming and, in a voice that would never make it onto a recording, sings some awful made-up song down low and soft.

Dead silence follows. Moving the Jeep into the left lane to pass a slower vehicle, Lyle rolls his eyes.

"You like the song?"

"No, but these two important words are here, okay? Be ready now." Lyle pauses. "Ready?"

"Uh-huh."

"Shut. Up."

❖

The small, second-story apartment is a sublet through the end of September, but is home for now. The place came furnished and is in Bret's price range, which is cheap. Lyle lies and says the construction job lined up for Bret starts toward the end of the week instead of tomorrow morning at six. That head, Lyle figures, needs a little time to heal. And Bret knows it's been a long day for both of them. It doesn't take a lot of convincing to get Lyle to spend the night, especially since their drive with some surprise road construction took over seven hours.

What does take some convincing is getting Lyle to take the full-sized bed instead of the couch in the small living area.

Alone now on the couch, Bret tries to sleep. He doesn't want to be alone with his thoughts, though, particularly as memories from what happened last night in his room cannot be quieted.

You must get lonely, yes? I mean, you must be on the road a lot. Different places. Do you have a girlfriend?

No, do you?

Well, kinda.

Pratt with those eyes, those hands.

Why is my shirt on the floor?

So it won't get wet if the ice drips on it.

And there other words—kind words—when the two stripped to their underwear. Pratt had lowered the light, had been both gentle and strong. And it was all so right for a few minutes. It was so good, wasn't it?

Bret stops, turns, shakes, shivers.

It wasn't good.

None of it was.

He wills the bad memories away by taking one deep breath, and then another. His fingers slide over his stomach, which is cold and hard even though it's under a blanket.

Turning on the couch, he redirects his mind to the conversation he had with Lyle hours ago. It was just the two of them. Lyle was becoming someone Bret could trust, and Lyle asked the good questions, the caring questions.

And he listened.

Bret smiles because Lyle's questions bounced around—school, home, life, dreams.

Answers came, but Bret guarded most of what he shared.

Lyle didn't. He talked about getting expelled as a nineteen-year-old sophomore from Princeton University. He talked about his former life as a voice in radio, which is a job he both loved and hated: loved because of the people he met, and hated because the music wasn't the good stuff—the good stuff, according to Lyle, were bands from 1962 to 1974.

"Nothing past 1974?" Bret asked as the two shared a baked cod and a salad from the grocery store for dinner earlier. "Now why is that?"

"No soul, young man. No edge." Lyle set down his salad fork.

"Would you go back into radio, Lyle?"

Lyle thought about it for only a split second. "With these knees, yes."

"But you're going to be a wrestling manager."

With a dead serious expression on his face, Lyle asked, "Now, who told you that?"

Bret licked the tip of his thumb. "More cod, Lyle?"

"Red? Who told you—"

"More salad, then?"

❖

Bret wakes to the sound of a loud *thump* in the apartment building's hall. Another follows, not as loud, but it's definitely coming from an area outside the door.

Bret smiles. "Welcome to the neighborhood."

Some forty-five minutes pass. While no other noise slips through the door, Bret can't get back to sleep. Restless, he goes to the fridge he stocked that night, pulls out the gallon of skim milk, and pours himself a glass. More noises come from the hall. After finishing the milk and leaving the empty glass on the counter, he opens the front door.

A very handsome dark-haired guy stands there in the second-floor landing holding one end of a forty-four-year-old sofa. He says, "Man! Sorry! I'm making way too much noise. Did I wake you?"

Bret can't believe what he sees. First John, now this guy. Setting down an end of one of the ugliest sofas Bret has seen is a slim guy about five feet nine inches tall. With a closely trimmed, soft beard framing the bottom of a boyish face, the furniture mover smiles at him.

"Maybe I should have said hi first," the midnight man says.

Bret doesn't make a sound.

The guy's thick, shoulder-length hair frames brown eyes that reach right into Bret.

"Yeah, sure," Bret nods, "the hello thing. Maybe you should have said hi first. And then there's the housewarming gift."

"The housewarming gift?"

Bret sticks one of his hands into the back of his shorts and shrugs. "A housewarming gift, you know? Maybe you could have brought over a 'welcome to the neighborhood' cake or a jar of jam for the new guy in town."

"A housewarming gift."

Bret feels the base of his neck flush. "I'm never really sure how this whole domestic thing goes, especially at this hour. Shouldn't you have with you a cake, jelly, or a spare carburetor lying around?"

"Oh, buddy, I got you. You're saying this couch here *isn't* a good housewarming present?" The man's dark eyes move away as he taps the couch's arm rest.

"You're staring at me," the stranger says when their eyes meet again. "I know," he taps the arm rest a second time, "this isn't your color."

Bret's new neighbor straddles the arm and sits down on it. "And yeah, you're thinking I'm kinda small to be in the furniture moving business."

"And you're alone."

"How'd you know that?" he asks.

Bret nods. "Somebody would have helped you with this couch."

Wearing a thin, tight muscle shirt—a wifebeater—he flexes his biceps and drops his voice half an octave. "Me, no, I've got this."

"And that banging out here a minute or two ago? That was..." Bret slides his fingers over his chin.

"Banging out here a minute ago? Really? Huh. Must have been the *other* guy. And now he must be, you know, downstairs."

"Uh-huh." Bret shuts the door behind him. "Downstairs."

Bret's neighbor slides down to sit properly on a couch cushion. "I have a confession to make to you, man with really muscular arms and a chest Superman would be proud of."

"You don't have a moving partner?"

"Yeah, that, but there's something else."

Bret frowns as he places his feet further apart, as if to brace for impact. "Something else?"

"I don't know the difference between a jam and a jelly."

"I don't either."

"But I do know something."

"What?"

"You are about to ask if you can help me move this old stuffed beast into my place. I'm going to say yes. I'll agree reluctantly, mind you, but I will say yes."

Bret hides a grin. "That's how this goes?"

"Uh-huh."

Bret asks, "Can I help you now?"

"Ah, shouldn't you ask my name first?"

"What's your—"

"Ryan."

"Ryan."

After Bret introduces himself, the two move the overstuffed piece of furniture into an apartment the mirror image of Bret's.

Once inside, Bret takes a look around. Ryan's apartment is a relatively small space, just over 700 square feet, but the difference between these second-story one-bedrooms is remarkable. While Bret's three rooms plus bath never leave the beige family—and it took a combined time of forty minutes to decorate the whole place, including some cheap furniture assembly—Ryan's space reflects chic, open, and warm living. Bold, creative touches punch the place. Light and airy pieces mix with earthy mosses and two flat brown walls. Even an uncultured eye, like Bret's, notices from the curtain tiebacks, which are three-prong rusted pitchforks, to the dining area place mats trimmed in rust and gold, that everything hits and strikes perfectly, intentionally, and artistically. Everything, that is, except Ryan's "new" couch and coordinating chair, which was the first sound Bret heard in the hall over an hour ago.

Tired, Ryan plunks down in the chair, which farts on impact. His eyes open wide. "Did this chair just..."

Bret laughs.

Ryan holds his forehead in his hand. "Great. A chair with gas issues." With his face down, he studies the horrible fabric. "My friends said I couldn't get these rare and amazing sidewalk finds. That's why I had to move them on my own."

"You rented a truck?"

"Rent one? Nah, I have one—a big, mean, ugly truck."

"You have a big, mean, ugly truck."

"Yep, we're tight, that old Ford 250 and me. Going on twelve years now." He draws his left ankle up over his right knee. Ryan is wearing tough-looking hiking boots stained with grass. "What else? I take care of a dozen people's lawns, cut hair for a living, and like men who don't easily sit down in a new place." He laughs. "Bret, you were supposed to sit down on that cue. Take the not-so-obscure reference and plunk."

"Plunk?" Looking toward the couch, Bret stays still. "But I'm afraid of it."

"A guy like you? Afraid of old couch cushions?" Ryan frowns. "You ain't scared of nothin'."

Bret smiles. "But what if it..."

"The likelihood of another furniture fart? Highly unlikely."

Bret takes a seat.

Ryan leans back further, spreading both of his surprisingly big feet on the floor in front of him. "Better."

Bret makes himself comfortable on the sagging disaster of a couch.

Remembering to get something, Ryan continues talking as he heads toward the nearby kitchen. "My Ford 250? I just replaced the drive-train in my old bomb, so we're good for another fifty thousand miles." From the refrigerator, he tosses Bret a bottle of water that hits him squarely in the chest. "I knew you'd want to know about the truck over what fabric I'll reupholster this vintage stuff."

Bret holds the bottle. "But I'm not thirsty."

"Then two for me. This furniture moving bit? Yeah, it's definitely water time."

Good talk follows. Friendly. Inviting. They stand at Ryan's front door not quite twenty minutes later. Ryan holds the door frame near his doorbell while Bret intentionally tries—successfully—to get a trace of what Ryan smells like. Bret notices that those same muscle-lean forearms are covered lightly with the softest swirl of hair. Short, dark chest hair peeks out from the top of his muscle shirt.

"I don't clip it," he says. "It's just always been kinda short."

Bret swallows. "I wasn't looking."

"You were looking."

Bret motions toward his door. This has been good, but remembering Pratt from last night, Bret closes this. "I should say good night."

Ryan, without asking, almost steps into Bret. Securing the small of Bret's back with one hand, he stands on his toes to get close to Bret's face. Intentionally, he leans forward to kiss Bret's lips, holds steady for one moment, and then drops down a few inches to plant a warm, gentle, damp kiss right on the base of Bret's thick, strong neck.

Bret backs into his own door.

"Bears don't mess in their own woods," Ryan says. "Us being neighbors and all, we shouldn't...shouldn't go at this." He starts to shut his door. "At least tonight, anyway."

"Well, good night, then."

Ryan stops. "And you're really not all that gay, are you?"

Bret shakes his head.

"Thought so."

CHAPTER NINETEEN

In the living room six hours later, Lyle stands over him wearing super-sized Houston Astros pajama bottoms and a T-shirt. He says the obvious. "You don't look like you've slept well."

The sun through the patio doors beams into the apartment just before seven a.m., which is nice because Bret's a morning person.

With a cup of coffee in his hands, Lyle leans over the couch to study Bret's sleepy expression. "How are you feeling?"

Hungover could be Bret's first response, but he hasn't been drinking, not even the bottled water tossed to him last night. He says, "Fine, thanks. I'm good."

"Wake up, then. I'm buying breakfast before heading on home."

Bret moves the soft fleece blanket covering him. "Coffee first and then a shower, okay? And I'm buying you breakfast."

Lyle steps out onto the little balcony behind the patio doors. "Sure. I've made enough Quick Start for two, am cleaned up and ready to go."

With what appears to be something safe to drink once diluted with hot water, Bret joins Lyle on the vacant patio.

Leaning over the railing, Lyle takes in the view of the parking lot below lined with ornamental fruit trees, each with a neat mound of colored red mulch around its sturdy trunk, and the small playground far off to one side. Lyle hopes Bret will like his new place.

Bret doesn't see a thing in front of him. Instead, he thinks of old furniture. He considers the space behind him. His mind runs through all sorts of different colors he could paint the vanilla and sand-colored walls if he owned the place. He sees reds or hues of blue, maybe a crisp summer green.

The walls aren't his, though, and neither is the furniture.

He's just passing through.

Still.

And he doesn't want to pass through. He wants to be home. With kids. He wants a home that smells all buttery from marshmallow treats in the kitchen.

Staring out into what he can't quite see yet, Bret wants good expensive sheets he can wash in his own damn washing machine instead of running through pounds of quarters per load in some dank apartment complex basement. He wants a backyard clothesline so when he and his man get close at night, those fresh brushes from the air-dried cotton bedding all around them will make them feel like they are in the clouds.

Lyle leans over. His eyes meet Bret's. "Where you been, bud?"

"In the clouds. Why?"

"Comin' down?"

"I'm not sure I want to, Lyle. I'm not sure I want to."

Maybe it's the fact that it's morning in Maryland and he's still on West Coast time, or his head hurts violently at times. Maybe it was flying with those two small boys two days ago, meeting John later that day, and now Ryan last night.

Everything seems to be moving a little fast for a guy who'd just like to find the love of his life, wrap his arms around him, and sleep not on a strange couch necessarily, although he likes its sandy-colored fabric, but in one normal, typical, everyday bed.

He takes a sip of his coffee.

Lyle says, "So, it's a little strong."

❖

The water feels good and right. It pounds his shoulders, back, the top of his butt. He washes Pratt away again, like he did the night it happened.

And he won't think of it.

He won't.

With his forearms resting across the back of the shower wall, Bret continues to let the water massage and roll over him. He remembers the good day he enjoyed yesterday with Lyle.

With the water hotter now, he sees in his imagination the one he hasn't stopped thinking about since meeting him last night.

Again he feels where Ryan's lips landed on his neck and touches that spot with his fingers. There, in his doorway, he just moved forward and planted one deep and long and good kiss that still numbs Bret's knees and heats him up.

Bret imagines Ryan with him. It is Ryan's hand that rubs and rolls the soap bar over Bret's upper body; it is Ryan's touch that makes Bret spread his legs further. With his nose pressed against Bret's shoulder, it is Ryan who makes Bret hard and excited; Ryan who has to kiss Bret now in the shower.

Bret loses his balance for a moment and stumbles back against the shower wall. The water sprays his belly, his feet. The knot in his stomach rises and tension builds. He moans.

He's at Ryan's door, and the kiss comes again. And this kiss, like the first one, makes Bret both weak and charged all at once. It's a kiss that makes Bret fire all over the shower wall.

❖

Ready for breakfast, they sit side by side in Lyle's Jeep as Lyle turns the key again. "Maybe one more try."

Bret says what Lyle won't. "I think she's dead."

"My baby? Nah."

Just then, Ryan appears on the passenger side of the Jeep where Bret is seated. Ryan leans over on the passenger side door. "I heard you trying to get it started. No luck, huh?"

"She'll go," Lyle says. "Give her another minute."

"Bret." Ryan leans forward. "Good morning."

Lyle looks at his passenger.

"We met last night," Ryan continues as he introduces himself to Lyle.

"So," Lyle asks in that awkward moment of quiet, "you two met last night?"

Ryan folds his arms over the passenger side's window ledge. "Kissed in the hallway."

Not to be shocked, though he is, Lyle immediately echoes, "Kissed in the hallway. Well," he nods, "that's good."

Ryan moves toward the front of the Jeep. He taps the hood. "Open it up. Let's take a look."

When he senses Lyle looking at him, Bret plays with the hem of his shorts. "I'll explain later."

Lyle hops out to join Ryan. "No, I caught what he said."

Bret stays still and watches what he can with the hood raised. He sees glimpses of Ryan's belt, which, in being thick and brown, wraps around Ryan's waist. Once, while talking with Lyle, Ryan slips his hand into his front pocket and exposes a hint of skin. Bret hopes to see some underwear, but doesn't.

He knows he should get out of the Jeep, but he's just been outed. Bret wonders, do many gay guys do that, just come out to someone they don't know and say inappropriate things?

It wasn't inappropriate, though.

But Ryan shouldn't have said anything, right?

Bret runs his fingers over his face. He does know what he wants. Opening the passenger side door, he stands and asks, "Well, what's the verdict?"

Lyle moves to stand behind Ryan. With his eyes opened wide, Lyle points both index fingers at his companion. "Do you know this guy actually pulls in ninety bucks for cutting hair? That's not ninety dollars *a day*, Red, that's ninety dollars *a head*."

"And it's your starter," Ryan says matter-of-factly. "I'm going to have to pull it."

Again Lyle points at Ryan and shakes his head.

❖

Lyle heads off to get a take-out breakfast for three while Ryan and Bret hop in Ryan's truck and head to the auto parts store.

"Say it." Ryan adjusts the mirror on the driver's side door by strong-arming it into a better position. "You're mad at what I said."

Bret's quiet for a second.

"Mad, or," Ryan continues, "or what? Just really, really quiet?"

Bret watches him. Some twenty strands of hair lift from the crown of Ryan's head from both windows being open. "No, it's good."

"Bull!" Ryan shifts the truck. "You're not saying anything."

Bret's voice is thin. "No, it was fine."

Ryan's eyes darken.

"I just don't know him, okay?" Bret stares at the dashboard. "I mean, we just met yesterday. And I didn't tell him everything."

"But you were ticked."

"Ryan."

"If this is to go anywhere, bud, you have to be honest with me."

"I wasn't ticked." *And who says this is going anywhere?*

Ryan knows Bret's lying. "I did it—I said what I did—because I don't get involved with closet cases. And you were pissed off. Or you are pissed off."

"You also said last night that you don't get involved with neighbors. So, what are you doing?"

Checking the rearview mirror, he says, "I didn't sleep well. I was thinking about you."

"You're sending a mixed message, Ryan."

Ryan looks right into Bret's eyes. "I know. I am. I don't know what to do except like you."

The two are quiet for a moment. After making a sharp left hand turn down a narrow street, Ryan asks, "How do you know Lyle, anyway?"

Bret swallows.

"Well," Ryan asks again, "how do you know him?"

"I wrestle."

"What?" Ryan asks.

"We wrestle, actually. We wrestle in the Mid-Atlantic Wrestling League."

"Mid-Atlantic what?"

"It's a professional wrestling league."

Ryan shakes his head. "You wrestle professionally? Funny."

For the second time that morning, Bret plays with the hem of his cargo shorts.

"No." Ryan shakes his head. "You wrestle professionally? Really?"

"Yeah."

"That's just off, man. Weird." They pull up in front of the auto parts store. When he pulls the key out of the ignition, Ryan shakes his head. "I don't get that, man, to be honest with you. I don't get that at all."

Bret puts his hand on the door latch. "All right."

"No, seriously. Each to their own, absolutely. You know, I'm a fag who cuts hair, but I don't get that whole thing."

"What 'whole thing'?"

Ryan steps out of the truck and walks around toward Bret. "That pro wrestling bit. Man, it's just gross, and mean. Visceral. Sorry, but that's just badass thugs beating on each other. That's just *violent*."

Bret stands still on the sidewalk.

He catches up with Ryan a moment later. Though they'll stand near each other for the next ninety minutes, Bret never gets close to him again.

CHAPTER TWENTY

With cushions from the couch, he leans against the rough-sided exterior wall and slides his bare feet through the patio's metal railing. He stares at the first star out there brave enough to show up against the lights of the nearby strip mall. It's dusk. The wide expanse of pinks and blues quiet down the day, leaving Bret both introspective and a little down.

Lyle's been gone for over ten hours now. The new starter Ryan installed worked right away and Lyle set off, glad to be heading home after what turned into an unexpected three-day weekend.

Both glad and bothered to be alone, Bret keeps thinking of Lyle, the first man he met off the plane. He's been a sudden and good friend, a caring guy.

Bret also remembers one of the last things Lyle said before leaving that morning.

"So, this kiss," the big guy had said as the two were saying good-bye just inside the apartment door this morning. "Well?"

Bret looked to the floor and Lyle's suitcase at his feet. He didn't know what to say.

Lyle understood, at least in part, and wanted what was best. He said, "Here it is, Bret. Because you were—and have been—quiet about it since Ryan told me about it, I'm going to go with being quiet about it to the guys in the league." Pausing for a moment, Lyle scooped up his overnight bag. "Is that what you want?"

Is that what I want?

Looking through the railing, Bret turns to see the first star again. He says the same thing he did when standing in front of Lyle. "Yeah, that's what I want."

With his fingers over his chest and a wiggle of his toes through the railing, he thinks of what he does want. For sure, he doesn't want to see John again. While he'll be out for a while with his bum shoulder, maybe he won't be back at all. And that would be fine.

Under his fingers, he feels his heart beating quicker.

And John, really, for as hot as he is, he's also ice. Yeah, he tries sometimes, but bottom line, he hides behind a wall.

But he did bring ice. Bret smiles at this. He carried that bag ice of ice from the convenience store.

As he rubs his forehead with fingers from one hand, he feels a small pebble land in the middle of his stomach. A second later, another pebble skids across the concrete flooring beside him. He rises a bit as a third hits the concrete again and bounces against the base of the patio door window.

"It's me," he hears from below.

Bret rises to his knees and hopes for a second that it's John.

Ryan waves a one-hand salute. "You don't have to move just yet. There are bigger rocks I can hurl up there."

"What are you doing?"

"I don't have your phone number."

"And knocking on the door would be…"

Ryan shrugs. "I'm like Romeo down here. This is more fun."

Bret says in a New York accent, "Fun and games, buddy, it's all fun and games until somebody loses an eye."

Ryan shakes his head. "A big wrestler like you? Nah, you'd be all right."

Bret frowns. "Did I say I'd lose?"

Ryan licks his lips and nods. "You're mad at me, about the wrestling thing. About what I said this morning."

"No, whatever."

Quickly, Ryan climbs the drain pipe near the balcony. Both slight and strong, he's adept at muscling his way up to the second story. Holding on to the pipe, he says, "You're not telling the truth again. You were kinda ticked there."

"And you're kinda crazy for scaling the building here, Ryan."

Ryan slips. Unintentionally, he drops down a few feet. With his face against the building's exterior, he says, "I meant to do that."

Bret steps over the railing and, with enough strength in one arm, pulls Ryan to safety. By sliding his arm under Ryan's shoulder, Bret is able to bring them both back onto the balcony.

The landing is not smooth. Ryan, who lands under Bret, quickly moves over his rescuer. With his legs straddling Bret, Ryan peers into his eyes. "Can I ask a question?"

"Um, sure," Bret replies. "I think that'll be okay."

He wiggles. "So, I do have your attention now."

Bret nods. "You're getting there, yeah."

"We're going to have to understand our differences," Ryan admits, "as just that, differences. Are you good with that?"

"Good with that? And when did we become 'we'?" Bret wonders.

"During the kiss."

Bret isn't quite falling for this. Taking a guy on his words alone cost him, and he won't make the mistake he did in Cincinnati. "So, the kiss, that's when it happened, huh?"

Ryan sets his fingers on Bret's lips. "Yeah, that's when it happened."

"How did that first one go again?"

Ryan puckers and slowly angling his neck, starts his descent.

Bret is strong enough to raise them both in a triceps press. "Oh, I remember now."

From this new position, with Ryan sitting on Bret's lap and nearly face-to-face, Ryan tries to kiss Bret again. Their lips almost touch.

Ryan stops inches from Bret's face. He wrinkles his forehead in a frown. "What is it?"

"Nothing."

Their lips touch. So unlike the first time they kissed, this is awkward, clumsy, and void. They try a second time, a third. Still nothing.

On the fourth time, a connection begins. Slow and weak to start, the two find each other.

It's good. So very good, Bret thinks, or hopes.

❖

The wrestling event for the following weekend is canceled on account of poor ticket sales. Everyone meets again the following weekend.

The site is actually a midsized banquet hall, complete with thin, gold-plated chandeliers.

Lyle takes in the place and says, "I postulate that this not-so-high-end lighting adds a certain ambience to the sweat, smacks, and sweet sounds of foul-mouthed fans cheering on a favorite wrestler."

Thunder chuckles. "I don't smell anything just yet, buddy, but you, ah, you just postulated, Lyle. Is there a need to check your shorts?"

Lyle shakes his head. *"What?"*

Bret whiffs. "I don't smell anything either, Thunder." He turns to Lyle and asks, "You good?"

"Both of you," Lyle huffs, "shut your word holes."

More juvenile banter bounces around as the three notice that there is no locker room. There are no showers. Instead, there's an adjacent banquet hall, smaller than the first, and, since they're the first three to arrive, they set their duffel bags there.

Reaching into his bag, Lyle presents the box of powdered sugar mini-doughnuts he packed.

Thunder's hand dives right into the treat. "You're feeding us so that we'll be nice to you." He shrugs. "That will work." He pops one in his mouth. "Hey, Red, do you even eat doughnuts?"

Bret finds the nearest chair, drops down into it, and laces his fingers behind his head. "Oh yeah."

Lyle smirks. "Liar."

Thunder pops another into his mouth and says, "Do you even know what they taste like?"

"I could postulate an answer for you," Bret suggests.

From his bag, Lyle takes one of his wrestling boots and throws it at Bret's chest. He misses.

❖

The quips Bret hears as he makes his way to the ring are always selective. Usually, he just hears typical cheers. Tonight, however, a fifty-year-old woman says, "He's hung!"

Bret steps into the ring. Vaughn is already there. This is Vaughn's second time in the ring and, with Bret tonight, he's scheduled to lose like he did the first time.

Without John wrestling, the Mid-Atlantic League has yet to hire another wrestler. Gail Jackson shared that they're looking for just the right product, but let no one know that they're saving needed money by not hiring someone new. Vaughn is cheap at his current hourly rate and is being exploited.

"Get him, Red!" someone cheers.

Bret plays the hero. His broad smile and open facial expressions easily win over the fifty or so gathered tonight.

Before the bell rings, Vaughn charges Bret back to the ropes, pulls Bret's hair and, after a few open-hand chops to Bret's chest, brings the younger wrestler to the canvas and applies what looks like a choke hold. Bret shakes one foot in protest, but Vaughn turns Bret from the ref and continues his assault.

Having practiced with Bret earlier, Vaughn lifts the hold and launches Bret's face into the turnbuckle, tugs at Bret's skimpy red, white, and blue trunks and, with momentum, folds his peer in half at the waist.

Quickly Bret escapes and scrambles to his feet.

Lyle, watching behind a shiny silver curtain, realizes Vaughn will never go back to just lighting and sound again.

Vaughn's slowness in life translates to a methodic pace in the ring. He trips Bret and slides the muscle boy to the bottom rope where, with his knee, he forces Bret's neck down in another choke.

Bret flails to this fake move.

The crowd, on their feet, starts yelling.

The ref, a sixty-five-year-old retired middle school gym coach, breaks the illegal hold and Bret, acting hurt, rolls out of the ring.

Moments later, Vaughn jumps down on Bret from the top rope. Bret catches him enough to make it look like a real good solid hit.

Coming to his feet first, Vaughn walks Bret's forehead into the metal post of the turnbuckle. On the ground again, Bret spreads his knees and sells. The crowd is on their feet screaming.

After yelling to a woman near the door, Vaughn tosses a limp Bret into the ring before both wrestlers are counted out. Scooping Bret up, Vaughn parades and throws him down to the canvas with a heavy thud. After impact, Bret protects his injured back from more damage, but Vaughn, seeing the weakness, attacks with a few sharp kicks.

On his feet again after some beating, Bret lands a few blows to Vaughn's stomach. For a few moments, the momentum remains in Bret's favor, but, as planned, Vaughn returns fire. Reeling back to show his incredibly tight abdominal muscles, Bret staggers to stay on his feet. Flexing his sweaty quadriceps and calves after each attack, he regains energy and traps his foe in the corner. With a quick lunge and well-placed feet for balance, he flips Vaughn over his shoulder. The smackdown, loud like a clap of thunder, rattles the dentures of the senior couple in the second row near the aisle.

It's all business for Bret. There is planned give and take in the minutes that follow, but Bret gains control over Vaughn in a series of showcase moves. Bad antics have Bret on his knees again, but as Vaughn goes for a pin, a sudden reversal has Bret coming out the winner.

❖

Tonight, it's a room for three. Just off the highway, the small old motel owned by a young family from Greece invites few unexpected weekend travelers. Vaughn, Lyle, and Bret decide to stay for the night on account of heavy fog some fifty miles into their ride.

The room is small and cheap. A roll-away cot becomes a bed for Bret.

One at a time, the three take showers. Lyle comes out of the steamy bathroom wearing XXXL pajamas emblazoned with a red hot chili pepper pattern. Vaughn laughs in such a contagious way that the other two join as well.

"You know, not everybody can pull this look off," Lyle says after the laughter finally subsides.

"You're the first to fail," Bret quips.

A pillow fight ensues and lasts less than ninety seconds. The youngest of the three pulls out first when Vaughn shouts, "This is just so gay!"

Lyle, with a sigh, drops down on the bed he's claimed and says, "Well, enough of that. Vaughn, go get beer."

"Me? Why don't you go?"

"Dressed like this?" Lyle checks a button over his chest. "Besides, it's your turn."

Vaughn looks at Bret. "Beer?"

Bret scans the floor for his shoes. "Sure. And I'll go with you."

Lyle reaches for his wallet and money. "I was hoping you'd say that, junior. Two's better than one—and it's an important mission, as you know."

❖

Lyle isn't much of a beer drinker—he'll take one or two down here and there—but had hoped Vaughn would go by himself so that he could talk with Bret. Concerned and curious, he wants to find out how Bret is doing with his new job and what's going on in his private life.

Scanning through the TV channels, he becomes more restless than usual after a night of wrestling. Hungry, he raids the back of his Jeep of its last three small bags of salt and vinegar potato chips and, upon turning back to the room, sees a towhead that reminds him of John. A moment later, he realizes it's a short, thin teenage boy.

The teen ducks into a room three doors down from where the three wrestlers are staying. Lyle misses his friend. Damn it. He does. It's been two weeks since he's seen or heard from John. He wonders how his shoulder is healing. Furthermore, he's concerned this injury will close him off even more.

Turning off the TV and staring into space, he knows how John physically pushes himself as a means of release rather than share what he's feeling. Now that he can't lift, run, or move well in the gym as a trainer, what will this do?

The two never—*never*—talked of Dax, so what Lyle knows came only in those very few times he either saw them together, or when one's name was mentioned in the company of the other. And that didn't really happen.

Except that the bastard somehow hurt John. Since John is good at hiding his emotions, however, Lyle never knew for certain what—if anything—went on between Dax and John.

Honestly, he wasn't sure if he wanted to. Even though Dax was known as a ladies' man, there was still something there. Still something Lyle couldn't quite name.

❖

When it comes to drinking, they are all lightweights.

Sloshed, Bret is on the floor between the beds. His knees are spread. His eyes are red. "Really, Vaughn? An animal shelter? You volunteer there?"

"How do you do it, man?" Lyle asks. "Doesn't it break your heart?"

"It would break my heart if I didn't do anything."

Bret and Lyle look at each other.

"Yeah, guys, I know," Vaughn says, "when I'm drunk, I'm profounderer."

"What? Profounderer?" Bret starts to say that's not a word, but Vaughn cuts him off.

"No, you love while you can," Vaughn says matter-of-factly. "I've learned that. And I'm your Cupid, so you remember that."

❖

Both six-packs are gone, and the lights are off. The quiet whirr of Vaughn's regular breathing is the only sound they hear.

"You're awake," Lyle says.

"Yeah."

"Big day."

"Yeah."

Lyle listens to make sure Vaughn's breathing remains constant. "You're seeing that guy, the whiz who cuts hair and fixes cars."

"Yeah."

"How's that going?"

Bret sighs. His head still spins from the beer, even though the side of his face is planted in the pillow under him.

Lyle smiles. "Oh. That good, huh?"

Silence.

Lyle gives it a minute. "Come on, tell your Uncle Lyle everything."

"It's late."

"And you don't have a lot of people to talk to, junior."

Bret turns. He can almost see Lyle's expression in the dark.

"Talk," Lyle says again.

"Well, I don't know. I don't. I mean, Ryan's funny and he's hot." He pokes his head up off the pillow. "You don't mind me saying that, do you?"

Lyle almost laughs. "Geez, he *is* hot. He's cute."

"Yeah."

Patiently, Lyle waits. A few more seconds pass. Lyle continues. "So?"

"It's just—"

"There's something. What is it?"

"Lyle, I don't know. I mean, I don't know. He's fine with me. We're close. With his friends, though, he's not this different person— he isn't—he's just not the person that fits with who I am."

"What do you mean? The sex is good, right?"

Bret squirms. *Did a straight man just ask if the sex between Ryan and me is good?*

"Is it?"

"Yeah, it is." Bret lies. They haven't had sex. Together, they decided to take this slowly.

But is it too slow?

"Bret," Lyle asks as he shifts his head in his pillow, "where are you, bud?"

"Well, okay, we went to this restaurant. Ryan's friends meet us there, and that's fine, and I'm solid with them joining us for dinner. Okay, but there's like this wedge that comes up—and it's me against them. I don't think the way they do. I don't act the way they do."

Lyle says, "Differences are good, though."

"Yeah, but...okay. So, we're eating, right? I, of course, have calories in front of me that I'm downing, whereas Ryan and his friends have seven leaves of lettuce on each of their plates. They fuss and they coo and make their catty remarks."

"You're not dating Ryan's friends, Bret."

"But when he's with them, Ryan's *just like them.*"

"And you're this klutz, this oaf?"

"Primate."

Lyle smiles. "You do have hairy pecs."

Bret groans. This is hard to explain, to let loose.

With all of his fingers linked behind his head now, Lyle closes his eyes. "Share it, Bret."

Bret flips onto his stomach and spreads his knees. "I just don't fit. I like him, I do. Man, he is *together.* He's gone to Spain and France and Belgium and plans to travel to Italy and Egypt this fall. He speaks French and Spanish—he says he's not great at it—but on the phone with friends he's made in Europe, he's fluent. And he has his hand in this charity and that cause. He hangs with his nieces and nephews every other weekend, and he loves, man, he just *loves* his job, though he says he's considering a degree in political science."

"He's a real catch, then."

Bret wonders, *But is he a real catch for me?*

"I know what you're thinking, primate, but time will tell." Lyle drops the extra pillow over his face. He thinks of John. "Time will tell."

CHAPTER TWENTY-ONE

S itting at the edge of the pool, John dangles his feet in the aqua blue water. Bret does all he can to not stare, especially when John leans back on his hands to offer more of his bare chest to the perfect September sun. For weeks now, his shoulder has been free of the sling.

Earlier this Sunday afternoon, the Mid-Atlantic League's Labor Day Lock Up went over poorly, just as it has for the past two years. People just aren't hyped up about mom-and-pop-shop wrestling matches on the last summer weekend—especially when they're held in the middle of a Sunday afternoon. Hoping for a better turnout, promoter Gail Jackson insisted on keeping the Buffalo date.

Now, just after four p.m., the pool party at the nearby motel starts casually. The promise of a great evening is ahead of them. Fluky years in the past have seen residents of Buffalo wearing their first warm layers on this early September weekend. This day continues to remain both hot and humid, however. Autumn seems months away.

Talk around the pool is shared by wives or girlfriends who've joined their men for the long holiday weekend. The mood definitely says party, yet the pace so far remains considerably low key. Wrestling is work and the guys are hungry. Food comes first.

Bret moves to stand near the grill. He keeps his back to the pool.

At first, Lyle doesn't realize what Bret's doing. He finishes the final drop from the can of soda he's holding.

"Good match, today," Lyle offers. "You did good, kid."

Bret wrestled Thunder. As a jobber, Bret lost to the larger man whose real battle, everyone knows, has been arguing with his wife for weeks now. It happens each weekend she joins him.

Despite their ongoing marital problems, one fact remains clear: Thunder is one great dad. He does love his boys, who are traveling without their mom for the first time.

Bret loves the kids as well, having entertained the hooligans one afternoon a while back when their parents were off "discussing." In fact, each time Bret sees the boys, he wrestles with them playfully. They tag-team him and demand scoop slams and kamikazes on the hotel mattresses.

"Good match, indeed," Lyle says again, bringing Bret back from a memory of the last time he tossed and turned Thunder's kids.

"What?"

"You and Thunder. Good show."

Bret starts thinking about the guy Lyle wrestled earlier that day, which is just where Lyle wants him to go.

"My match," Lyle says after a minute where he seasons the meat on the grill, "that was easy. That little blond stick, that beanpole pencil neck...eh, he ain't got nothin' on me." He'd wrestled John. "It's good he's back, right?"

Bret nods awkwardly.

"He's a good guy, Bret. You should know that."

Intentionally staring at the grill, Bret nods almost as clumsily as he did a second ago. Bret remembers seeing John's backside before John entered the ring to wrestle Lyle. He remembers John's swagger, and that damn smile.

Bret tries to swallow, but his tongue gets stuck.

Gail moves in to stand beside Lyle now. She's come to spend the weekend with her wrestlers and she's glad to be out of the city.

"What?" she asks Lyle as she links her arm with Bret's. She tilts her head to one side just enough so she can play with one of her hoop earrings. Gail is large with masculine features like height and broad shoulders. Some women may dress equally well, but no woman dresses better than Gail Jackson. She is stunning, even when outfitted rather simply for tonight's barbecue.

"What," she asks Lyle again, devilishly. "Who is it?"

"It's Carla," Lyle answers. "Thunder's wife."

Gail eyes widen. "That's—"

"Yep." Lyle shakes his head in the direction of the far gate opposite the pool. "That's her."

"Well," Gail says, handing her drink to Lyle, "I'm off to see this up close."

Annoyed with Gail's intrusiveness, Lyle shakes his head as he turns the first of the steaks over.

Bret misses the nuances between a husband and wife who are

some thirty-five feet away. As he takes in the whole scene, he sees that John misses what's going on too. When their eyes meet, both men look away.

Holding his empty soda can, Bret stares down at the low, flopping flowers lining the fence around the pool. He takes a second can of soda from a nearby cooler, chugs it, and crushes the can in his hand.

He sighs. Breathes. *Just walk over, sit down and say hello, nice and easy, eye to eye. You've seen him shirtless a half dozen times now. Yeah, just say hello. Just join him there by the water. It's no big deal.*

He imagines John sneaking up behind him and sliding his arm around him to get another drink.

When his stomach tightens with nerves, he realizes he shouldn't be thinking this. His face shouldn't be flushed; his pulse shouldn't be so strong.

Bret turns. He wonders where to go. Maybe he could just get away for a few minutes.

Lyle heads off first, however, to check on the beer keg around a corner.

Keeping his feet still though he's ready to bolt, Bret eyes the handle of the closed grill lid, though John's still in sight. He's just rubbed his hard stomach with his thumb.

Bret swallows. He shouldn't be thinking what he's thinking.

Lyle's back. "Ryan," he says, "I wonder if he'd like this."

Ryan? Oh, Ryan.

Lyle takes a drink from a beer he has no intention of finishing. He just went to get it so Bret would have a moment to squirm alone. "Yeah, you should invite him."

"*Another* wrestling weekend?" Ryan asked just two days ago when they were eating dinner.

"Yeah, buddy," Bret said, "I told you this."

"Buddy" is Bret's name for Ryan when Ryan annoys him, but Ryan finds it endearing.

Or does the guy who now cuts Bret's hair like being called that? *Buddy.* Bret frowns.

Out of the corner of his eye, Lyle catches the expression on Bret's face and smiles as Vaughn replaces him for a turn at the grill. With Lyle now by the pool, Vaughn sits quietly on the ledge facing the cooking center.

Bret spreads his feet and drops down to join him. Vaughn senses Bret is hurting, or sad.

Side by side, knee to knee, Vaughn wraps his hand around Bret's inner thigh. The sudden intimacy catches Bret off guard.

"You'll be okay," he says before standing to attend the grill. "You just need to trust this."

"This?"

Vaughn doesn't say another word.

❖

The heat between Bret's legs remains. Bret didn't know he looked like he needed comfort or companionship.

He stands. *What is this? I'm fine. Totally. Ryan's great, and that's enough. Dammit. It's enough.*

Thinking a walk would be a good idea, Bret takes the long way toward the motel's lobby by navigating through the back parking lot. He heads to a grassy area that hasn't been mowed in a few weeks.

As he stares down at his feet, he realizes he's run out of places to avoid what he's feeling.

Shoving his hands in his pockets and sighing, he doesn't welcome this. He doesn't want this. He allows himself one minute—just sixty seconds—to give into what he's been fighting and avoiding for weeks.

Thoughts of John.

He wonders what John wears to bed. Shorts, briefs, boxers, nothing? Does he sleep on his side? His back? His belly? How many pillows does he like to sleep with? Does he touch or liked to be touched when he sleeps?

It's the simple things he's curious about, like what music he listens to, what movies he likes. Does he like to hike? What does he eat for breakfast? And who would pin whom?

He walks as he wonders. A daydream of the two of them side by side on a beach at dawn, and later in the surf, the tide strong and teasing, waist-high water tugs at them.

He sees the two sides of John: the one in the ring, all brash and showy, and the silent side. He closes his eyes and catches just a glimpse of his fantasy of John wet beside him in the surf sporting a big, bright smile.

That's the John so tucked away.

Something tingles down Bret's shoulders, his arms. He swallows hard. He knows now that he is just like John.

Bret thinks of his own silent side as he rounds a hotel corner. He looks down at the macadam. Hell, he's hiding now.

There's a noise to his left. Laughter. He hears the punch line of a joke that doesn't make sense because he never heard its beginning.

❖

Gail notices Bret has just returned. She watches as his hands settle deep into his front pockets. After studying him for a minute, she sees how his eyes seem to be looking around, but he doesn't see a thing.

Lyle, who wondered how good a cook Vaughn actually was before returning to a job he actually enjoys, shuts one of the grill's lids after the second round of steaks is ready to be served. He asks, "Thunder and Carla?"

"Yeah," she answers flatly, almost in a sigh. "They fixed that up. Not a big deal, really."

With a peculiar look in her eyes, Gail returns her attention to Bret. When their eyes meet, he bobs his head twice. Awkwardly, he sits at a table facing a wide, flat lawn.

As Gail keeps her attention focused on Bret's back, Lyle gives her a moment before asking, "Okay, what are you thinking?"

She doesn't look at him. "More information first."

She senses Lyle moving to stand behind her. She likes his size compared to hers and tilts her neck.

Ready to keep playing the game, she faces him. "Tell me more."

"About?"

"Well," she says after barely bringing her drink to her lips, "I was thinking that all the fireworks were over for the season, but now I sense something else. Something that is probably greater—or at least more eruptive—than Thunder and Carla."

"Really?"

She continues. "Lyle, this is bigger than some blah blah married couple's spat about not spending enough time with each other."

"Uh-huh," Lyle responds flatly.

"Carla and Thunder? They are two dull fish in a pond. There's just nothing *happening*."

Lyle flips the two new steaks as he watches Thunder and Carla take two seats on a concrete bench near the pool. "What are you getting at?"

"That boy." She points, getting back to business. "And that one."

Lyle looks into the crowd.

She waits for him.

"Oh, you mean—"

"Precisely." Gail doesn't let him finish. "Now tell me again what happened between them."

"You mean, when they wrestled?"

"Yes, about the match, their first and only match, so far. Start from when they met and then what happened during and after their time in the ring. Leave nothing out."

"You sure?"

"Lyle!"

Leaving a lot out, Lyle shares with Gail when Bret first met John in the locker room.

Gail considers this as she makes her own connections. "You're good, Lyle. You're good. That match in Cincinnati generated a lot of fan interest. I heard about it for weeks. Lyle, if we bring that tension to the ring again...these two boys...that will *really* sell. The money we could make." She shakes her head.

He doesn't answer.

"Look at them. They don't know how to do it. They don't know how to start. Two shy boys. They can barely say hello to one another. And I don't blame them. It must still be so awful to be gay."

"You know they're gay?"

"No." Gail presses her lips together. "But what else can it be?"

"They're good guys."

"I know."

Lyle begins to catch where Gail's heading. "So if they can't do it themselves, then someone has to do it for them."

Gail thinks about quitting her job, but what would be the fun in that? No, she really couldn't picture herself anywhere else. More money and a vacation would help. Despite the fact that she's not good at her job and knows it, she wouldn't put herself in another place.

"You are the Cupid here, Lyle. It was your idea first. You set the first scene."

"Vaughn is the Cupid here."

"What?" She pretends she doesn't hear him. *Vaughn?* She thinks. *Really? That idiot?* She takes a sip of her wine. "Oh, it is love I'm talking about, Lyle. No one should hurt. No one should be alone, especially these two. They're like golden retriever puppies—one red, the other yellow."

Lyle frowns. *Puppies?*

"And we can do this. We can pull this off."

"How?"

"You've done the initial work. It's not moving along, though, not quite."

"So," Lyle says, "we bring them together again. In the ring."

"Yes, but not yet."

Lyle thinks. "Tonight. With Carla here, she and Thunder will need their own room, their own anniversary suite. And Bret, who rooms with Thunder…"

"Will need a new roommate."

Lyle opens the lid on the grill. "But John already has a roommate."

"Details we will work out."

Lyle faces her. "So you're really not—"

"What?" She laughs. "No, Lyle, this isn't about ticket sales. Well, not completely. But yeah, this will sell—bringing their frustrations to the ring will sell, definitely."

"But—"

"But that's money, the outcome, or by-product." She presses her lips together for a moment as if seeing something not yet there. "No, Lyle, look at them. Really look."

In baggy board shorts John still sits with his feet in the pool. He's talking to a girl in a slight bikini. And Bret? Well, Bret moved away to find Thunder's kids and a soccer ball. The boys were more than happy to play in the open field with him.

Gail continues. "Lyle, see them with your heart, not your eyes. Feel what's going on around them and between them. What one will give to the other will circle back again. These two tough guys. See who they are, and what they can give each other."

"Bloody noses. Black eyes."

"Lyle. This is something that needs to happen."

Lyle doesn't trust her completely. Something makes him want to watch Gail. However, he nods. "You're being sincere, aren't you?"

"Don't go that far."

"I wasn't."

"I know."

CHAPTER TWENTY-TWO

It's Vaughn who walks up to John with the news about rooms being switched tonight. The electrician turned wrestler finds John in the hotel lobby about an hour after they'd all eaten.

John, who'd been watching major league baseball on the large-screen TV near the front desk, doesn't wait for the elevator to take him to the third floor, although he's just pushed the button. Fidgety, he shifts his weight from left to right, ducks down the hall a few steps, and bangs open the door to the stairs. Taking two or three bare metal steps at a time, he bounds up one rise after another. He's in a hurry, but why?

He gets into the room and plops his duffel bag on the bed. *This is not a big deal. It's really nothing.*

Clearing the bathroom sink of his toiletry bag, he catches sight of himself in the oversized mirror behind the sink. He looks nervous, agitated. His fingers find some curls over his ears until he realizes what he's doing. Staring at his eyes, he leans forward and sets his hands on the edge of the long counter. He meets his eyes in the mirror a second time. He swallows.

Bret.

He wants this. He doesn't want this. Since the time they first met in the locker room, since that morning when they all had breakfast in that restaurant… He forces thoughts of Bret away, but they come back.

The receipt to the ice bag he bought for Bret's head is still in his wallet.

He can't throw away that small, simple white piece of paper. No, he wants to remember. He wants to hold the feeling he had in the hall outside Bret's door.

But this is wrong and it's dangerous.

He can't love someone. He can't even date someone. He'll mess this up.

But there's Bret whenever he closes his eyes.

Damn. Bret. Damn.

John turns from the mirror. Paces. Catches sight of that little wastepaper basket and thinks again of the ice. He should let this go. He turns to see his face again in the mirror again. *Tonight? This, this is no big deal.*

But it is.

He runs his fingers through his hair trying to neaten the curls, then changes out of his board shorts into jeans. Good jeans. He paces more.

Pulling the bottom of his T-shirt up to his nose, he realizes his skin smells of chlorine from the pool. He strips, showers, and dresses again. Same jeans? Yes. No. Yes. He finishes packing.

He walks slowly in the hall. On legs he's convinced are numb or hollow, John reads Bret's green eyes from his memory. For the first time, he feels their loneliness and sorrow—emotions he realizes Bret tries to mask.

Maybe the lonely, transient feel of this hotel enables John to see this side of Bret. It's either that, or he can see now how they are both empty and alone, each waiting—just waiting—to be touched.

John tries to keep his focus in front of him. Instead, he sees more of Bret.

And then he catches himself. No. He's not falling.

He imagines Bret has a girl he doesn't know about, or the handsome guy will have a girl real soon. Yeah, John will just happen to find out tonight that his new roommate has a steady someone, or maybe be engaged.

And he's here now. Just like that. Standing right in front of the door he needs to knock on since he doesn't have a key card to his room for the night.

Exhaling, John ignores the flutters in his stomach as he leans his good shoulder against the door frame of his destination. His fingers are hard to keep still, but after a couple of quick and loud knocks on Bret's hotel room door, he tucks his thumb into one of the belt loops on his jeans. One shin crosses over the other. A cool cowboy stance…sure, that's what this is.

Though he's anything but cool.

The door opens. Bret. He's barefoot. Thick, muscular legs, thin soccer shorts. The T-shirt he wears is neither thin nor tight but showcases his build because he is just *really* put together.

Face-to-face, there are no words, just looks—anxious, confusing, mixed, guarded. They stand some five feet apart, but are somehow much closer.

"Well, hi," John offers after a few seconds. Looking down, he lets his left hand find the back pocket of his jeans.

"Hey." Bret nods.

"So," John barely says since his voice is trapped deep in his chest. "Lyle called."

Bret doesn't know what to do, what words to use because he smells John's intoxicating, stirring scent. "Yeah…he…Lyle, he, he called here too."

John peels himself away from the door frame. "And so, you know."

"Yeah…so, come on good. I mean, this is good. You're being here, th-that is." Bret tries to hold on to the doorknob and misses twice. "Yeah, come, come on in."

The new roommate scoops up his bag and walks through both the nervousness and the heat between them.

A moment of silence follows after the door clicks closed.

John scans the room. The drapes and bed coverings are the same muted autumn and oatmeal colors as the one he just left, but for some reason this space seems smaller, and it's not just that Bret is here. The beds are closer, the aisle way tighter.

"It's not the biggest space," Bret offers.

"Yeah."

Another moment of silence slips between them as they both examine everything in the room except each other.

John fumbles with a hotel information card by the phone on the nightstand. His fingers tingle. Butterflies circle in his stomach.

Bret just watches. It's just the two of them. No crowd, no pool party.

John, keeping his eyes on Bret's bare legs and feet, doesn't know what to do or say. Nervous and knotted, he can't say anything. Locked inside, he can't try.

This is Bret, though. While scared of being hurt again—yeah, John admits he's scared—he can't reach out. He doesn't know how.

Not like this.

Not with Bret, so hot and handsome, so close.

Equally nervous, Bret tries to be funny. "Hey, you better not snore, bud. That's it between us if that happens."

John nods.

Bret continues. "And if you talk in your sleep? You're out on the balcony."

John wonders how he'll ask his roommate about his dating situation. Realizing what Bret just said, however, he glances out the window. "Hey, there's no balcony."

Bret acts distracted but is not.

"Ah, Bret?" John motions toward the window. "Not to repeat things here, but there is no balcony."

"Oh right." Bret's heart keeps beating too fast but he's able to say, "I was thinking of a makeshift hammock."

"Makeshift hammock."

"Sure. That snoring thing. You know, if you do the beluga whale imitation, we can use the cords from the drapes and knot those around the four corners of your sheet." Bret continues, "See, if your sounds shred the wallpaper here, we slip you and your new bed through the window."

John stands near the window. Reaching into the neck of his T-shirt, he rubs some tired muscles along the top of his shoulders. "An awesome outdoor experience, for sure."

Bret nods. "Good ventilation."

"Great view."

Bret moves closer to John. "Of the sheet, or of your knees as they come close to your face?"

It's working. Bret makes it easier for John to talk. "I do have good knees."

"Nice."

"No, good. I have good knees. No one really calls them nice."

Bret lets a perfectly timed pause follow. "I'll have to remember that."

"Pen and paper by the phone."

Bret raises his index and middle finger to his forehead. "Up here. I've already taken note."

Their close proximity warms them both. "Sure there, Bret? I did drop you on your head pretty hard when we wrestled."

"No, you *thought* you dropped me on my head pretty hard, Johnny."

John smirks but keeps his chin low to conceal this. He reads the University of Oregon Soccer logo across the front of Bret's T-shirt. He takes in the hard curves of his roommate's chest and, not knowing how to drop the following question into conversation, just shoots it out there. "You have a girlfriend, right?"

"A girlfriend?"

"Yeah."

"No."

John won't process that now. He'll wait. Still nervous, he says, "I saw you with Thunder and Carla's soccer champs. You guys were in the field behind the barbecue. Looked like fun. You are good with kids."

Bret wonders how many more times John's brain will bounce with what he's talking about. "You're getting nowhere with that flattery."

"Still with the sheet and the drape cords, huh?"

Bret folds his arms to his side. "Wait. Let's back this up a bit. Do you have a girlfriend?"

"Yeah. No."

Their eyes meet and lock. They glance away quickly to defray the jolt inside each of them, but it's too late. The shock is there, the anxiousness, the fire, the fear of what could happen.

Neither moves because they can't. It's just too close in here, too soft and quiet now, especially with no one around them.

Moments pass. They should say something—hell, anything—but the words they both think of falter. Bret thinks of Ryan, of how smooth he'd be in this situation. He wonders if his sort-of boyfriend would like John, and realizes that Ryan is anything but a sort-of boyfriend. Being neighbors is the only thing that keeps them going, and at that they are barely moving. Other than some serious fooling around, there's been no sex, and there hasn't been any fooling around in over a week—almost two weeks. Slowly and surely, Ryan is moving them into friendship territory.

There's more to this, but he won't go there. Not now. Not here so close to John. He won't think about that night.

No, he won't go there.

After a few sidelong, nervous glances, John sits on the bed that isn't rumpled. He faces the bed Bret claimed earlier, and it's difficult to say what's been on his mind. "You are good with kids."

"What? Nah. They're just—" Bret doesn't finish.

"You *are* good with kids. I see you with them after matches. They light up around you."

John's words feel good.

"You have it too. They ask for your autograph, every time."

The awkwardness comes again.

"Nice party tonight," Bret finally says.

John swallows dry air. "Yeah. It was nice."

Lapses fall here and there as they talk. They listen to each other very closely yet are careful not to let the other know how intently they are following along.

They surf the television channels and click through the numbers again. Thirty-one different stations and nothing to watch. They settle on a sports/news program, one that shows highlights from the past games of the week. Neither says another word. Instead, they both thank God they can be this close and quiet together.

CHAPTER TWENTY-THREE

Some thirty minutes later, Bret flips to another channel and finds a professional wrestling broadcast.

"Oh, wow," Bret says, still standing in front of the old, small TV. "That's...that's Sport-a-torium!"

John looks closely and can't believe what he's seeing.

Bret leans forward. "It is! Right there in Wheeling, West Virginia. Look! It's that guy Thunder wrestles sometimes. What's his name again?"

John, who'd been seated on his bed, rolls onto his stomach to come closer to the little screen. With a pillow under his chest and elbows on the mattress, he spreads his knees out like a frog. Positioned like this, his ass is *way* too touchable now. "Something with an 'R'...Rod or Roy or..."

They watch as Thunder enters the ring. Neither says a word throughout the televised match. During the following commercials, however, John says, "It's kinda wild to see it on TV, isn't it?"

"Yeah, but something isn't—"

John finishes for him. "Isn't the same somehow. It's not as athletic, or something." Feeling like he sounds like an idiot, he swallows.

"Not as intense," Bret adds.

Silence slips in again.

John sits up in his bed. He knows the answer to his next question, but asks it anyway. "You wrestled there that night, right?"

Bret can't remember. There have been many, many nights in the ring since he's come east.

John remains quiet because about five weeks ago he went to the Sport-a-torium alone. No wrestler knew he was there, but he not only remembers Thunder wrestling that night, just as he had seen on TV, but also he saw Bret locking up with someone named Ace, who was at the pool party this afternoon. A few inches shorter than Bret, Ace carries a linebacker's build with a bit of a belly. Bret won the match.

Bret wore deep red trunks that night with matching red and black kneepads and boots. The intensity he had in the ring when he and John wrestled was there—or almost there.

During the match, John was sitting by a woman who said, "That red one...now he's hot. *Hot.*"

And he was.

Angled and sleek, determined and athletic, Bret easily controlled Ace, who was about their age but looked a good five to ten years older. There were scripted times, of course, when Bret's challenger had the upper hand. More moves followed. At one time, Bret hopped up to the second ropes in one corner and flexed for the viewing pleasure of the fans.

All John could think of that view of Bret was *I'll take him now.*

John still remembers what the woman beside him said, because he was thinking it too. "I'm seeing this in my dreams tonight."

Bret passes the TV set and moves to stand closer to John. "How'd you know who Thunder wrestled that night, John? That guy, Rod, he was only there once. Remember, he just up and retired or something like that."

"Oh." John frowns. "Right."

Bret calculates. *Yes. It had to be.* He taps his fingers to his jaw. "You were there."

John doesn't answer.

"With your shoulder still sore?" Bret stands and faces him now.

John feels a lot of heat in his face and his groin. He looks at the television. The commercials end, but so does the wrestling. It's a new hour and time for a new program.

"John?"

He looks away. "Yeah, I was there."

Did you watch me? Bret wonders. *Did you show up that night to see me?* He asks these questions with his eyes. John knows what he's asking and nods.

Dropping all his guards, Bret comes even closer. His eyes are wide and tender.

Shy, John looks down.

"So, about your shoulder, tell me because I wanna know. What happened?"

John looks right at Bret's crotch. He can't help it. And even though Bret is in soccer shorts, John stares and sees the outline of what he saw that night. He wants to reach out and hold Bret around the waist, between his legs. Just hold him.

Bret turns and asks again. "What happened there with your shoulder?"

"Nothing."

Bret shuts off the TV.

"It's nothing, Bret," John says into the quiet some thirty seconds later. He lies. "It's nothing."

Bret sits beside the TV on the faux wood credenza. He stares at the carpet. "You didn't hurt it when we wrestled that night. So, what happened?"

John isn't about to tell him he was taken out by a hit-and-run driver. Definitely he isn't going to tell this great-looking guy in front of him that he was thinking of him when the accident happened.

"John, ah, how'd you hurt your shoulder?"

"It was a bad night."

It was a bad night. Bret remembers that fraternity guy, Pratt.

"Your door wasn't locked," John says. "In fact, it wasn't even closed all the way. And I didn't see much of your pj's that night. In fact, you weren't wearing a whole lot, if I remember."

Bret swallows. "It was hot. You know air conditioners sometimes."

"What happened?"

"You first. Your shoulder?"

John opens his hands as if that gesture alone can explain it. "Some things happen."

Neither one says another word. Walls go up in what little space they have together.

Bret retracts to where his toothbrush rests in a cup by the sink. He picks it up and starts brushing his teeth.

When he finishes, he comes back and says in a tone that is all business, "I usually shower in the morning. And since tomorrow is Labor Day, I don't need to set an alarm. But if you need to wake up at any time," he moves toward the clock on the tiny wedge of a table between the two beds, "feel free to set the clock."

The space between the beds is tight but it's definitely wide enough for them now that they are so far apart. John will not say he came to the

Sport-a-torium to see Bret. He won't tell him that the scent of Bret on his skin was the last thing he remembered before getting walloped by a little red car.

And Pratt is back in Bret's memory. Just like that. Sure, Bret tries to keep that buried. He tries to move on, put that experience behind him.

But it's here.

From across the room, John studies Bret's thick legs and says, "No, that's fine. Having no alarm…that's good."

John moves from his bed to stand near his duffel bag. He pulls off his T-shirt. The muscles down his back are deep and exact. He turns, slides off his jeans, and steps out of them. Bret is drawn to John's underwear: thick, soft cotton. He tries not to look, he doesn't look, he can't look, but he has never seen John like this—not in this light, not with this softness.

His chest tightens. If he could be honest with himself—which is hard to do because he's just so damn confused—he'd admit he'd want to touch John tenderly over his wide shoulders and slide his fingers down John's arms. He would angle in for a kiss and, face-to-face, he'd tell him he's been thinking of him, maybe more than he should.

And more words would come—good words—not this stupid stuff about hammocks, alarm clocks, and showers. No, if he weren't trapped in his own pain, if he could figure out how to get out of his own box, he'd say what it means to have this time alone with John and be this close.

Bret turns, lowers his chin, and closes his eyes. He wants to bring his nose to the front of John's underwear and smell, just smell him.

John moves to the sink now.

Bret wonders, *Should I wear my soccer shorts, or just my underwear? John's in his briefs and I want him to see me. I do. Dammit, I just do.*

Bret listens to the sounds his roommate makes. John brushes his teeth and washes his face. There's a tired sigh. The sound of the faucet, and the sound of the towel hitting the counter. All of these common, typical everyday sounds are wonderful for Bret. He spreads his legs, strips off both his soccer shorts and underwear. He slips into the cool nylon shorts again and cups himself, enjoying the freedom. He slides the sheet down lower and lower. He flexes. John will soon see him like this.

When John steps away from the sink, he's more than half-swollen in his white briefs and tries to ignore it. "Lights? Bret? Do you want anything left on?"

Bret doesn't answer.

John continues. "I usually leave a bit of the curtain open to let the parking lot lights shine just enough to find the bathroom in the middle of the night."

Bret doesn't want to say anything because the boy in John's voice comes through for the first time. Maybe there'd be more.

From Bret's silence, John wishes he hadn't said anything. "I know. Dumb, huh?"

"No, I'm the same way."

John turns all the room lights down. He passes Bret's bed and heads toward the window. Their room faces nothing but woods, and here on the third floor facing a stand of timber, privacy isn't a problem.

"This good?" John asks as he parts the curtain a bit.

Bret is mostly in the dark, so he can easily watch John. Somehow, just being this close is fine for now. "Yeah," he answers. "That's good."

John stays put for a while. He looks out the window. When he hears Bret roll toward his direction, he answers before Bret even asks. "I'm just looking. It's pretty out there. Where I come from…well, this is just nice."

John lowers the curtain and pulls it so a few inches of a silver light cast a strip across the room. The darkness brings them closer, as if under one blanket.

Back at his bed, John faces Bret. "My shoulder," he says quietly, "it's okay."

"I shouldn't have asked."

"Nah, it's good you did. It's all right." John swallows. *It is all right.*

Bret, who has been on his side facing away from John, rolls to his back. Minutes pass.

Here, in the darkness, they realize they are safe. No one will hurt or take away from them. No one will dominate or control, threaten, rob, abuse or destroy. Knowing this, they lay their shields down, one heavy piece of metal at a time.

A few more minutes click along on the little clock between them, but so much time passes. With eyelids low or closed for the first time here in the same space, their first dreams of the night mix like brackish water with the last thoughts of the day.

Turning toward each other, both men slide to places in their pasts. Parts of their history are rewritten or recast in a different way because, even in beds some three feet apart, the two are close. Their lives start to mend, reconnect, or fit in a way that didn't before. Without either knowing how many times the other's heart has been broken or the number of nights they've spent alone, they find each other. They neither touch nor speak, but understand what can't yet be put to words, and that is simple and true: that it is just damn good to be alone together.

John lifts his head off the pillow. "I was hit by a car. This little red thing. I was standing on a corner and wham, the next thing I knew, I'm on the street and my shoulder is off its hinge."

Bret opens his eyes. "Wow! Really?"

A softness to John's voice comes through. "Really."

Bret wishes he were close enough to smell the crux of John's underarms. He wants to straddle him, take in John's scent. He imagines being on top of him, his legs folded on either side of John.

John, on the other hand, begins to heat up for a different reason. He pulls his sheet down further and, as a habit, he naturally rests the top of his hand just inside his underwear. "That car, it's no big deal."

"Did the police get involved?"

"Nah."

"The driver? Did you meet him? Did he even get out of his car?"

"I don't even know if it was a guy driving."

Bret slides onto his back. "That must have really hurt."

"It's good."

"It's good now," Bret corrects him. "And here mama thought wrestling like this would be dangerous. She doesn't know anything about you and cars."

John won't think about this mom. He's not going to think about his pretend mom, either.

He just wants to hear Bret's voice beside him, warm and close.

And he'll think about his roommate's soccer shorts on, and then off.

❖

They wake in their own beds, hours later, neither remembering the last words shared. It's Labor Day.

In the gray morning, where do they go? What do they say? Neither knows how to be close again. John walls himself up because that is what he knows; it's what he's done in the past. And Bret? At some point over the night, he received a voicemail from Ryan saying to hurry home, that he's really been missed.

Unlike the last time, there's no group breakfast that morning. By seven a.m., John heads back to his apartment in West Virginia and Bret meets a fellow wrestler in the lobby for a ride back to Frederick. After saying good-bye at the door to their room, they don't speak again.

Gail calls each of them the following Wednesday morning. They are to wrestle each other the weekend after next in Philadelphia.

CHAPTER TWENTY-FOUR

He must hurry. Five minutes is all he has to change and stretch. He quickly finds and opens his locker. Boots, kneepads, and elbow pads fall out of his duffel bag. He places them on the bench beside him. Almost set.

The tape, where's the tape? He fumbles through what he's unpacked. His fingers don't work well.

He stops and tries to concentrate. He finds he can't do this. Too much has happened too fast. What distracts him most is he keeps imagining John, who arrived about five hours late to tonight's match.

As he continues looking for the tape, snapshot memories of what happened a moment ago replay in his mind.

Harried, John had rushed up to him, having first asked Gail if the two of them could still wrestle tonight, despite him being so late. While checking to see if this "new" last-minute main event could actually happen, she sent John to find Bret.

"Give him a heads up," she said to the West Virginia wrestler, who had never, ever been twenty minutes late to a venue before, even when traveling great distances. "Tell Red what you know, and what you and I are trying to do here."

When just the two of them stood face-to-face, Bret took in John's Adam's apple, his square jaw, his blond whiskers, and his pale lips. When it came to meeting John's bright blue eyes, Bret understood more than just the long trip the latecomer had just made. Something else was said without words. *I just want to be close to you again.*

With tape now in hand, Bret stares into his open locker but does not see a thing in front of him except the memory of John's neck, and those whiskers.

And those pale lips that were soft.

And kissable.

Mike, an older wrestler who's just come back from the showers after his match, catches Bret's faraway expression. As an in-your-face guy, he needs to know everyone else's business. "So, you are gonna wrestle him after all."

Bret, who's busy, doesn't give Mike much in the way of a response.

The gruff guy presses. "What, Johnny boy just shows up, at the start of what *should be* the last match, and you're going to lock up with him *tonight*?"

For distraction and cover, Bret slips off his shirt.

Mike continues. "You should be dressed and warmed up—both of you. Coming at this with no prep and planning is a little dangerous, isn't it?"

"Right." Bret kicks off his shoes, loosens his belt.

Mike starts to walk away. "To wrestle someone without going through the moves beforehand? I sure wish I was that young and dumb again."

Bret straddles the bench he's on and opens his duffel bag up further. He is nervous. Excited. Minutes, just minutes remain.

"Bret?" Mike asks, realizing Bret hasn't been listening to him.

"Yeah? What is it?"

Mike walks away. "Nothing."

With Mike gone, Bret remembers Gail's face when she came up to John and him in the hall. After having just checked with the sound guy to leave the microphone on for the intro to this one new final match, she stood in front of both of them. It was all a go, but she asked one last time, "You two are sure about this?"

Both answered at the same time. "Yeah."

It took Gail a moment to process what she heard. As the corridor buzzed with fans buying refreshments, she made sure to look at both of them. "You were scheduled to wrestle, but that was assuming you'd both be here hours in advance to practice. So listen, boys. You're no good if you're hurt."

They both nod in agreement.

"So really, yes?" She couldn't see either of them at the moment because she was getting what she really wanted. "You're gonna do this, and do this safely?"

Bret shakes his head now that he's alone in the locker room. They'll be careful, for sure. But as far as being safe? They can't practice what they will do tonight. There is no time. No details have been worked out for their match. Neither knows what the finishing move would be, nor who will win.

On his drive east from West Virginia, John wound up in a bad patch of road that caused two back-to-back tractor-trailer accidents. John sat on the Maryland interstate for more than four hours as a result. When the highway finally cleared, he raced the rest of the way to Philadelphia. He was too late, of course. He and Bret missed their place in tonight's lineup. Bret wrestled Vaughn as a substitute. Now Bret would have to wrestle again and they'd go last, since the last scheduled match had started.

There on the locker room bench, Bret senses someone behind him. It's Mike, he figures, coming back with another wise comment.

"What are you lookin' for?" In new royal blue wrestling trunks with two white racing stripes on each hip, it is John who stands beside him. He's barefooted. His white boots are under one arm.

"Ah," Bret sets his bag down. "Nothing."

"We should get—"

"I know." Bret cuts him off quickly, nervously. "We should get going."

John sits beside him and, with socks on, moves to lace up one of boots.

"So, John, you're okay? That accident. That was pretty close."

"Yeah."

"And five hours in your car."

John shrugs. Greg never cared for him like this, or Dax. Something warm rises in his throat. He swallows it down, but it doesn't quite go away.

"And you," John says, shifting his boots under his arm. "You've already wrestled Vaughn tonight. You sure you're up for another?"

Nothing is stipulated in their contract one way or the other, but it's been known that each wrestler wrestles only once per night, unless something is staged calling for everyone to come rushing out to pull apart wrestlers in the ring—or one or more wrestlers ambush another in the ring. Even in big-time wrestling, where highly paid wrestlers fly all over the country and into Canada, this isn't done.

Bret will be a first.

John checks again. "You are sure?"

Like I would ever say no to wrestling you? To seeing you close? To have you all tangled around me?

"Bret, you sure?"

"So who wins tonight, you or me?" Bret keeps his voice low, so no one will hear how much he cares about John, or can see how glad he is that John arrived safely.

John nods. He steals a whiff of his wrestle partner—faint, hidden, almost undetectable—but it's enough that his stomach tightens. His fingers tingle.

Bret turns. "So?"

John nods. "Since I won last time, you take it."

"We're last, the main event, so we should give them a good show." Bret steps into his high-cut metallic gold wrestling trunks. He wore white and blue striped square-cut trunks for his match with Vaughn—and those are soaked through with sweat.

John can't look at this sight, even though he wants to. He wants to take this picture of Bret with him into his memory for all the lonely nights that will follow, yet he keeps his face down and turned away until he's sure Bret's thin golden gear is in place. Like Bret, he keeps his voice dry. "So, you gonna say something about this good show of ours? Curious here. What's your plan?"

Bret hides a smile by keeping his voice somber. "You're the one who came in five hours late. Out there on the road, did you think of something?"

"I had my mind on something else." *Someone else. Red hair, pale freckles, tall, handsome.*

They fall silent, like they did when John first arrived in the hotel room they shared two weeks earlier. John sits again and neither wants to move right away. They don't want to be apart. If they could just stay here, if they could just be allowed to be together with some quiet, uninterrupted time—even just for a few minutes—that would be enough.

John wants this moment to count. He sees the tape on the bench beside him, picks it up, and rolls it in his fingers.

Bret thinks about whether or not to use it. He'd rather not wimp out, but he did hurt his wrist last week in the gym. He wrapped it earlier when he wrestled Vaughn.

"Here," John says, handing the tape over.

"What? I don't need that."

"Then why—"

"I just had it with me, that's all."

John keeps his voice warm and soft. "Then why did Lyle tell me about it just a minute ago?"

Bret dismisses this with a shake of his head. "Oh, yeah. Fine. Last week at the gym, I—"

John sees it's swollen just a bit. "I won't grab it."

Mike is back. "Princes," he jokes goodheartedly, "it's time to go."

The joke backfires.

"Princes?" The hair on John's neck rises. Especially since he's close—maybe too close—to Bret, John stands from the bench where he was seated and snarls, "Princes? How 'bout shutting the hell up?"

For some men, heat begets heat. Mike's own short fuse lights and he reacts. "Oh, prin*cess*."

Deftly, John moves toward Mike. They stand face-to-face.

Mike cools it. His tone is different now, older, wiser. "First up, you should just be ready, that's all. This is serious. And second, this prince or princess bit? Chill with that, pretty boy. That something like this has you all charged up and in my face, guy, you've got some figuring out to do."

John clenches his fist and locks his jaw.

Mike starts to walk away. "And don't think about hitting me, because you're not mad at me—you're mad at yourself." He takes one quick look at Bret and, without a word, says the same thing to him. "You two know what you have, just name it."

With a click of a nearby door, Mike is gone.

John burns. *With what we have? With what we have? We don't even get two minutes together without being interrupted. What we have is a dream, maybe. It's not real.* The anger he felt toward Mike turns toward himself, and then Bret.

"The hell with this," John says. "The hell with all this talk. We figure out the match as we go out there."

Bret too is angry—but at John. *What was that explosion? Where'd it come from? And so fast? And over what?* He realizes he was wrong to let his feelings to grow.

So damn wrong.

Turning to the row of lockers, Bret hates himself for falling for this spitfire who burns easily and fast. What, a future here with this guy? Even a date? Ha. That's a laugh.

A real laugh.

This isn't working. This doesn't work. Tim at camp all those years ago, and that night with that slimeball Pratt? And Mr. Romance himself, Ryan?

He's just a fool for this. For all of this.

Yeah, he does hate himself.

"So." Bret voice carries a knife in it. "We figure this match out when we get there? I don't see a problem with that, princess."

John fires back. "Sure? You're the fag whose wrist hurts."

"And you're the fag who said you'd leave it alone. I didn't ask you to, John."

"Shut up."

Bret squares off in front of him. "Or do you mean to say, see you out there?"

Too far gone with his misdirected emotion, John knocks over a nearby folding chair. "Oh yeah, see you out there, faggot."

Bret's words bite back. "You're damn right you will."

CHAPTER TWENTY-FIVE

They will wrestle each other so hard that they will actually be fighting themselves. Each will give the other punishment neither deserves, but they don't know another way. No positive experience, guide, or recall of how to connect in an open, honest, or trusting way with someone they are interested in has worked for either of them before.

So, it's this.

From opposite corners of the sports complex, they take their separate entrances. Neither wrestler wants to be first in the ring. This pause adds to the tension. The crowd notices that both Bret and John see each other from a distance of some one hundred feet. From opposite sides, the two approach at the same time, first slowly, then with quicker footsteps. They both step into the ring at the same time and as the announcer starts to read the card, Bret grabs the card and the microphone. With a forearm, John elbows the announcer out of the way as Bret tears the card in two. When the referee attempts to step between them to start the match, both men shake their heads. They lift the official and walk him over to the top rope. Rather than be tossed out, he opts for a much safer route. Gladly he slips away and leaves.

Before dropping the mike out of ring, Bret says, "Philly—you wanna see a fight?"

The crowd roars affirmatively in response.

Bret nods. "Then you got a fight. No ref and no rules. Just action. This blond *prince* here? Your boy in blue? Only one man will stand at the end, and that's me."

John shakes his head at this and with a hard slam he introduces Bret's back to the nearest turnbuckle. A hard chop to Bret's jaw shows that John is not kidding.

There is no retaliation from Bret at first. John takes control of a man tired from wrestling some thirty-five minutes earlier. As he lays

Bret out, move after move, he fights old demons. First, it is Greg, not Bret, who suffers an arm bar. Greg is gagged in a front chokehold, not Bret. Greg gets his legs knotted and the wind slammed out of his lungs. It may be Bret's body that hits the mat each time with definite thuds, but to John it is Greg taking this long-overdue punishment.

And then there's Russ, followed by Dax. John burns with anger as he remembers how he was foolishly maneuvered and manipulated. He remembers what was taken from him. Damaging punches land on Bret's abdomen. It's an attack Bret first rolls away from, yet he finds himself trapped in again and again. He slides to the rope, but there is no escape.

His knuckles now raw, John wipes the sweat from his face with his wet hand. He catches his breath.

John grabs each of Bret's ankles and drags him to the middle of the ring. He thinks of what Mike said when he raises Bret by his feet and showcases Bret's ass.

He is angry with himself. Everything that he's hoped for has slammed him again and again. It hurts. It hurts so damn bad. Men are pigs—dumb ass pigs.

And he's one of them now.

Bret hits the mat with one hand. "No."

John's always been the underdog, always been the one to have something taken from him. Sensitivity? Kindness? No, now it's payback time.

I'm not a prince, John thinks as he folds Bret's limp body under his and sits on Bret's chest. On top and in total control, John spreads his legs further and puts more his weight on his seat. Sweat pours down his abs and through his blue trunks. It pools at the V of Bret's neck. John smells his own crotch from here. He scoots up to sit higher on Bret's chest.

"Take it!" he yells to Bret.

John hooks Bret's feet and repositions himself, allowing Bret even more of his crotch.

With nowhere to go, Bret takes in the smell of what's in his face.

In having Bret under him, John hears in his mind a fan yelling "Crush him!" but now no one in the house says a word. Amazed by what they see, they are actually quiet, as quiet as they have been all night. On a subconscious level, they seem to understand this give and take with the wrestlers—that John, for now, has earned this top position.

John gets up and sees Bret sprawled and motionless. He wants Bret to feel more of his power, his muscles and his strength. He wants to give him more. And he wants to be close, body on body, because that's the only way he thinks he'll ever connect with a guy. He scoops up Bret and applies a bear hug. When John squeezes Bret, the fronts of their trunks rub together. Their nipples tease each other's chests. In one obvious moment between just the two of them, their balls rub together.

On the release, Bret slides to his knees. John's crotch is right there and after his face falls forward for a deep breath, he immediately finds himself on his back over John's shoulders. He's facing the lights above. John parades him around the ring, stroking Bret's inner thigh all the while.

Stretch out more, John thinks as his legs begin to quiver. *Give me more of your relaxed weight. Trust me.*

Their bodies do communicate because Bret understands what John asks and does go limp, which increases his body weight over John's shoulders. John grunts. Primal and unguarded, the sound is not thought of or planned; it is just released with heat and energy.

John's steps become more labored. The jostles only excite Bret, who feels such a longing for John in his groin, despite what happened in the locker room earlier. He too realizes this is the only place they will connect. He relishes his balls when they shake.

John drops them both. The short, wild ride to the canvas is a sensation like a surfer coming to the sand after the wave releases him. It awakens all the blood and his muscles even more.

Though not hurt at all, Bret stays down as John climbs the nearest turnbuckle. It's the move played out five million times by pro wrestlers. Just before John hits the canvas, Bret rolls out of the way. John doubles over in seeming pain while Bret staggers to his feet.

My turn, Bret thinks as he gains momentum and applies moves that stretch and twist John. It's a showcase of muscle and talent, and the crowd, rallying behind Bret, responds with thundering cheers.

Anyone timing this would know they'd been locked up and rolling for thirty-five minutes—about ten minutes longer than the second longest match of the night. They are as wet as two buds who've spent the afternoon at a water ride park, but what's more surprising is the canvas itself is now visibly damp from their sweat. Mid-September in Philadelphia still means air-conditioning, and tonight the system hums in perfect working order, but the two are just so hot.

From the corridor, Gail paces. *Will they stop? Do I send someone in to stop them? If so, when?*

She sees Lyle. Ready to check into the hotel for the night, he's dressed in his street clothes. "Okay," she says, "now plan this. What happens next?"

Not understanding, Lyle frowns until he realizes Bret and John have not stopped since his match ended. "What? They are still—"

She doesn't let him finish. "Yes, they are. They are still going at it."

From a business point of view, they cannot afford to have either wrestler hurt. From a quick gauge of the crowd, Lyle realizes that the house is duly impressed, and that more is not necessarily good, it's just more.

Bret hammers John, and Lyle, a good hundred feet from the ring, feels the pain in his gut. "We stop them."

"How?" Gail wonders.

Lyle is choked up when he sees what both men have done to each other. He talks quickly. "We just get them out. Separate them. Tip the scales. Get a guy in there along the apron."

"Who goes in? Who's still dressed to wrestle?"

"No one," Lyle answers. "We're all out of the locker room. It's me. I stop this."

"But—" Gail's final word is swallowed by the roar of the crowd who cheers Bret because he pretzels John into a move that should be a submission hold.

Lyle makes his way down one of the two aisles. While just in the ring in what was supposed to be the main event, he doesn't know how the crowd will respond to him because they won't know why he's there.

"Move it, man!" someone yells to him. "We wanna see!"

John sees Lyle. His face is determined to take what Bret gives and give back that much more when he can.

A few fans scream for John. Most, however, still side with Bret.

In sensing what could happen, the fans boo Lyle. He makes his way around the ring searching for the microphone. He sees the cord. The mike itself has rolled under the ring.

With it in his hand, he thanks God it is on and still works. He yells, "Boys! Enough! Time's over! You're at a tie!"

Bret doesn't stop.

Lyle shouts again. "Enough!"

When Bret turns to see who's calling, John clamps a sleeper hold on Bret. This is one of pro wrestling's "fake" moves, designed to make an opponent lose consciousness.

"Enough!" Lyle taps his wrist indicating that time is up.

In John's arms, Bret is acting now, staggering as if quickly losing air. From behind, John can smell Bret's hair and breath. Both feel hot against his face. Inviting. Necessary. Wanted. Not wanted.

Without thinking, he thrusts his hips into John's back.

Wanted. Bret is so truly, deeply wanted.

But he isn't. This won't work. None of it. *No dreams, John*, he tells himself. *No hope.*

As quickly as he's able, Lyle climbs the steps to the ring and, through the middle rope, hurries to break the hold John has on Bret. With this accomplished, he pries the two apart.

The mike never made it into the ring. Lyle must have dropped it. His voice carries, though as the crowd waits to see what will happen.

"Enough! It's a damn tie!"

Somehow Bret and John's bodies do talk to each other again because in one wordless exchange both know what the other wants. They go after the obstacle that will keep them from wrestling each other. Sensing his own danger, Lyle grabs both John and Bret by their necks and keeps them still, but both bust the hold. They take Lyle down with high-flying kicks to his chest. John jumps onto Lyle while Bret sees that the microphone did make it to the top step.

With Lyle on the mat, Bret thinks of the circus show this has been made into by the demands of the crowd. He also figures Lyle's the one who put them in the same hotel room last time, and that those kicks to the chest? Yeah, maybe he had that coming.

Playing the fans along, Bret uses the microphone cord and begins to tie the large man's heavy, strong legs. John joins when Bret gets to Lyle's hands. Together they work quickly and when Lyle is out of commission, they square off again.

An end means separation and neither wants to be away from the other, so they circle. The crowd rises. Noise is deafening. They cannot charge; they are too weak. They cannot think; they are too exhausted. It is all instinct now.

Because of this, their stares are uninhibited. They are also surprisingly familiar, almost comfortable. Having been repeatedly trapped in each other's arms and legs, having been held between the other's crotch and armpits, the two know each other in ways few men know other men. And here, face-to-face, they learn more. They can trust. Worn down now, fighting their own anger out of each them, they open themselves more deeply than ever before, and they do this because both know just how strong the other is, just how much the other can take, and hold.

Bret raises his arm to apply another hold on John, but John catches his arm by the wrist. *The wrist. My way to win*, he thinks.

He doesn't know what to do. Does he grab it? Does he let Bret win? Their eyes meet again. Then neither knows what really happens other than a horde of wrestlers from the league pry each of them apart because the intensity of the holds between them is dangerous.

Some kind of all-man wrestling action takes place for a minute or two, as Gail had asked. A few shots land on Lyle, for instance, but Bret and John who are just too damn fired up, are carried off, each in opposite directions.

Chapter Twenty-six

W hat floor?" the sixty-something-year-old man in the elevator asks once John steps inside.
"Six."

The metallic doors slide to a close and the gentleman pushes buttons six and eight. John notices that the gentleman's mid-weight suit fits with tailor-made precision. John swallows a dry lump after he figures the man's crisp maroon tie costs more than he'll spend on gas on this trip.

In the slow ride up from the hotel lobby, neither says another word. John realizes in standing beside this blond-and-silver-haired man who could pass as a relative that he wants what this man has: a wedding band on his ring finger. Companionship. Partnership. Someone to love. Someone to hold.

And what he said to Bret before the match tonight? Where did that come from, and why? He hangs his head low.

In doing so, John also notices this business executive's expensive watch and brings the two extra-long pillows he picked up in the lobby closer to his side. Thinking of his roommate already in their room, he hopes for a special night and plans what to do with the extra pillows in his arms.

John will be intentional in going for what he knows he wants and now cannot deny, and that is Bret. To see him like that, in the ring, to be that close, to be that strong, raw and sensual, yes, *yes*, he wants Bret. He rests his chin on the pillows that he brings to his sore, battered chest. Closes his eyes. Yes, he wants Bret.

And he needs to apologize. Again, he thinks about the stuff that happened in the locker room before they wrestled. The words said. The anger. Yeah, he really goofed that up, made a mess of it.

John steps off on the sixth floor and thinks again about this one king-sized bed as he carries the extra pillows down the hall.

Neither said a word about their surprise sleeping arrangements when they arrived at the room. Neither mentioned trying to get another room, or even offering to sleep on the floor. No words were spoken. Tired and unfocused, Bret reacted first by simply setting his duffel bag down on the floor. John, equally zoned, followed suit by dropping his gear near Bret's.

Even, though they didn't look at each other in the locker room or even in the hotel lobby, it didn't take long for John to realize Bret was in pain. That's why he went to get extra pillows to help stabilize Bret's injury while he sleeps.

John wants to hurry, yet each step down the hall is measured and slow because his legs have never been more difficult to move.

As he turns down the passageway to their door, he shakes his head and feels something warm inside, literally right below his heart. It's churning. He moves the pillows against his tight abdominal muscles.

He is tired—incredibly tired—but the churning inside increases and becomes a fluttering. Butterfly wings brush against the inside of his stomach walls when he thinks of how close he'll be to Bret, how easy it will be tonight to simply hear him breathe.

❖

John left without explanation, and with his roommate gone, Bret stares at the door and realizes he should not do what he's about to do. He should not—*should not*—do it.

But he can't help it.

I'll be back in a few minutes was all John had said.

Bret listens. Not a sound filters in from the hall, nothing. When he bends over John's bag, a sharp pain shoots up his wrist. He ignores this. With his other hand, he brings John's bag to the bed. Awkwardly he unzips it and finds what he's looking for. He just wants to hold what he's only been able to peak at, from afar, before or after their matches— and that's John's underwear. He settles his fingers in and over the briefs slowly and with care, as if he is touching John, who is wearing them. He feels their light weight, and then slides his hand into the front pouch.

Guilt rises. This is wrong, a violation, but he checks the size on the waistband—it's 32, just like his.

Looking down at John's open bag, he thinks of the endless times John has packed. He'd heard about John's background through Lyle.

Foster home after foster home. New place after new place. Again, he realizes that he shouldn't have gone rifling through someone else's things without permission. Quickly, neatly, he folds what he's taken out and grabs his wrist after the bag is zipped up and beside his own again.

To make him feel at home, that's what I need to do. Yeah. Make him feel safe, secure...

Though he is tired, an idea comes to him. He steps into the bathroom. Twisting the dial on the shower wall to let hot water fill the tub, Bret guesses his roommate could be as sore as he is, and a bath would be welcomed.

In a short time, the rising heat from the water permeates Bret, standing near the tub. Even, though it's hot, he sinks his good hand into the water that will lap and splash, soothe, touch and caress John.

With the water running, he doesn't hear the door. John is standing behind him with pillows.

Not understanding, Bret squints. *Pillows?*

John presents what he's carried up from the lobby as a gift, and feeling foolish, brings them back to his chest. He looks down and mumbles, "I, um, I was thinking of these, for you."

Bret still doesn't understand, so John presses on, almost painfully. "Yeah, your wrist there...it's bothering you. Maybe these can help."

John lifts his eyes. They stay steady when they meet Bret's. No other words are needed. Nothing else could be said more completely than the gesture itself, and Bret now understands the thought behind it.

In the intimacy John creates between them, though, Bret cannot speak. In a room as small as a hotel bathroom, he can't shrug this off, or say *John, you shouldn't have.*

Bret lowers his eyes and accepts. "Thanks, man."

John steps out of the bathroom. "I'll leave you to some time here."

"No, this..." Bret looks into the tub. "This is for you. I thought... well, there's not a whirlpool tub where we wrestled tonight. Not a hot tub here. So..."

In disbelief and surprise, John barely shakes his head. "You, you did this for me?"

Bret nods and passes John at the bathroom door. They are close here.

John follows Bret out into their room. "We were kinda rough on each other."

"Enjoy the heat," he says as he raises his arm and thinks of his wrist. "I'm goin' to get ice for this." He heads to the door.

It clicks open and closed. Not another word is said.

❖

Alone now, John puts his hands on his forehead and then slaps his thighs. "I shoulda got ice for him instead of pillows." He shakes his head. "Stupid. Pillows."

He sees what he brought up from the lobby there where he set them, and has an idea. He's a little nervous about it, but with luck he thinks he can carry it off. All he needs is a cube or two. Grabbing a towel from the bathroom, he sets the thick terry cloth on the bed and, with the bath water now turned off, he strips.

For a moment, he just stares at the water. No one has ever done this for him, no one. He smiles.

Once inside the bath, the water is amazing. When swirled into waves by his hands, the water caresses and lulls him into a place of bliss. He spreads his knees. The water laps his inner thighs. He strokes himself. With his eyes closed, he imagines Bret is here with him, face-to-face, nose to nose. One's eyelashes brush against the other's cheekbone. Naked, warm, perfect, close, they soothe each other's souls without a sound. And the kiss…the kiss that follows isn't intentional. It does not have a clear starting point. Instead, it just slowly, slowly happens.

They find themselves in and against each other's mouths. Together they taste such sweet and rich sensations they aggressively explore, probe, and tease. It is all give and take, give and take, again and again, over and over, for hours on end.

He sits up and realizes he was just *gone*, asleep for a minute or two. As he leans back, the tiles that catch his wet shoulders are cool.

As he closes his eyes again, he thinks about how he wants to know all sorts of things about Bret. Curious, John wants to hear about Bret's first bicycle, his first day at school, his high school prom, his years in college, and what he'd like to do about becoming a teacher.

His eyelids get heavier again. Peaceful, John pictures Bret in a white room. His wrist, his arm, and his shoulders are protected in the softest cotton. Wearing nothing, he is resting on his stomach. And John, equally naked behind him, stretches his arm over and around Bret's bare chest.

When Bret's rib cage rises and settles, rises and settles, like that, John swears he's as close to heaven as he can get.

CHAPTER TWENTY-SEVEN

A middle-school-aged boy stands at the ice dispenser at the end of the hall. The machine regurgitates enough ice to fill the plastic bucket the boy brought with him. He turns, spots Bret, and drops his soft jaw. It's a look Bret has seen before. The boy must have seen him wrestle tonight.

Bret walks up to him. "Hey, buddy."

This cat's cool. He's seen the world and says so with eyes holding neither inhibition nor too much interest. "Hello."

Bret can't be too friendly. He doesn't want to alarm or make the kid uncomfortable.

"Hey," the boy continues, tentatively. "I saw you. Right?"

Bret lowers his eyebrows dramatically and points his finger like a gun. "I don't know, did you?"

The kid laughs. "You got hammered!"

Bret puts his pretend gun back in its pretend holster, licks his lips, and nods a bit. "I thought I did some hammering too."

"Nah, he had you!"

Bret mimics his inflections. "Nah, I had him!"

"Didn't!"

"Did!"

"That blond guy? The one you wrestled?"

"Yeah?"

"He was all over you."

"That's how you saw it, huh? Not the other way around?"

They look at each other. Where Bret can be shy around John, to someone this kid's age, it's all natural, and easy.

"Let's put it this way," the boy continues, "you were the pizza sauce and he was the cheese."

"He was totally over me, huh?" Bret crosses his arms, remembering the term *over* is used for the one who wins the match. He starts to laugh, but, because he's really sore, it hurts to do this. "And, bud, where did you say you were sitting during this match? In like New Jersey or something?"

"My mom lives in Jersey."

"Well, I'm glad you showed up tonight."

"With my dad, sure. We had fun."

Bret gets his ice and the boy starts to head down the hall, then turns. "Hey, mister? Can I ask you something?"

"Sure." Bret welcomes the question.

A pause follows.

"Well, guy," Bret says with his ice bucket full, "what, what is it?"

"Why do you hurt each other?"

"Why do we—"

"Yeah. Why do you hurt each other?"

It's as if Bret's been hit again, this time out of the ring. He doesn't know how he answers his young fan. Jumbled words fall out of his mouth but they do not make much sense.

Not understanding a word he heard, the boy asks again, "I mean, do you have to do that?"

Bret passes the room he shares with John by some four or five hundred feet, though he's not entirely sure how this happens.

❖

Hit. Hit by a kid.

Hitting…and hurting.

Hurting each other.

With the ice bucket, Bret keeps going and sits in an alcove just off the lobby. It's a space he shares with a small table, two boxy chairs, and a flat rack that holds brochures for sightseeing in Philadelphia.

The question the boy asked at the ice machine rolls in his head. Thinking about it, he stares into the lobby, which is completely empty except for one desk clerk with a silky blond ponytail staring at his computer screen.

Why do we hurt each other?

He can't go to John. Not just yet. Not with this.

As his whole hand sinks into the bucket, he does what he needs to do, and that's to remember who he is, and where he came from. His father and the only grandfather he knew, the one on his mother's side, come to mind. Both Army men, they would have approved of Bret and his wrestling, if they had lived to see it. They died three days apart, however, both from lung cancer.

Their lives and their deaths diminished his mom. Both men made it clear to her in thought and in action that her role was to serve them. Without them, she never did find another direction. She did date another abusive man, who, in turn, found someone younger and even more submissive. Bret had started college at this time. His mom would never have dated the loser had he been around. Or so he hoped.

It's not that he doesn't want his mom to be happy—to find and have a life of her own—but living for the past six years in a two-bedroom house with her divorced sister Dora isn't what he'd call living. Rather, it's settling.

Or hiding.

Bret swishes his wrist in the ice. *Hiding. Like I'm doing now.*

Like his mom, Bret did as he was told. For a boy, even a teenager, there was no choice under that one roof. He was going into the armed forces and that was that. He would be damn well prepared for anything a sergeant threw at him in boot camp. No, he would be more than prepared; he would be ready. Both father and grandfather made sure of that.

"Tougher," they would say when his mom dared even a mild protest, "Bret has to be tougher. He's not going to be a pussy." That boy of theirs was going to be a Navy Seal, an Army Ranger, or one of the damn best of the Marines that Corps ever saw. That boy of theirs would get a greater ride after he got out of the service than either of them sure did. "You could bank on that, missy," they'd say.

Both men died before Bret came to the age where he would have to enlist. On his eighteenth birthday, the first day he could have contacted the military, neither he nor his mom made any mention of what Bret's father and grandfather wanted.

But that one word still haunts him. It cannot go away. He doesn't hear it anymore, not even in his dreams, but *pussy* is still something he fights against being called.

But being raised with bloody noses and broken fingers because, after all, he did need to toughen up, Bret never intended to cause another guy pain. It's not what Bret signed up for. It's not what he wants, or wanted.

Yet it happened.

Why do you hurt each other?

The only way Bret knows how to get close to the man he's interested in or cares about is to wrestle. To him, wrestling is a way of knowing another man in a playful, sporting way, and the harder he wrestles, the more he shows his love—his masculine love, if there is such a thing. Any other way to express or demonstrate this tenderness to a man is unknown in his world.

That's why he stopped at the door to his room with John holding fresh ice some thirty minutes ago, and then moved away to this little room off the lobby. He didn't know how to do it. He didn't know how to be with John as a man to a man. Even though most of his experiences with Ryan were good, he didn't know how to connect—*really* connect—with a guy, other than to wrestle.

Pussy.

A knot tightens in his stomach. He doesn't want to hurt John—ever—it is so much the opposite. He wants to show him and give to him—give to him all he is. He wants to hold John so closely that the sexy blond guy knows, he just *knows* with every fiber of his being that he is desired, needed, appreciated, and loved.

Bret stands. He is the only one who would ever call himself a pussy now; his father and grandfather are dead.

And he is not weak.

He is strong in what he wants, and he wants John. Despite the words they shared before locking up tonight, yes, he wants John.

❖

The note on the floor just inside their room has the time, 9:10 p.m., handwritten in pen and reads, *Bret, where are you? Where'd you go? Stay put if you get this. I'll be back in the room in fifteen minutes or less. I'm out looking for you. Are you all right? John.*

Just when Bret sets the note down on the long, low dresser, John appears at the door. When he sees Bret, his face washes from worried to relieved.

John shuts the door. "Where—?"

"I should have told you."

"Nah, it's all right." John tries to play it cool, but he's not convincing.

"No, I should have." Even though nothing is new here, Bret still can't believe just how handsome John is. For a moment, he loses his train of thought. "I should have told you, but you were in the tub and I just went for a walk."

Care and concern mark John's expression. *A walk? Why? Where'd you go?* As if regaining his balance, which he seems to have suddenly lost, John puts weight on both of his feet, one at a time. "Your—you iced your wrist, right?"

"Yeah. It's good. Good."

They idly mill about the room, each so aware of the other. This is hard.

Neither knows what to do.

Deep from his gut, Bret wants to just take him right down on the wide mattress. He'd position them so they are face-to-face. Topping John, he'd tell him what he thought and realized while he was gone.

Instead, his chest is tight. To release some of the tension, he says, "I should have told you." He pauses and nervous, he repeats. "Where I was going, I should have told you."

"It's all right." *But it isn't,* John thinks, worried like he used to be when he cared for a man. *I wanted to know where you were.*

Bret sees the towel on the bed and doesn't understand why it's there. "Listen, there's something I'd like to talk about with you."

John comes to stand in front of him. "There's something I'd like to do for you, and let me go first. All right?"

Bret tries to speak.

"And the towel," John says over Bret, "that's part of it, part of what I have planned."

"John—"

John quiets Bret by almost putting his finger to Bret's lips. It's a move that makes both of them take a step back.

Anxious, John takes the empty ice bucket that Bret had set down and tells him to stay put. He heads to the door. "One minute and I'm back." At the door, he turns. "Just one. And when I get back, we'll talk, sure. There's something I want to share with you too."

CHAPTER TWENTY-EIGHT

On their bed, Bret barely sighs. Of all he has seen of his wrestle partner, John's hands are something he hasn't studied until now.

More thick than thin, John's fingers are long. With big knuckles, they remain wide right to his nails. Strength rests in his hands. Bret feels this in what John is doing.

Working just over Bret, John hears the quiet sigh from the sleepy man beneath him. Having done this with his clients before, John is very intentional with each strong, sure stroke.

"This should make it feel better," he says in his low, confident voice. His breath is warm on Bret's face. "We're just moving some of the swelling, some of the stiffness."

Bret doesn't respond, at least in words. Instead, he opens and trusts himself more with his feelings. To be cared for like this and be able to watch John...to stare deeply into his blue eyes or lower his own eyes to study what this hot guy with him is doing...it's just amazing. Damn amazing. John is touching him in ways well beneath the skin.

For the last ten minutes, John has been sliding one ice cube at a time over and around Bret's wrist. Two towels cradle Bret's injury, soaking up the water from the melting cubes before it can reach the bed.

Bret has been placed on his back for his treatment. To get the ice completely around Bret's wrist, John often raises Bret's arm and sometimes holds Bret's hand. Both are aware of this.

John, who'd been beside Bret at the start, now straddles him. He squeezes Bret's sides with his legs.

They remain dressed in their jeans and T-shirts, but the awareness of their bodies so close to each other makes their comfortable fitting clothes tight in the biceps area, the chest, the thighs and the crotch. If John were to look, not that he has, he'd see that Bret is hard.

"This isn't something you have to do," Bret says as if he's had one beer too many. "It was hurt before tonight's match, not during."

John varies his expression just a little, but stays quiet. Though tired just like Bret, he keeps on with his work.

Bret senses this and tries to get him to stop. "This ruins your tough-guy image."

John puckers his lips. Bret's attention is drawn to them when John makes the "shh" sound.

"Jeopardizing your future in pro wrestling," Bret continues.

Still John gives no audible response. Instead, he circles an area just below Bret's thumb.

Seconds pass. Bret continues to stare at John's lips. This is just so perfect now, so tender. "So, doc, how'd you get so good at this?"

John wrinkles his forehead but does this teasingly. "I'm a trainer, remember? Sprains, strains, snaps, and a good number of cracks? Yeah, true, I don't have a degree in this kinda stuff, just experience. So rest now. Be quiet."

Bret slips his free hand under his head. He does not want this to end. "Tell me about this 'experience,' and about your being a trainer."

The scent of Bret's underarm makes John weak, dizzy, vulnerable. Reluctantly he begins to tell Bret about his job. He acts guarded or annoyed as he does this, but it's a bad act because for the first time with a guy—especially one like Bret—he is playful, not reserved. His dry humor comes through first with his voice, then his expressions. As he finishes sharing with Bret what he did after his high school graduation, John intentionally holds the last sliver of an ice cube still.

John now slides in beside him. "Lookin' good on your back there, bud. Just like in the ring tonight."

Bret repositions his hips. "No way, I *had* you."

John's eyes light. "Who, you? Other way around with the action there." He calls attention to his chin by scratching what does not itch. "I had you."

"Not what I heard."

"You're not listening to the right crowd, then."

The angle of John's head, the attention to his lips, and the playful glow in his face is all there. Unhurried, they are lost in each other for a moment and, inches apart, both would swear they are closer—and this proximity is what they've dreamed of. The first kiss is close, but recedes. The idea of kissing comes again, and again. Each time, it just barely passes.

Bret picks up the conversation again. "Oh, I hang with the right crowd."

John moves the damp towels to the floor with a toss from his hand and sets his head in the pillow next to Bret's. "You must have hearing troubles, then. Clearly." He frowns his boyish expression, one where his chin wrinkles. "That must be what it is."

Bret wants to smile. "Hearing troubles?"

John raises one of his wide, warm shoulders in a shrug. "Yeah, let's think about this. Your hearing was last checked when?"

Bret doesn't answer.

John turns. "Or is it just your active imagination?"

"Yap, yap with your floppy jaw there, Johnny. Your best muscles are those around your mouth. The king of the ring? Well, you're lookin' at him."

John raises his eyebrows. "Um, Johnny?" He laughs. "First of all, no, and second, king? That's me. Listen, as I guess we are going to have to do this again. I *so* had you."

"Active imagination…yeah." Bret rolls onto his back and imagines John's lips on his neck. "Did some doctor actually diagnose that for you?"

"Some doctor? No, I had the crowd with me, remember? Scrawny dude, the fans screamed my name. No, Red, I'm the champ here."

Bret smiles from the inside. The heat over his sternum feels right. He drifts along for a minute, happy to be where he is. "Champ? Now, that would be a good name for a dog, and you were like a hurtin' pup with the ways I had you."

"No way."

Bret continues. "But as for the obvious winner tonight? It's all me, bud. *All me.*"

John settles his chin in next to Bret's shoulder.

With his eyes closed, Bret says, "About those fans?"

"Yeah?"

Bret drops his fingers so they're *just* a half inch from John's.

John rises just a bit. "What is it?"

Bret waits a moment. There is no hurry. That they can just be this close? That's the connection here, the glue, what is true and right. In time, he shares the story of his time with the boy at the ice machine. He tells John every detail, especially the joking, but he leaves out the boy's final question.

They are quiet for a minute until Bret turns toward John. They are face-to-face. "There's something else, John. Before I left the ice dispenser, the boy asked me why we hurt each other."

"What?"

"He wondered why we beat each other up."

John disagrees. "We didn't beat each other up." Then he pauses and realizes they did. He swallows the taste of guilt as it creeps up his throat. *We did beat on each other. We pummeled each other, over and over.* He looks into Bret's eyes, "So, what did you tell him?"

Bret is falling asleep. That scent of John's, and his body heat like a wool blanket, makes it tough for Bret not to drift off.

"Bret?"

"I'm not sure what I told him, but I've thought about it. That's where I was. Out there thinking."

Bret draws his hand up to his chin. Unconsciously, John mirrors the action.

They mean to talk more, each of them. They'd engage if the other led, they would share more or try to share more, but neither can fight sleep any longer. After all that wrestling and being pried apart, they really are just *that* tired.

They each drift off, their foreheads just touching.

❖

John stirs a few minutes later. He is so close to Bret, so wonderfully close. In moving, he wakes the quiet one beside him. Face-to-face, Bret's eyes seem so bright, so inviting.

Bret sees a question on John's face. "What?"

"After you got the ice, what did you think about?"

Bret, still climbing back out of his first dream, untangles the words to the question he just heard and somehow scrambled in his head.

Being this tired makes him unguarded. He opens his eyes right down to his soul and speaks this truth. "You. I thought about you, John. You're important to me. You know…" A long gap slips in. Sleep comes close for a second time, but he fights it. "I was worried when you didn't show up to wrestle tonight." *Actually, I was really worried.*

"You were?"

Speaking openly in a moment filled with a tenderness he could never have imagined with any man, most especially this totally hot one here, Bret waits a moment. He considers what it is like to cross from wishful thinking in the past to what is really, truly happening here now.

While his hands stay still, though he longs to slide them over the side of John's face, he continues. "But you're here now, so close and safe, and everything is all right."

These last words touch John's soul.

There is no more for now. They did pound each other and stayed up much later than they ordinarily do, especially after a night of wrestling. To be together, though, to share this time, they made it last as long as they could. Despite a hot bath and an iced wrist, they are still hard and worn out in so many places from exertion. Face-to-face, however, as they share the same air, they do what each has longed to do, and that's sleep together, one so close to the other.

It takes just moments. Suddenly and soundly, they drop off into sleep.

CHAPTER TWENTY-NINE

They do not stir for hours. John wakes first, simply by turning to his side. It is shortly after four a.m., but he does not know this because no clock rests on a nightstand in the room. He thinks about finding his watch in his gym bag. That idea slips by quickly, though. Instead, he turns so that his front is to Bret's back. Reaching around, he slips his warm hand down Bret's warm and fuzzy stomach—ah, nice!—and daringly slides his fingers into the waist of Bret's jeans. He finds the waistband of Bret's underwear and holds tightly.

Bret has wood. John can feel the smooth, warm head against his fingers. He lifts his head off the pillow. *How can he sleep so hard?*

As if to answer the question not asked, Bret moans and turns so that he pins John's hand beneath himself and the mattress. To stay with Bret as he moves closer to sleeping on his stomach, John is now covering at least half of his sleeping partner's back. John slides his knee between both of Bret's and, without thinking, humps him once, twice.

"Are you awake?" he asks Bret.

No response, just steady breathing.

The floor lamp in the room remains lit because neither had planned to fall asleep so suddenly. John considers shutting it off, but that doesn't happen. Wrapping his hand around Bret's erection, he means to do more—and will do more—but closing his eyes, he's back to sleep again.

❖

John's heavy. When he's over him, however, Bret can't imagine a better blanket or way to sleep. He arches his back and enjoys how John's sleeping weight stays right with him.

He opens his eyes. Squints. The light over there by the curtains. Why did he leave that on?

And why is he sleeping in his jeans?

Before he can answer his question, he realizes where John's fingers are. He rocks his butt against John's crotch and drifts back to sleep. That comfortable. That right.

❖

Damn. John has to pee.

Once back from the bathroom, he sits down gently on the edge of the bed and watches this man in front of him sleep. Soft and smooth, Bret's expression is open now, tender, vulnerable. His fingers barely curl in front of him.

Thoughts of just jumping on him and stripping him down to nothing fill his mind, but now, oddly, something stronger wraps around him; it is as warm as when he was curled behind this handsome and hot man who, in good, expensive, and key places, smells like one of those good soaps or body washes he comes across sometimes when passing through the men's locker room at the gym where he works.

Bret. Dang. He's here. *Here.*

And that's what has come over him, that Bret is here, and that he can simply watch him.

Rising from the bed to finally turn down the light, he looks through the glass to the parking garage well below and sees no one. The black sky is lit with an ugly orange cast from the security lights mounted not only to the building but also along the weed-lined sidewalk in the distance. Surprisingly, six floors up do not give John much of a view.

He's still wearing the clothes he put on when he went out to look for Bret who took *way* too long to get ice. He is quiet as he thinks about the boy Bret told him about there at the dispenser.

And that question.

Like Bret, only he doesn't realize it, John doesn't know another way. He doesn't know how to get close, how to touch Bret so that Bret knows he loves him, if there even is such a true thing between two men.

Sure, there is sex. Earlier tonight, he could have stripped his shirt and angled his muscles in the light, exposing more of his torso by lacing his fingers behind his head, pulled out his own hard-on when they were in bed earlier. He's done that before. He reminds himself he's been a whore. Louise Amsterdam gave him her money and her bed and that red slingshot as a gift, a birthday present. And before that, with Greg, he prostituted himself on that borrowed and beat-up twin mattress in that piece-of-shit trailer. With his shirt off and legs spread, he teased Greg and never gave thought to the fact that what he really wanted was never there. As it turned out with both Greg and Dax, he was a blond sack for pounding.

So yeah, there's sex. Empty sex.

And then there's Bret. Bret with his handsome, sure, bright smile. Bret who drew a bath for him. Bret who sleeps so quietly now. Bret who just makes him feel like he's alive when they are together, whole, happy.

He cares so much for him, and wants to do more. He sees the two damp towels on the floor beside the bed. He picks them up. The ice chips, massaging his wrist…he shakes his head. It just didn't work; it didn't—or hasn't—worked *enough*. He's wanted this one thing since he's lived with Greg: a home, a home with someone who loves him.

John puts his butt against the sink counter and leans back after wadding the towels and tossing them on the counter. He slips off his T-shirt, which he realizes is damp from his own heat when sleeping, and folds his arms. He understands every couple is different, unique, complicated, and wonderful—every twosome is exceptionally particular, of course. From what he's seen of Bret, he knows neither can just give away trust. That is not how they were raised, or who they even are.

Someone passes in the hall. It's so quiet that John hears every sound until the fan in the heating and cooling system under the window kicks on and sends the sheers under the curtains for a short ride. They whirl and wrap around the heavier fabric that John closes.

The sheers that are now motionless behind him remind him of wedding dresses and bed ruffles. In all of the homes he's lived in, he does not know this delicate or refined world or how to embrace it. How to be open and expressive is a mystery.

He should have kissed Bret, though. In bed together, yeah, they were so close. He just should have kissed him.

But he didn't.

Soft light from the window now spills onto the bed and John finds his way back to where he belongs. On top of the covers, Bret is on his side wearing a green T-shirt and jeans very similar to John's. A good bit of his T-shirt is wadded under him, so it is tight over Bret's muscular shoulders. Inches of his lower back are exposed. Slight dimples take either side of his lower backbones. John wants to kiss them, rest his head against them as if Bret's whole lower back and butt is one hard, curved pillow.

He slides under the covers that Bret hasn't pinned down and is so thankful to have his partner there. When he brings his face close to Bret's, Bret says, "Grandpa said not until I was done. Not before."

John touches Bret's face.

"Just the wood pile in the corner."

John scoots up toward the head of the bed. He thinks about pulling his pillow up for his bad shoulder to rest against but he just leans against the particle board bolted to the wall. The long top crosspiece digs into his skin but he doesn't mind. His attention has moved onto what he wants more.

Being a wrestler, John knows how to maneuver someone else's body. He uses this to his advantage. In one precise yet gentle move that involves both his legs and his left arm, he plunks Bret down almost on top of him. Bret's pillow, as planned, stays behind so that Bret rests his head against the contours of John's bare chest. The still sleeping man curls his arm around John's rippled side. In his dreams, Bret nuzzles his chin and rocks his hips once, twice against John's thick thigh. A moment later, Bret folds his arm between his own chest and John's lap, resting his elbow just to one side of John's crotch. His muscle-heavy arm, along with his head, becomes deadweight.

John sighs. With this one incredibly hot, remarkable man so close to him, he thinks of one word: *perfect.*

Minutes pass. With the hand closest to Bret, John reaches for and holds his partner's shoulder at the deltoid, the small capping muscle right at the top of the arm. Bret's musculature is so hard, so pronounced. John leans forward. Slowly and gently, he kisses the top of Bret's head. Content with his nose in Bret's soft red hair, he closes his eyes and waits for sleep that will come again. He is still tired, still worn out from the pounding action in the ring. Arching his back to bring even more of Bret's weight on him, he thinks about tonight, about what happened between them—not just in the ring, but before. He tries to remember what happened in the locker room after he came up to Bret who was busy looking for his tape. What was that guy's name again, the forty-year-old wrestler with the mouth?

A cold sensation spreads within John. His blood thickens to gelatin. Mike was the wrestler's name. He had called them Princes.

With his eyes still closed, he remembers getting up in Mike's face with the intent to hit him and hit him hard. *Princes.*

Dax had once called him one. It was during a fight, one of the few they had because they rarely talked. It wasn't the word itself, of course, it was the situation—the whole situation.

John closes his eyes. Dax. It never should have been; it just never should have happened. His blood moves again, but does so only with the sting of regret.

With a content smile, one that enables him to breathe in the lingering scent of shampoo in his wrestle partner's hair, John realizes he hasn't stopped sliding his fingers over Bret's back. For lazy minutes on end, he loses himself in doing this and then snaps back when he remembers that one of the last words he called Bret before they fought in the ring was *faggot.* He knows gay men can be hard on one another, even though he's come close to a gay bar only once and has never lived a culturally gay life. There are shoppers and one-timers, cheaters, game players, liars, and while the same can be true of heterosexuals, the boy's question comes again, only a little different. *Why are we hurting ourselves?* Bret and John did it physically in the ring tonight, for sure, but in other places—from bars to beds, from being caddish to cruel, truly cruel, the oppressed oppress.

John hears the word again. The word he shot out before he wrestled tonight. *Faggot.* His heart stops beating. He squeezes Bret, holds him even more closely, and wonders why gay men keep hurting each other.

Silence comes instead of an answer. John looks toward the window. It's funny now that he's closed the curtain on the outside world. It's safe in here.

❖

The mattress moves. He figures that it's Bret's knee jiggling his. Yet there's an aroma. Coffee. Eggs. Toast. *Is that breakfast?* He opens his eyes to see Bret turning away. Catching a side view of Bret's arm, he simply stares at the pronounced muscles that make up Bret's upper back. John's sleep mate pops off the bed and is back again almost as fast. Their eyes meet. More of their loneliness washes away.

They smile. In doing so, such light comes, such peace. Both know what they are doing, or want to do. Bret comes closer and bends down over John. He sets his elbow and forearm alongside John's shoulder and head. He stretches down even further.

It's time, they say to each other with their eyes. *It's time to kiss.*

Bret lowers his eyes, drawing his eyelids down, but John doesn't move. Bret senses this and opens his eyes again.

I want you to see this, John says without a word. He picks his head up and meets Bret's lips with his own.

Neither moves for what could be an hour or more. In truth, it is just seconds, but they are seconds that will last indefinitely because finally—finally—both are out of options, defenses, and denial. There are no more walls between them. Nothing gets in the way of the sure, steady draw that has pulled them so strongly for so long.

And it happens. It just happens. It flows smoothly, naturally, inevitably. As if they are saying hello to one another for the first time in a different way, they nudge and prod, burrow and intentionally explore getting to know each other like this.

They start gently and tentatively—even politely—but that changes. Hunger and want surface and take hold, driving them into one another harder and harder, and then, like a lull in a set of ocean waves, they relax.

Their lips part with a very loud noise. Both smile at this.

"I wasn't sure—wasn't sure if I should do this." Bret looks to the heavy white paper bag on the bed beside him and then stares warmly into John's eyes. "But I wanted to. I bought us something to eat this morning."

John thinks on this for a moment. "Thanks for breakfast too."

Not understanding, Bret frowns.

John sits up and leans toward Bret. "I was thanking you first for the kiss. We did that you know."

Bret frowns. "Kiss?"

"Yeah, that. The lip locking thing. You. Me."

"Oh. I hadn't planned on that right off." Bret glances up at the cheap headboard, then back to John. "It happened on its own."

"Did it, now?"

"Yeah. It did."

Scratching the side of his head, John gives a handsome, boyish grin. "Show me, how'd that go again?"

They kiss a second time. It is even deeper than the first, even longer. Bret stretches out over John for a long time and winds up on his back with John over him.

"Food," Bret says minutes later when his stomach gurgles.

"And I have to really pee," John counters as he climbs off Bret.

John runs water at the sink, hoping the gushing sound will soften his morning wood for Bret. He doesn't hear the door knock.

When he finishes in the bathroom, Bret is not alone.

John stares. It can't be. It just can't be. It's been so many months since he'd seen him last at his wrestling school. John really hasn't thought much about his pro wrestling teacher since he and Lyle finished his school in West Virginia, but there he is. It's Russ.

Neither Russ nor Bret sees John at first. They are busy talking like they know one another. From the bathroom, John approaches slowly.

"And yeah," Russ says, "when I saw you this morning buying breakfast, well, yeah, I couldn't wait to tell you—to tell you both." John's former teacher looks at his student. "And there he is. Hey, John, how are you doing?"

"Russ?"

They shake hands. It is awkward. Too much has happened and then again not happened between them, but Bret misses most of it. Still watching both of them, he says, "Yeah, John, when I was out getting food, I ran into your old coach here."

"Hey guys, eat," Russ says as one of his hands finds the back pockets of his jeans. "Don't let me hold you up."

Bret opens the bag. "Russ here wanted to talk with both of us—together."

Russ and Bret take the corners of the bed and John sits in the room's only chair. As the two begin to eat breakfast sandwiches, John says he likes to check up on his grads and was in the audience last night.

"That was an awesome match," Russ says. "Never saw anything so raw, so really damn powerful. How you planned that all out. Pretty incredible."

Neither Bret nor John looks at each other. They know Russ is taking in the fact that there's only one bed in the room.

"And I wasn't the only one to take notice," Russ continues, "And that's why I'm here right off the bat this morning. I wanted to be the one to tell you that a major scout also saw you last night. You definitely have his interest and he's passed this along to his boss, Howell Launders, the president of New World Wrestling. How does the idea of trying out for NWW strike you?"

New World Wrestling, or NWW as abbreviated, is major league wrestling. Televised weekly, Howell Launders's NWW is seen across the country, in the five provinces of Canada, and in parts of Mexico. Money is deep. All first-class travel expenses are paid, including incidentals such as tips. Binding contracts, promotions, and product endorsements are all a part of the lucrative deal, and these big-time wrestlers easily make five to ten times more than wrestlers at their regional level.

"And Howell wants to see you two," Russ says. "I had Vaughn keep the ring up. Howell will be here in, well," he smiles, "when do you guys plan to finish eating?"

CHAPTER THIRTY

I don't need to see you wrestle," Howell says exactly ninety minutes later, "I just need to see you."

Standing on the floor in front of the ring in their street clothes, neither Bret nor John moves.

Howell thumbs through a thin file. His attention stays with the papers inside. Without looking up, he says, "Tell me about wrestling. Sell this. If I were watching you two, what would I see?" He looks up from his work with little time to waste. "What?"

The following pause disappoints Howell.

"Well, we can really go at it," John says flatly, knowing already that his answer is not enough.

"I know you 'go at it,'" Howell responds. "That's why I'm here."

Bret and John nod uneasily.

Howell sighs. "What I'm looking for now involves seeing if you fit what I'm seeking to develop. So, that said, imagine this scenario: I'm a charged-up fan and I've paid good money for this upcoming match. Who do I see when you two guys are in the ring?"

"Like our personalities?" John asks.

The moment Howell rolls his eyes is when Bret comes in on the save. "We are clean-cut athletes. We don't prance around or stall. We lock up and give a lot of sport to our wrestling. A lot of strength-showing moves."

"Clean-cut," Howell wonders. "You don't do cheap shots and tricks? Bad-boy antics?"

Both answer, "Not really."

"That's actually boring," Howell says, "from a marketing standpoint, that is." He sets his file down. "So groin shots, kicks to each other's nuts? You're not into that?"

Bret and John squirm. It's as if they've just been kicked themselves.

"I don't need badasses," Howell confides, though he isn't speaking the truth. He's always on the hunt for off-the-wall, rough-necked bad boys the crowd will love to hate. "I have enough of those big jerks, thank you very much. But I'm looking for something I think you can give. I need sportsmen. And you two are built very similarly. As I started just a minute ago, let me see that. Just your shirts off."

Both look toward each other, but not in the eye. Sterile, cold, and embarrassed, they toughen this up with a show of manufactured confidence. Each pulls off his T-shirt and stands like a side of beef to be inspected.

Howell completes his task in one perfunctory glance. "Yep, that will work. And this is what I'm thinking. Bret, is it? First, you shave your chest...that you haven't yet, well, that isn't done. And second, we dye your hair to match Jake's here."

Bret says, "John. His name is John."

"Oh, John, sorry." Howell apologizes, but doesn't mean it. He's not sold on either of these wholesome wheat Sunday school boys and shows that he is too much like Gail. Neither Bret nor John likes this. "We change your names, anyway. You're going to play brothers."

Lyle, who's been standing beside Howell this entire time, moves forward. He remains silent.

"No," Howell urges, turning toward Lyle. "Don't be quiet, Lyle. I sense you have something to say. Say it."

"Brothers, sure, that's a good idea. Or they can be friends," Lyle suggests. "That's what I was thinking."

"Friends?" Howell frowns, thinking, *How limp is that?*

Lyle senses he's losing Howell and adds quickly, "But either way..."

Howell won't overlook any possibility to make money. "Yeah, fine. We will test that theory too. Regardless, you two would be teammates with the same look. And I'm thinking lifeguards. Ripped, tanned, ocean lifeguards. Maybe even with white oxide on your noses. You come out in board shorts, one or two waist sizes too large to show just how tight you are in the abs...and hinting under those shorts, yeah, when you strip down to wrestle your opponents...red Speedos."

Red Speedos. Not trunks? John looks away without moving his head. He sees the birthday gift he received from Louise Amsterdam, the one he had to wear for Greg after Greg left him behind in that grocery store parking lot after he...after he... John swallows. In a way, he hasn't left anything behind. A whore, he's right back where he was.

"Yeah," Howell is thinking out loud. "Definitely red."

"A hot color," Lyle adds. "No boots, no knee or elbow pads. That wouldn't go with their beach look."

Howell speaks as if talking to himself, still pretending that he's interested. "And that adds a sense of vulnerability to these two pretty boys, an earthy quality. Natural."

"Another way is just to twist the standard," Lyle offers, knowing that this is his only time to spend with a big wrestling exec. "Keep them in more standard gear, but have them come out as...I don't know... anything from medical students to garbage collectors. How about lab or science geeks? I see goggles, coats..."

"Go on."

"Real tech moves. Totally in sync. Precise, scientific wrestling."

Howell's eyes light. Lyle doesn't know it yet, but he's just landed himself what he's wanted, a great managing job with New World Wrestling.

Lyle shrugs, although he senses that Howell likes what he hears, if not sees. "They're just options."

"Good options," Howell says in correction. They conclude this short meeting when Howell says he has a good deal to consider. He admits he likes what he's heard about last night, but will have to get back to them in no less than three weeks. As John and Bret fumble back into their shirts, Howell asks to speak with Lyle privately.

Standing alone ringside, both Bret and John think the same thought at the same time. *That's it?*

❖

Thirty minutes later in a first-class restaurant not far from the hotel, Howell presents Lyle a dream job. After the two discuss responsibilities, salary, and even private stock options in the NWW, the president of the ten-million-dollar company sets his elbows on the starched linen table cloth. He waits a moment for Lyle's complete focus.

When he has it, Howell asks, "They're together, somehow, aren't they?"

Lyle doesn't share what he suspects. "Who's together?"

Tapping his fingertips on the table, Howell does not engage

extraneous conversation. "There's something there, between them. Explain what you can about this because I've hired you for your ability to read people. Are Bret and Jake lovers?"

Lyle appreciates Howell's candor. "Right from the start, from Bret and *John's* first match, I picked up on something reactionary, almost palpable between them."

Howell's patience is tested. "And you're not answering my question about their being ass-pounding faggots because…"

"Because it's not yet known." Lyle looks at him directly. "I don't believe they know themselves, at least completely."

Howell gestures for and receives the check from a lovely server whose poise reminds him of his eldest daughter, a freshmen at Penn and the real reason he's here in Philly this morning. "So, they're figuring themselves out." He thinks on this. "Yes, it makes sense. That's what my scout saw last night. They are working this through."

"Exactly."

A distant look sweeps over Howell's dark eyes. He mulls over the conversation he's had so far with Lyle. "Well then," he says, "as my granddaddy would say, 'the pickin's just right on these boys.'"

Lyle catches a lump in his throat. He glances toward their server now at a different table and hopes the hot feeling inside cools. It does not.

Howell sips his drink, clinks his ice cubes. "You're ticked at me, Lyle."

"You're direct. That's good."

As he slips his credit card into the sleek leather holder containing the check, he says, "Wrestling? My vision of wrestling exposes our primal nature on one very real, very visceral level. It's about as raw or unexposed as we can get with one another. We have good prevailing over evil—or evil over good—played out in vivid detail. We have injustice, betrayal, even robbery. And the bottom line? Lyle, it's clear. Fans relate to the oppressed or the oppressor. Think about it."

Though worried about what he'd do with John and Bret, Lyle nods. "Everyone is hit hard at some time. Job, money, boss, spouse, family."

Howell continues. "And while most of us can't—and even shouldn't—hit back, there's still an element deep within us that's just brutal. This is seen in our wrestlers. Your concern over exposing these two? Yeah, that will be done. Every wrestler I have is exposed—literally. Dirty, down, and sometimes nasty. That's what makes this."

"But what about—" Lyle doesn't finish because Howell holds up his hand.

"About homosexuality? It's a tender subject for some, sure. And sadly, I believe there's a push and pull that will see itself relived in a generation or two to come. Factions on far sides may never agree, but my job is the story, or the creating of the story, and I want to do that well." Howell lifts his sloe gin fizz. "Do I know exactly how this unfolds for your two pretty boys there? Of course not. A good bit has to do with what they bring of themselves to the ring. Can this be told incredibly well? Of course, that's my goal."

"'Incredibly well'? You mean cheesy, raw, juvenile?"

Howell smirks. Finally someone is on to him.

They leave the restaurant but continue the conversation as they wait for Howell's car in the parking garage. Lyle says, "So, you'll let them be gay?"

Howell is tired of this. He doesn't really care. "I'll let them be themselves."

"That's not an answer."

Howell looks for the valet. Waiting is not something he pays to have happen. "No, truthfully, it isn't an answer. You've caught me there."

Lyle rolls one of his shoulders forward, making it seem like what he's about to say is done in confidence. "I knew John before he started wrestling professionally. I'll protect him to the end. And I'll do that for all of them. It is *their* best interest to bring forward, even encourage. That's management, or my management. I won't have them manipulated."

Howell studies Lyle as if he's seen him for the first time. Perhaps he really has. His eyes lock onto his new employee when he says, "I have made one of the best business moves in five years by hiring you. You won't see this management style through, we will. But know something, Lyle, something all of your romance and deep, heartfelt emotion smacks squarely against again, and again. It's a big, bad world around us."

Lyle is a little annoyed, as if the alcohol in his own drink turned sour. "Howell, I hear you speaking on a platform to your constituents. 'A big, bad world'? What are you saying?"

With a purr, Howell's car arrives, a Mercedes 900 series. "I'm saying that we will see. That's not a lack of commitment on my part;

that's me saying we engage what we have. And again, and hear this: I am in the business of showing people stories, and I will do this as best as I can. Exploitation is a low word I don't honestly appreciate. I hear where it comes from with you and I am not offended. With that in mind, we will tell this as it happens. Will it be groundbreaking?" To answer his own question, his voice becomes reflective. "You know, God, I hope so."

Lyle shakes Howell's hand. "We've said enough now."

"I agree." Howell tips the valet and steps into his car. Over its top, he says, "And we will say more later. This needs to be done well, so very well."

"One more question?" Lyle asks. "Are you going to hire John and Bret?"

Howell shakes his head. "After talking with you now, I honestly don't know. I need time to consider other options that I'll share with you this coming Monday morning. But if it's not with those two muscle boys, then homosexuality and pro wrestling will meet again with different athletes. And we'll take that as it comes. One story at a time, Lyle."

"Deal."

❖

"Deal," Bret says as he hands his menu to their server, who saw them wrestle last night but won't recognize them until he's alone a minute later in the kitchen. Both Bret and John wear baseball caps pulled down low on their heads after having just met Howell and Lyle at the ring.

John echoes what Bret just said. "A deal it is, then."

The two had decided to split a large chicken-topped veggie pizza because the calorie-loaded breakfast sandwiches they ate while Russ was in their room were not enough.

"Growing boys" is what Bret's military grandfather would have said had he been alive to see this. He understood the need for food as nourishment, especially to hardworking bodies. Homosexuality would be something he wouldn't understand, at least at first, but he would approve of their appetites. As an Army sergeant, he knew that a young man ain't worth a damn unless he eats, and eats often.

"And salads?" John asks Bret. "To start?"

Bret smiles and nods. He traces the top of his drinking glass with his finger and thinks his tough-ass grandfather would like John, for sure.

"Okay, guys, I'll be right back with your greens," the server says before winding his way through the crowd to place their order.

They watch him weave around small, tightly spaced tables that stuff the long, narrow restaurant in a part of town that, unknown to Bret and John, is gay-friendly. An early lunchtime crowd begins to pack the popular place and the couple sitting nearest the wrestlers instantly know what Lyle, Gail, Howell, and others sensed but could not immediately name: that the fit between Bret and John is not just obvious but complete, flawless. In their late thirties, the two closest to the baseball cap boys just celebrated fourteen years together and, as athletes themselves, one being a rower and the other a swimmer, they *knew.* One short, nondescript glance between them confirms that Bret and John share what they have—chemistry.

As they each realize this, they cannot help but overhear what John says in amazement. "*That* was Howell Launders! Wow."

"Yeah," Bret responds more quietly. "Wow."

Neither Bret nor John took time to talk about what had happened right after their time in front of the ring. Instead, hunger pushed them across the street to this little restaurant revered for good pizza.

Keeping his eyes on Bret, John frowns. "He's a lot bigger on TV."

Bret laughs. "Yeah, I thought that too."

"But still, *Howell Launders*. And the NWW? Just…wow."

Bret smiles because it's good to see John happy. "We didn't see this one coming, did we?"

John scans the room and notices everyone but the two he should: the couple at the next table. "Yeah, I didn't see this coming, Bret, at least not yet. But we're good at this."

Bret is silent.

With his chest puffier with pride, John continues. "He seemed to be pretty sure of us. But I did think there'd be tryouts or something, didn't you?"

Again, Bret remains quiet. Something inside him locks, then pings. It's not hunger, though he certainly is ready to eat. It's more vague and troubling than the need to down half of a large pizza. He tries to ignore this sensation, but he can't. It returns. Is it loss? Regret?

John goes on, too lost in his fast-moving thoughts to notice Bret.

"I didn't think it would be like this, just meeting him. Guys out there in leagues like ours believe this is a dream come true."

Bret's stomach tightens, then he realizes that this...this isn't his dream. Wrestling at this highest level is not where he wishes, or even wants, to go. Instead, there's a classroom out there, a grade school door with his name on it. A roster of twenty-one students' names, *his* students' names, a grade book, lesson plans. A lopsided child-made ceramic mug on his desk that holds pencils.

Scanning the restaurant hoping that something will distract his thinking, he sees the two seated near them. Handsome and strong, each man has short dark hair and strikingly clean-cut features.

Bret deliberately pays attention to what he's feeling. He senses some sort of a parallel between the four of them. While eating his salad, he wonders how these two met and what their relationship is. As he questions this, his memory draws immediately to John and their first kiss this morning—that one incredible, necessary kiss—and then, just like that, he knows. He knows. They are, in one way, what Bret and John could be.

To confirm this, he glimpses at both of them and then quickly looks away. Yes. He's right. As weird as this does sound to Bret, these two are their possible future.

All of a sudden, John's voice, which has not stopped, tunes back into Bret's frequency. With a little surprise, Bret realizes John is in mid-sentence.

"...when really, that's all there is to it." John's eyes meet his.

Bret shakes his head. "I'm sorry. Say that again?"

John, finished with his salad, drops his strong chin and pretends rather poorly to pout. So damn handsome, though, he doesn't succeed. "I was talking about how the NWW is a dream job. To some, this is it. Guys long for this."

Bret looks down at his simple place setting. Without peering into John's blue eyes because he thinks he knows the answer to his question, he still asks, "John, wrestling pro, it's your dream?"

John leans back quizzically, then, with the energy of a teenager, quickly plunks his elbows on the table. He forgets those moments in front of Russ's school sandwiched between those two Cape Cod houses with sun-faded toys cluttering their tiny front lawns. "Oh, yeah! This is everything. The money and the fame...all right, no movie-star status, but first-class travel? For free? And the fans?"

Bret stares at a safe place just beside John's shoulder and again thinks of his mother and all she relinquished to be the wife of one bastard and a daughter of another. He thinks about the decisions she's made, the compromises all couples not just go through but somehow endure, the best coming out stronger, the rest feeling bitter or more brittle with each passing year.

Again, his attention is drawn to the couple sitting nearest him. He sees now that one has his knee between the thighs of the other. *What have you been through?* he wonders. *How do you make it work?*

Bret glances at one of the men in the couple, the one who had met his eyes just a few minutes earlier. That man, who Bret now sees has flecks of gray in his hair, is looking at him again. He says to Bret through his silence that being a man and loving a man is by no means easy, but worth it.

Bret nods and draws his attention back to his drinking glass. The NWW…at least for a while is a go.

The funny feeling in his chest is pushed away. He will do this. He will definitely do this with John.

CHAPTER THIRTY-ONE

While waiting for their pizza to arrive, John notices where Bret's attention has been. For the first time, he becomes aware of the two sitting beside them. He doesn't see what Bret does, at least at first. Instead, he translates the positive impression these two give into competition. He literally sizes up one of the muscular men and then the other and bets that he could take them in or out of the ring. Then John wonders whom he will wrestle in the NWW or, rather, who will he and Bret wrestle.

He's excited. Waiting three weeks for Howell to make up his mind, though? Man, that will seem like forever! Three weeks. The start of October. Halloween matches will start and they'll be *lifeguards*?

"Hey, Bret," he says, "what do you think of that beach idea? You and me, lifeguards?"

Bret's been thinking about finances to finish his degree and knows unmistakably that the fast track to cash is to join with John in the NWW.

John bounces his chin left and right. "Hello? You, over there? Lifeguards?"

"Yeah, sure, why not?" Bret responds, but only halfheartedly. "I bet we even get whistles."

"And you'll be blond."

Bret shrugs his shoulder. "We'll be teammates. Imagine the guys we'll wrestle."

"I had thought of that, actually just a minute ago. There will be big guys, *way* bigger than you and me." John senses that Bret isn't altogether with him. "But we'll practice beforehand. Everything all worked out. Winner, loser, the holds, finishing moves. Not like us—not like the two times we've gone at it."

Bret does not say what they both know, that some of that wrestling is real and painful, that bones break, men get hurt.

"We really do go at it," John says almost as an afterthought.

Without thinking, Bret adds, "In the ring, yeah."

John shoots a quizzical look and wonders, *What's that supposed to mean?* No sooner does he form this question than his answer comes. He remembers them tangled up in the ring just hours ago. One human pretzel made of the two of them. So much of Bret's body folded both under and over him. He remembers one move, the bear hug, where he could feel Bret's heart beat against his chest. Bret's breath—in, out, in, out—seemed to stroke his neck, almost massage it. And how Bret had relaxed then and there in his arms. How, for just a moment, he gave in, surrendered.

With the crowd favoring him, John remembers another hold, with another chance to get close, *that* close. Bret's chest. Bret's nipple hovered just over his face—just there to lightly chew on, taste, tease. It pressed to his chin, against his mouth. And then, in play, his own crotch quickly straddled John's neck.

At the table, John swallows and tastes something numbing in the back of his throat. It's desire. He smiles but his lips do not move. Instead, a tear comes to his eye. Bret.

Leaning forward in the restaurant's chair, Bret jokingly moves his head side to side. He knows John is lost in thought and he tries to bring him back. "Helloooooo? John? Where'd you go?"

John's eyes focus. After this happens, he waits three seconds, maybe five. There's more he wants to say now, more he wants to share, but the words are trapped at what feels like the top of a funnel. Finally, he's able to state what is obvious. "You're hot."

Bret dismisses this by putting a frown across his forehead. He sets his left index and middle finger on his forearm, as if taking his own temperature. "Nope. Ninety-eight point five degrees, bud. Average, not hot."

"Just the ways about you, Bret. That's what that scout of Howell's noticed. He saw your heat." John leans forward by putting the palm of his hand against his own crotch. He locks his shoulders. He's blushing. "About this heat of yours. About us. Together, really together. Just a question here, can we…" He is suddenly nervous, shy and courteous. "Do you…do you think when the pizza arrives that we can get it to go?"

❖

They're in Bret's car on their way back from their meeting with Howell. With the pizza boxed and on his lap in the passenger seat, John wonders about the three weeks. "Is it really going to take that long? I mean, he seemed to be pretty sure of us. He hardly looked at us with our shirts off."

"That felt a little weird."

"Yeah, but that's how it is. Not a big deal." As soon as he says these words, John knows it is a big deal. He experiences the same sinking feeling Bret has in his stomach about the NWW. John ignores this however, or tries to. Unlike Bret, he didn't have one home growing up, nor did he have two of four years of an undergraduate degree in education completed. Money would bring comfort. "I think we're going to go, Bret. I think we're going to go."

Bret stares ahead as a distant red light changes to green, making another piece of what was holding him back on this decision break away. He scrambles to think about the two guys who sat so close to them back at the restaurant. How he could not name but could rather sense what one gave up for the other, and how, like any couple, they compromised and negotiated their relationship escapes him now. He has not done a partnership of any kind before and does not know what to do. The only thing he's certain of is the pit in his stomach deepens. He swallows. This does not accomplish anything because the catch in his throat returns.

"Yeah," Bret says flatly with a squeeze of the steering wheel as they ride through the crossroad of two opposing routes. "We're going to go."

❖

This life isn't real. Hotel lobbies with fake plants, dank elevators, dark halls, cigarette butts littering the sidewalk around glass exit doors that never quite come clean, white sheets that are almost blue they are so thin.

He wants to stop. In thinking of John and of the times he can be with John, however, Bret takes the steps anyway. Their room is now just six floors and one long hallway above them.

We are going to go, he says to himself again.

"You're quiet, Bret," John says when they reach their floor.

"You too."

"Thinking about that lifeguard whistle." He leans over and bumps Bret's shoulder with his own. "It's going to be okay."

"Sure."

They stand at and then walk through their door a moment later. Everything inside is as it was when Russ was there. The few slices of pizza that weren't downed in Bret's car a few minutes ago are set on top of the TV.

"Those guys we saw," John says, when he moves the pizza box to a more solid location, "back at that restaurant, you know, I think they were together."

Bret is careful to watch his words, not go too far. "They looked happy."

"Yeah."

Both stop at the same time, about ten feet apart. Bret says, "Do you think we could be that happy?"

"If there are two whistles, sure. If not, I'm not sharing."

They meet in the middle of the room, a few yards from both the dresser and the bed. Enough talk. John's forehead finds, nuzzles and rests on Bret's shoulder. In turn, Bret instinctively hugs John.

In this warm embrace, John whispers, "Just be here. Be here for me. Just don't move. Don't move at all."

Bret complies. The silence that follows is sacred. John moves his forehead closer to Bret's warm neck. Breathes the whisper of soap Bret used before going out to buy breakfast hours ago. His nose barely brushes against the cotton collar of Bret's shirt. All that muscle so close. All that strength.

Slowly, so very slowly, Bret begins to rock his hips left and right, left and right. It isn't noticeable at first, in fact, it's barely there, but like a lake lapping the beams of a dock on a perfectly flat August afternoon, a rhythm starts, a slow dance.

Bret moves his foot forward just an inch or two. John slides his back. Their fingers lace and lock and, face-to-face, they circle.

❖

John's stomach gurgles. They break just enough for Bret to look down, then meet John's eyes. He smiles and almost laughs. He is as bright as a boy at a major league baseball game.

"Yeah," John says with a crooked smile. "That, that was me."

Bret realizes yet again that this time with John is not a dream, that all of these whirling feelings are good and true and right, he sets the muscles in his jaw, revealing a serious expression. He reaches for and holds John again. With perfect timing, he says into John's ear, "I can get you another pizza if that will keep you busy down there."

"No, I should be pretty good."

Bret breaks completely, sits on the bed and motions for John to do the same. "Please, John, sit with me."

They are side by side, shoulder to shoulder. Bret sneaks his arm under John's and curls his fingers over John's thumb. He pulls and strokes what his fingers hold and says, "Listen, okay? All I know is that I have not had this…this…everything feeling. It's like—and I don't know if this will make sense—but I'm just trying to say that you just feel good to me, John, even when I'm not touching you."

With his free hand, John reaches for and strokes Bret's neck. There's a flash of a moment when all that badass wrestling comes between them—when the world they knew of punching and pounding slips between them for one second—but the touch is warm and healing and penetrates so deeply that dark places in Bret's past are cast in light. Those times, those damn times when his father or grandfather made him chop wood with a splintered ax in the dead heat of summer, those painful, lonely times when his high school or college guy friends would get lucky on dates with girls and he'd be alone in his room not sure why he wasn't feeling moved the way they were, yet had to study manuals on how to assemble a rifle so that he would know, damn it, he would just *know* how to put one together not just to have a heads up in the military but in case disaster struck home in northwest Illinois. All of those awful times soften with John's strokes.

Bret lets out a wordless, soundless cry of pleasure. With that, John's lips are on him and somehow through him. They reach inches below his skin. John slides around and tops him. Bret's back sinks into the mattress and, only as a wrestler knows how to do, John effortlessly maneuvers Bret into the center of the mattress with one strong yet gentle move.

They laugh and playfully wrestle. Without ever setting a foot off the bed, they slowly, surely, and methodically put each other into holds that position themselves in the best places for touch, for deep strokes and for kissing. They bend, contort, and power into and out of locks that require strength, skill, and a great deal of creativity. And they are there, somehow, not on the mattress but the mat. Sometimes they hear the distant, muffled crowds of the past cheering or booing for them—good-guy versus bad-guy antics are relived and replayed and they interchange these two roles seamlessly—until they both wind up in just their underwear.

It's then that John knows. Like the sound of the snap of fingers, he knows. He says, "You don't want to do this. You don't want to wrestle in the NWW. This big deal with Howell, traveling across the United States, different cities, and TV coverage…you don't want to do this."

An alarm sounds in Bret's chest. "I didn't say that."

"You didn't. I know."

"John—"

"You didn't say it. I just feel it. Your body somehow said it to mine. You don't want to do this."

Bret reaches for John's forearm. "No, I will. I will do this. We will do this."

"It's not your dream, Bret."

"But this is good. It's exciting. And the money. We could use the money."

John has a distant look in his eyes. He's thinking. With what Bret has and hasn't said since their time with Howell earlier, it's clear. How he missed it then, damn, he was just too busy himself, too consumed with his own wants.

"Money," John says, "for you to go to school. That's it. For you to teach. To become a teacher. That degree. Your degree."

"Yeah, but that's someday."

John moves Bret's thick thigh and sits so that their hips touch. Bret's chest is open to John in this position and he strokes Bret's pecs.

"John," Bret says, "someday. Teaching kids? Yeah, I think that will happen for me someday."

"You think that will happen, or you want that to happen?"

Bret doesn't immediately answer.

John looks him in the eye. "You want it to happen."

Bret can't lie. He stays quiet because he wants John to have his dream.

"We definitely couldn't do it long term," John finally says.

Bret sits up. "You've talked about wrestling in the NWW and what it means to you. This will make you happy. So we go, we go with this."

"Bret, we don't have it yet."

"But when we do…"

John stretches out, drops down to the mattress, and hooks his hand with Bret's.

Bret leans over him. "This doesn't have to be either/or. We can do both, especially at first."

"What?"

"We can both go to school."

"Me?" John shrugs this off. "School?"

"Your touch is better than you know. You heal with your hands. I'm sure you're a great physical trainer. At the gym where you train people, you enable them to reach their goals. Think about this. Just think about this for now, but you'd make one hell of a physical therapist."

"Bret, I don't—"

"Shh. Just think. That's all."

"Isn't there something else I could be doing?"

"And you had in mind?"

They kiss.

"So," John asks a lazy minute later, "we have a plan? We're good to go?"

Bret squeezes John into a cradle and laughs. "Good to go."

Walls keep coming down. As they wrestle and hold each other again, barriers are broken, forgotten, or paved over with new and healing feelings. Yet when it comes to the point, when it naturally and instinctively comes to the time for one to ride into and enter the other, John again senses something in Bret that Bret himself doesn't want to admit, or even think about. He hasn't been penetrated since that night with the college guy. Ryan, a gentleman, has played the good, understanding boyfriend, but there's a truth Bret conveniently forgets: there hasn't been penetrating sex between them.

John is on top now, his erection pressing against the front of his underwear. Oh, he wants to take Bret, just take him for the physical ride so that Bret knows that he's loved, that he's connected, fully connected, to John.

But something is still there. Something is still hurting, still in the way.

"Why'd you stop?" Bret asks. "I want this."

John shakes his head.

Bret is confused. He stares at John's chest as it rises and falls, and then into those bright blue eyes. "John?"

John doesn't answer. He doesn't know the words to use.

"Hey, guy," Bret says, "I don't understand. What? Is it me? Do you want me, like this?"

They are face-to-face and John, sitting back now, sets his knees against Bret's ass. Both of Bret's legs are up and resting on John's shoulders.

"John, answer."

Blue eyes that were calm and clear a second ago show a storm, and John looks away.

Bret still doesn't understand.

With great intention, John moves slowly to bring his face closer to Bret's. He sighs. "Those two guys? Remember? At the pizza place? They have something, I think, something that we have, that I have. It's…" Again, he struggles with the words.

"What? What is it?"

"Bret, I know. I just know you, maybe a little bit differently than you know yourself, but…I feel like I can really sense things within you."

"Guy, let's just go. Go at this."

John shakes his head. "Bret, stop. You're hurting. You are. This isn't the time to go further. It feels like I have my wood up to my face, but this isn't…not yet."

Frustrated, Bret's eyes fuse with anger. "What? We sleep together. We, we strip each other down to almost nothing and you climb on me ready to go and it isn't time yet?"

"I know."

"You don't know anything. You don't."

John now shows a bit of anger too. "Bullshit. I knew about you and wrestling and teaching, didn't I? I sense it with you. It may take me a little while, but I get it." He rolls his eyes and then brings them back to Bret's. "Listen, what I'm saying is not a game or a line to get your bare ass in the air for me to pummel, no, it's deeper than that. Better. No, that guy…I mean, there was a guy…the night I hurt my shoulder and ended up in your hotel room by mistake. I passed him. I passed him in the hall. He was wearing a frat shirt.

"I didn't think anything of it then. Man, it's just coming to me now. But there was something that night. Something between you two. And I can tell that it wasn't right. It wasn't good."

Bret is silent. He wants this. He wants this time with John, this connection. *That guy? Pratt? He didn't...didn't...*

He did. He took from him. He hurt and he violated. It was never an issue with Ryan because with Ryan he was just meat, and they were nowhere near this intimate, this close.

Bret's stomach knots.

John reaches for and strokes Bret's hair. "It's all right, buddy. Let it out."

Bret's a pressure cooker. Intensity pushes against memories and feelings he's ignored or pushed far away. Damn of all embarrassing things, he starts shaking.

Caring like this—and hurting with him on this—John's eyes water. "Trust me on this. Let it out." Holding Bret, he whispers, "I'm going to be here for you, and with you. In this and through this. Trust me."

Bret doesn't. He can't.

Yet.

Minutes pass and John winds up beside him, holding him closely. He doesn't say what he could, and that is he isn't ready either.

CHAPTER THIRTY-TWO

University students buzz in and around the campus eatery like bees to a nest. They need to be seen and heard making nearly constant noise, even if that noise is nearly nonsense, like Professor Garr's crooked tie in molecular biology that morning, the best use of declension pronouns during a school paper meeting, feminism in Ibsen's *The Doll's House*, and whether or not the atomic weight of magnesium should be considered when pouring shots of tequila.

Bret takes his time as he walks through the crowded, shiny black tables that are strewn with food trays, textbooks, and bodies around his age that are bent over and occasionally around chairs at funny, complicated angles. He swallows nervousness and wonders, *Do I belong here? Will I make it?*

A beautiful girl approaches. Her pale pink lips and long, graceful neck hold his attention. Smart, she is a cut above him. He knows it. He can't talk to her. He wouldn't know the words to say.

Two other girls follow. They are all white teeth and giggles and chatter about metaphoric imagery…or at least that is what Bret thought he heard.

A guy who just dumped his tray saddles up beside him. Blue eyes, skinny. He's tapping his notebook as if listening to music. No earphones, though. Bret catches his attention, but only for a moment. He fails to get the directions he needs from this swarthy guy who, in passing, totally gives Bret the cold shoulder. A star-struck sophomore from the Democratic Women's table, however, points him in the right direction. He is out on the wide sidewalk a moment later.

It's an amazing autumn day at the University of Cincinnati, but Bret cannot see this. He does not notice the first gold or red leaves swirling down around his feet. Also, he also doesn't see two sociology professors smiling warmly at him, for they, like their colleagues, wish the best for new students.

He comes to a busy corner and waits with a pack of other students who are all silent. The whirl of wheels from an approaching skateboarder magnifies before the light changes and, en masse, the group makes their way from the heart of campus.

With his eyes wide and busy, Bret does look like a new student. Looks can be deceiving, however—at least this time. He didn't enroll, of course. That's not the plan.

The crowd around him disperses before the first tree-lined residential street. Bret worries now. His palms sweat. His throat tightens and dries.

I can do this, he tells himself as he pays attention to the uneven sidewalk. *I can do this. Just find the damn house with the damn colors and knock, knock, knock and stand face-to-face with that snake and it will be over. Over.*

Around a bend, Bret sees the first fraternity house, or is it a sorority house? Do college women even have houses? Where he went to school, there was no fraternity or sorority system.

Two more Greek houses face one another at the end of the street. Both colossal structures have big, boxy additions that butt up against what were once grandiose fronts. Each displays its colors through windows that would be inviting and almost pretty if they weren't cloaked with cheap or very ugly curtains.

And there it sits. A gray battleship parked at the end of the next street. He sees the royal blue and gold on the front yard sign that are the same colors on the Greek shirt of the fraternity brother who... who...

Everything that happened that night is back.

His knees contain air.

With difficulty, Bret crosses to the edge of the well-worn lawn that, when the breeze whirls a certain way, smells of beer and charcoal from a nearby barbeque area. He lies out loud when he says, "I am ready."

He makes his way to the front door without feeling the sidewalk beneath him and knocks. Nothing. Music comes from one of the upper rooms, but it is really faint.

A frat brother comes up behind him and correctly accesses what he sees. He says, "Dude, you don't knock. Not at this time of day. Just come in."

"Okay."

"So, who's your guy?" It's another brother who asks this question after a moment. The one who led him into the once-grand foyer has taken the stairs two at a time and did not look back.

Bret says, "His name is Pratt."

"Pratt." The brother pushes the long sleeves of oxford shirt up to his elbows and shakes his head.

"Yeah."

"Pratt," he says again, this time as if it's the punch line of a joke, "he's been suspended from the university."

As if hit and not expecting such a punch, Bret doesn't know what to do. Suddenly he feels as dumb as those four made him out to be that night.

The brother at the door has come from the kitchen and carries a bag of microwave popcorn. Bret senses the guy in front of him is a bit of a loner and chooses his individuality deliberately.

"Yeah," the college guy says as he reaches for a few popped kernels. "Pratt's out of here for the rest of the semester. Stupid ass. Drugs."

Bret's tongue literally sticks to the roof of his mouth.

The brother politely ignores this and introduces himself as Dan and asks, "Are you are in one of his classes?"

Bret shakes his head. "Not quite."

"Well…" Dan says, not sure what to do next. "He has an address with his parents, and that's where he is, I think. I know he lives near Cincinnati. Call us in a few and one of us can look that up for you."

This isn't supposed to happen, Bret thinks. *All this way. The hours in the car, the knots in my stomach, for this? This sudden stop?*

"What," Dan asks, "it seems like you're…" Dan doesn't finish his question.

Lost, Bret turns toward the door.

"We don't do or sell drugs, if that's what you're thinkin'," Dan says.

Bret falls in on himself just a bit. He didn't know what he would find here or what could happen when he stood face-to-face with his attacker. But he came because he's in love with a man and knows now that love itself is strong.

When the door whines to a close behind him, he thinks of one of the wrestlers he first met when he trained out in Washington state. He was an older guy whose name Bret does not remember, but he had had extensive knee surgery that, in the repair of the cartilage tear, involved the cutting of one nerve. When Bret saw the five-inch scars on either side of the man's knee, the wrestler shrugged and said, "It's numb now. It will always be numb."

Bret lumbers down the final porch steps and notices what he did not see earlier. Marigolds that edge the entry are still beautiful. Summer cannot be far gone, or that far lost.

He doesn't know what to think, doesn't know what to do. Should he hang around the campus to find something somewhere that will just make sense or go home?

This answer comes to him when he sees one single marigold plant, a deep orange one that flickers with red. It had been broken months earlier. Totally lopsided, it grew around its damage and still flowers.

Unlike the last one he stood in front of, this is an unpretentious door. Its bright teal color reminds Bret of the Amish doors he passed on his way here to West Virginia.

It seems like home.

And there he is. John. In the now open doorway. Suddenly standing face-to-face, neither says a word. Neither moves.

Bret never knocked. John, who just popped open the door and holds the keys to his car in his hand, swallows. This isn't real. This isn't happening. *He's here. Oh my God, thank you! He's here.*

The silence weighs too much at first because neither heart beats.

Stunned, John thanks God again.

From the silence, Bret asks, "Is it all right?"

"All right? Yeah!" John reaches through the awkwardness and surprise and hugs Bret. It's a strong, masculine hug, one where only their shoulders embrace.

Dazed, John shakes his head. "You're here!"

"Your address is listed with the Mid-Atlantic League. Finding this place was as easy as reading the map."

What follows between them are a bunch of half-started sentences and fragment endings. There's a quick tour of the apartment John still shares with two roommates. In a short time, they settle on the couch in the living room, each with a beer bottle's neck choked in his hand.

"Cheap beer," John apologizes.

Bret stares out the window in front of him. *It's time*, he thinks. *Time to tell him.* "I went to see him. That frat guy."

"What?"

"I went. I went to the university out there. I remembered the colors he wore on his shirt. And I found him."

"Bret."

"Well, I sorta found him." Bret takes a hit off his bottle.

John doesn't process all he hears because, as Bret is talking, he sees the two of them as a couple now, an average, normal, everyday couple sitting in the middle of his living room. And it's all right to reach across and find and stroke Bret's thigh. It's all right—it's just perfectly and normally all right to massage those muscles.

Bret senses that it's okay too and continues. "But he wasn't there. He'd been suspended. But I went there, John."

"Bret, why?"

"To find something, or let something go. I don't know."

"Yeah?"

"You did it, John. You told me once you went back to Greg the day you graduated high school. You faced him, and what he did to you, again."

John shakes his head at what Bret has misunderstood. "No, I wanted a future—a future I dreamed would or could somehow happen." He shakes his head. "I didn't go back to level anything. I went back because I wanted him."

Bret moves closer. "The scar on your shin. The flagpole and the ceramic frog."

John can't believe Bret remembers details about his graduation day. This incredible, handsome man remembers how he ran from Greg, ran so far and so fast that he tripped over a flagpole and a damn silly ceramic frog to rip open his shin.

Shaken, surprised, or just so happy, John shakes his head. This is hard for him to wrap around. Bret. He, he remembered what John had said one time...*just one damn time*...and then he went that far...he went *that* far...*for them*.

John knows he needs to be intentional and make this moment count. He leans forward and then stands. He takes two, no, three steps to his left and crouches down in front of Bret. Both men have long legs and Bret spreads his knees as John comes in close, their faces almost touching.

"Bret, I wanted to be in love. With Greg it was just a dream, a wish that reality crashed. And the hole left after that wreck..." He finds curls over his ears, then lets them go. "How you met me, remember? I was still so lost, so broken. But you found me." John touches his chest. "Here."

"John—"

"And you, going all that way to that university."

"I did it to be ready for us," Bret says calmly. "I did it for us to be together."

John knows the kiss will come; it will connect them even further, but there is no hurry. No locker room or set time to check out of a hotel comes between them. No doubt, fear, or anger stands in the way. Without interruption or audience, it is finally, yes, finally, just the two of them.

❖

It is natural, obvious, necessary, comfortable. How it starts, how it flows. One hand slides here, another there. Warmth, closeness, squeezes, probes. They taste the beer on each other's lips. The kisses themselves have words—playful, hungry, intentional words. *I want you. I need you. This feels so good. Don't stop. Don't you dare stop.*

Neither will ever remember how they made it from the living room couch to John's bed—did one carry the other, did they slide along the floor, did they walk with one hugging the other from behind... unknown. Most of their clothes lay tangled on John's bedroom floor or between the sheets, but how this happens remains a mystery. Because they've wrestled together so much feels so familiar, but the further they go, the more they find not only their partner, but also themselves. The man underneath squeezes, strokes, and outlines the butt and back muscles of the one on top, then they turn side to side, switch, rub, and roll again.

Their combined scent of sweat, desire, testosterone, and force draws them achingly closer and closer. Hands, hair, muscles, surrender.

At a time and a position when they are nearly face-to-face with John under Bret, John cranks his neck and almost reaches the base of Bret's jaw. His lips touch Bret's skin when he says, "I love you, Bret."

Not wanting to miss this opportunity, Bret pulls back. He barely shakes his head and frowns theatrically. "What? Oh, I'm sorry, I couldn't hear you."

John plays too. "Got it. Don't talk with my mouth full."

There's a pause. Bret breaks it when that gravelly low bedroom voice of his says, "So, curious here..." He frowns again. "You were saying?"

Then it hits. It really hits. There can be no more words. It has to come, and come now. The momentum burns and drives, drives fast. Knees bend over thighs, hard chest to hard chest, arms lock. Thrusts take over, powerful and demanding—needed, important, planned and taken wildly.

After the fitted sheet tangles around them and John's voice is almost hoarse from pants and deep, low groans, Bret enters.

And he's there, there inside with one breath that mixes in the air with John's. John can feel Bret all the way up and between his lungs and the rocking starts. It is slow and gentle and perfect and picks up with rhythm and want and desire. Higher and higher and lower and lower John rides the mattress while Bret rides him.

Holding Bret's face, John takes in the sight of them now, sweaty and muscled, so wonderfully, closely tangled. Bret's head slips through John's fingers. He dives to kiss John's neck, shoulders, nipples, belly. There is nothing to guard now, no more walls or separation.

"I love you," Bret whispers without giving thought to speaking. The words just happen. With a low and sultry voice, he says it louder a second time, louder, right from his soul. "You, I love you."

"Bret!" John arches his back.

The temperature climbs higher, higher as the blood coursing between them gets hotter, hotter. Perfect tension fills their shafts followed by the silent half second before the sudden, explosive rounds of wild emission.

It doesn't stop. The rivers don't stop until the shots concentrate with each burst releasing the most amazing liquid bond. One, they are one.

❖

Slowly and intentionally, Bret rocks against John for the final random, unpredictable shots—electric, pulsing, incredible, tender, unhurried, amazing.

The motions stop. Healing silence settles over them like a sheet. This pure quiet seeps into their pores; it caresses their muscles, penetrates their souls.

Bret swallows a moment later. The sound is loud to both of them, and as the quiet comes again, John reaches up and strokes the side of Bret's ear, his face, his head.

The moments are lazy now, drunk. Before sleep takes them, Bret realizes John has one arm comfortably to one side. He reaches for that arm while holding John's other wrist. Slowly he brings both of John's wrists to rest just over their heads.

John smiles. He knows what Bret is doing.

Just before dreams set free and drift them both to deep and tranquil places, Bret slowly counts, "One, two, three."

He nuzzles even closer to the one he loves and says, "Pinned."

CHAPTER THIRTY-THREE

It's different now. Neither says it but the change is there. Bret and John still roughhouse, they still act all tough and gruff in the ring, but it is an act even the young ones who stand with mouths agape can see through. The elementary school boys know that, like the blond and red-haired wrestler, they can still pretend, still get close, and still push and shove one another just because that's the way it is, and always will be, with boys.

But with these two, unlike with the other one-on-one lock-ups they've seen tonight, yeah, something is different.

Three minutes into the match, John has scooped up one of Bret's legs. He covers him for the pin, but this is way too early in the action for such an easy win. Bret easily bucks out from his prone position and scrambles to his feet.

A woman with a Santa hat cheers for her young Kris Kringle dream man. "You don't take that there, red hot!"

Christmas is exactly two weeks away, and as it stands now, this is the last match John and Bret will have this year. They've known for over a month that Howell Launders and the NWW have opted not to contract them. While Howell himself said that he is still considering them in the immediate future, John and Bret know this is not going to happen.

"You're too clean, guys," Lyle shared with them after they'd received the news. "Wrestling up here isn't going in that direction. There's no way you'd be that psycho, wacko, or plain weird, trust me. It's not for you because neither of you flaunt that much or even realize just how sexual you are to those who watch you. If anything, we'll split you up and make you jobbers. We'd have you wrestle the big, the bad and the ugly, and up here, with you losing these matches as planned, your futures won't be very long."

This news hit John the hardest, of course, but only at first. There was a low day or two, but by the end of the week, he'd moved on to what really mattered for the both of them now.

At the start of the next week, he rifled through and found applications for Bret to go back to school at four universities renowned for their teaching programs. Bret applied to two. One already said yes for this coming spring semester, starting January twelfth. The school that would work best for both Bret and John has yet to get back to him. It's likely that he could start classes in just over a month but they have to wait to see what credits from his previous college will transfer.

Of the news from Howell, it's Bret who still feels this, Bret who still wants John to reach his dream of wrestling and earning the big money. They already feel the strain of their budget. They can't afford to live together because they'd have to sign a lease of at least nine months and they don't know where they'll be at the start of next year. John needs to keep his full-time job as a trainer at the gym. That's a given. They decide Bret should hold on to his construction job in Maryland through the end of December. The pay is higher there than what he'd get in West Virginia, partly because no one is going to give him a similar-sized paycheck for working only a few weeks.

But they have each other now, in the ring, and tonight they'll drive to Bret's place for the weekend.

The same woman in the Santa hats cheers for Bret. "You give it to him, honey!"

A moment later, when Bret maneuvers John into a camel clutch, a move where he's sitting on John's back, and whispers into Bret's ear, "Give it to me, honey."

Honey? Bret wants to laugh—*honey* is *definitely* not a word the two share—but to keep this somewhat serious, or at least to pretend to keep this somewhat serious, he buries his mouth even further into John's hands, which cup his chin.

The cobra clutch is a move designed to stretch out an opponent's back. John doesn't actually apply more pressure; he just repositions himself to make it look like he is. With a free hand, Bret slaps the canvas. The crowd catches on and joins his cadence. John, acting worried and distracted, looks about the house. Three rows back, he sees two young guys with the same short haircut as he has now. While the rest of the fans around them are yelling, they're both quiet.

A couple. He knows it. Just like those two at the pizza restaurant all those weeks ago. He's glad they're here. He looks down at Bret and with his head between his forearms, he playfully rolls his love left and right.

The crowd's cadence continues, however, and John knows he has to let Bret power his way out of the hold. The cheers escalate as this happens. Once free, Bret jams a couple of powerful elbow shots to John's midsection. With John bent over in seeming pain, Bret grabs the back of John's head and with a good bit of momentum, charges forward and drops John face first onto the canvas.

It's actually Bret's elbow that blocks the hit, but John, acting stunned, flops onto his back as if he's a fish on the bottom of a rowboat. He jolts around.

With the crowd behind him, Bret wraps up one of John's legs, snakes his own leg around John's powerful calves, and drops to the canvas in a figure four, a stretching move that tests the strength and endurance of John's leg muscles.

John shakes his head as if he's in pain and slides them both to the ropes so he can break the hold. As he inches his way closer to the edge of the ring, Bret applies more pressure. When he repeats this, he takes too long to clamp down again and John, as planned, reverses the hold. Now it is Bret who feels the pressure.

It feels good to stretch out like this, John thinks, *to work my muscles, and Bret's. To get the crowd involved. To play the bad boy.*

"Let him go, you bastard!" one older man shouts to John.

"Come on, Red!" another fan cheers.

Bret acts as if he's giving it all he can and that, power wise, what he has isn't enough. He drops his head to the canvas. His tight, hard, muscular ass is in plain view of most, but it is John who has the best view. He smiles. It appears as if he's laughing or mocking his opponent, but really he's amazed this has all happened. Bret. Bret. His love. The man he showers with, eats with, sleeps with. The man who has to have the right side of the bed, who falls asleep some nights literally in the middle of a sentence, who twitches and elbows John when he's having a bad dream, who likes to have his hard shaft held in the minutes before the alarm goes off and they go at it hot and heavy with morning sex. Bret. Who always wears at least underwear at all times unless he's sleeping, who can't stand to have the sheets tucked in under the mattress, who wants not just one puppy someday but two, so they can keep each other company.

John looks down again at Bret. That ass. That incredible sculpted ass. He's happy; he's just so damn happy.

"Let him go, you pig!" a woman screams at him.

Never lady, John thinks. *This one's mine...and God, I'm keeping him. Oh, I am.*

Bret slides them both to the edge of the ring, and just as he's about to clamp his hand around the bottom rope to indicate to the referee to break the hold, John grabs Bret's foot and seems to twist it.

He doesn't, of course, but Bret is forced to slap the mat again in seeming pain.

Suddenly Bret rolls over and kicks out of the hold. He clambers to his feet and wobbles around. He raises his elbow as if to drop it across John's chest, but just before impact, John scurries out of the way. The force of Bret's impact has Bret holding his new injured area.

Thinking quickly, John comes in from behind and picks Bret up and sets the muscle boy on his shoulders. He parades Bret around. To keep himself steady up there, Bret sets his hand on the side of John's stomach.

Man, is this move hot, Bret thinks. Even the crowd silences. *It's total trust in John, in his muscles, in his strength.*

John doesn't drop Bret to the canvas. Instead, he walks him to one of the turnbuckles and takes his time locking Bret's feet so that Bret hangs upside down. John leans his crotch in against Bret as he does this and Bret, looking up, has the best view of John.

John. Always so sure, always so strong. Always able to make the hard decisions fast with no turn-arounds, no regrets. A man who moves forward. John. They'll be together in the truck soon, the truck John bought from a guy at his gym for a steal and that John says will help in the move when they head off to Bret's new school.

A few days ago, when John last spoke to Lyle, he shared that he bought a classic Ford F150. "It's an old beater with incredibly low miles," he said into the phone. "An old gentleman's farm truck, you know? The hood doesn't match and one of the doors is dented, but it has a bench seat that's great for getting in all close to Bret."

John charges forward now and tackles Bret with a shoulder to Bret's exposed midsection. The hit was supposed to be hard enough to free Bret's feet and have him flop onto the canvas, but it wasn't hard enough. Bret's still stuck.

Not to keep Bret upside down for much longer, John hurries. He tackles Bret again and it works. Bret rolls over John's back and lands with a thud on the canvas.

Neither really remembers all that happens next. Close holds, bear hugs, body-to-body contact. Sweat, muscle, fun. They slide into and out of moves seamlessly. They know each other's body so well.

Minutes pass and they know their time is almost up. John, the heel (or the bad guy), is to win the match. After he has Bret in an abdominal stretch, he leaves Bret dazed and standing almost in the center of the ring. John runs to one side of the ring, turns, and races for the opposite side. As he gets close, he jumps feet first toward the top rope and catches the rope precisely at the arches of both feet. This catapults him toward Bret. Bret is hit hard and, in one thud, goes down. There is no more movement. John hooks Bret's leg and covers him for the pin.

Stunned, the audience has never seen a move like this before. It's dangerous because John could miss the top rope with his feet and go sailing into the metal dividers that keep the crowd safe and away from the ring.

But the crowd loves it. The cheers and boos are mixed about half and half, and with his arms in the air, John parades around the ring, drops down, and waits in the hallway for Bret.

Together and away from the crowd, they smile and laugh with each other. They joke as if both won after a big game. They hadn't seen much of each other before the match because Bret had to work his construction job and both knew it would run late. On the bench in the locker room, they talk and talk in what has become their crazy banter until they realize that the main event wrestlers had already finished not just their match, which didn't last long, but also their showers.

John looks to his left. "Showers are empty, Bret."

"So is the locker room, John."

There's a pause. John thinks of sex and asks, "You wanna?"

"In the shower?"

John bumps Bret's shoulder with his own.

"Okay," Bret responds as John's three or four steps ahead of him. "The showers it is, then."

❖

After a wet, steamy time together, they towel each other off slowly, dress each other with care and, noting the time, pack their separate duffel bags side by side. They are quiet in this, and the silence feels good, right. How normal it all feels, how natural. In just being near each other, the memories of love in the shower still connect them, even though they aren't touching.

After a distant car horn blows, both glance up at a high, narrow window above a row of lockers at the same time. Light snow is in the forecast, but should fall after midnight, a good two hours from now. They do, however, have a road trip in front of them. They aren't staying in the hotel with the other wrestlers because they are saving money.

As they walk back through the hall, they round a corner and see the last refreshment stand closing for the night. A wide, table-height shelf lines the opposite wall and there, among two dozen chairs, is a single, handsome thirty-something-year-old man with six, seven...no, eight grade-school boys who still have too much excitement and energy that magnifies when they see Bret and John.

The boys crowd around their heroes and start asking the wildest questions. *Are you two friends or enemies? How do I get to be a wrestler? When you got hit in the stomach like that, did it hurt bad?*

"Guys," their guardian for the night says in a kind voice, "one at a time!"

There's a pause and the boys' questions fire off again, one on top of the other. *How big are your muscles, anyway? Does it really hurt to be a wrestler? What do you guys want for Christmas?*

The last question made them all quiet. It was the unexpected—the innocent, simple one—that hushed them all.

"Well?" the boy asks again with a shrug. "Wh-what do you w-want from Santa?"

"Santa?" one of the more streetwise ones asks, his forehead all wrinkled at such a stupid question. "You know that's just a load of—"

"Santa." Bret cuts him off.

"Yeah," the younger boy asks. "Whaddaya want?"

The boys don't quite know where the red wrestler will go with this. Each quiets down.

"Let me see..." Bret says as he bends down to get closer to the boy, a Latino with eyes so heavy and round that it's all the pro can do to keep his heart beating regularly in his chest. "What do I want?"

Bret keeps his arms to himself yet makes an inquisitive face, one that lets all the boys know that he not only has light in his soul, but also a bit of magic in him. "Now, that's a tough question. Why don't you go first? Tell me what you want."

"A compass."

Bret doesn't expect that answer. "A compass, why?"

John lets whatever is tugging at him from within have its way. Before Bret even starts to piece this together, he read the scene. These boys don't have a home. This guardian of theirs with a big Adam's apple and kind, soft brown eyes is their only hope for something special this December.

Bret, who is still a little lost with the boy's response, repeats his question to the one in front of him, who is suddenly shy. "So, you want a compass, huh? You gonna be an explorer?"

John remembers his compass, the one he still has. It's the only remnant from his broken childhood. He chokes up and knows more fully why Bret loves kids the way he does. But there's more. Since Bret, he knows why he now loves kids the way he does.

John finds his voice, which surprisingly doesn't work for a moment. "He...he wants a compass, Bret, so he knows where he's going. So he doesn't get himself lost."

Bret and John's eyes meet and Bret knows, without another word said, what John is talking about. He both knows *and* feels what John has been through, and what these boys are going through.

The guardian, whose shirt has been washed too many times, steps in. "Now, Jonas, ask the man what he wants."

John comes forward. "Jonas, is it?"

The boy, whose back has been to John, turns. "Ye-yes."

"Cool. I'm John. And I know what I want. I know what I want for Christmas."

"What?"

"I want to give you my compass. I have one, have had one since I was your age. And see, I want to pass it along this Christmas."

"What? You wanna give me your compass? Why? Does it still work good?"

John nods. "It does."

"Cool! But why, why give it away?"

John looks at Bret then back at the boy. "I know where I'm going now."

❖

The truck has good tires. John's thankful for that, though the snow is only a few flurries falling here and there. The interstate is dry and traffic seems light. Bret is asleep, worn out from wrestling tonight, great, connecting sex in the shower an hour ago, and a long, difficult week at work. His head rests on John's lap, turned a bit toward the steering wheel.

He's had a long week, John thinks as he cups his hand around the top of Bret's shoulder.

In response, Bret nuzzles his head into the warmth of John's lap and sleeps more soundly.

Minutes so amazingly steady and sure pass along with the mile markers now. John cries just one single, clear tear as he stares ahead. He knows that love, just down the highway, will keep them both company on their ride.

EPILOGUE

Seven years later

The sun streaks through the south-facing windows in their safe, boring, typically nondescript four-door car. There, in the passenger's seat, the low, angled swath of light engulfs John's lap with the golden glow only a late-August afternoon can bring.

Bret notices this as he hits the turn signal left to pass a slower-moving car in front of them. Even though John's the driver with two speeding tickets and a warning—which, John insists, are trumped-up allegations—Bret accelerates in their pre-owned, midsized Toyota Camry. As the six-cylinder car John loves and Bret secretly likes slides into the left lane and easily passes what John would call a clunker (which is anything with wheels that ardently obeys the speed limit), Bret can hear his grandfather yelling from the grave the same four words he heard when he cosigned there at the dealership this past fall: "Should have bought American."

Without a vehicle in front of them now, Bret notices that the light on John's lap is warming something within him too. Keeping his focus on the road, Bret appreciatively understands yet again just how the sight of every sultry fiber of the one soul in the passenger seat beside him still rocks him so hard, sometimes with just one short sidelong glance.

Taking his attention off the quiet interstate for a moment, he glances at the child-size cup in John's hand. With a smile, he asks wryly, "So, you like watermelon drink, huh?"

John's eyes meet his. He responds with a shrug. "Who knew?"

Bret angles the rearview mirror to look into the backseat for a moment, just as he's done every so often for the past twenty minutes or so, and then glances at his partner, whose quadriceps muscles really fill out the jeans he's wearing. "You're a man of mystery."

After biting down on the red and white plastic drinking straw already gnarled by little teeth, John grins. "That's me."

The two are silent for a moment, each in thought about different parts of the day. From the quiet, John holds playful energy in his voice. "About the bet we made earlier, listen. I called this right. *I* have this."

Holding back his own smile, Bret does not respond because he knows he's won.

"Bret, you did not win." John scrambles to find a way to turn this around to his advantage. "No way. I want to call a judge in on this. There's a technicality."

"A technicality?" Through the mirror, Bret checks on their passengers again. Both of their little boys are soundly asleep. "There is no technicality. I won the bet. *You* owe *me*."

John cringes.

"And my prize?" Bret stares ahead. "I'm going to go with you cutting their fingernails."

"No!"

Bret laughs.

John squares his shoulders to look at Bret. "Nail cutting? Me? This is so not going to happen."

Bret grips the wheel and playfully changes the subject. "So, that drink there, bud? It's really watermelon flavored?"

"No distractions. Bret, come on, you do a better job there with the kids. With me and those clippers, truth now, they could lose a little finger."

Bret pretends to adjust an air vent that he actually doesn't move.

Knowing Bret hasn't changed the flow of air on the driver's side, John continues. "I'll take bath time for the rest of the month, all shampoos…and, tell you what, I'll take them to that plaster place again. But cut their nails? Dude, no."

Bret passes three "clunkers" in a line. Now that they are on the open road again, he sets the car's cruise. "Wait, *you'll* take them to the plaster place? You? This means you're serious." Over his sunglasses, Bret makes eye contact with John. There's a moment they could kiss, but don't.

Reaching between Bret's legs, John gives Bret's thigh a squeeze. He rubs one of Bret's inner quadriceps muscles as he says, "I'm not worried about that stinkin' plaster place. I'm thirty years old. I own a successful gym. I'm not scared of that mean old lady who runs that little store. I ain't scared of nothin'."

"You are."

John laughs. "I am."

A quiet moment slips between them as each takes in the view of the landscape. From his lap, Bret finds John's hand.

John laces his fingers with Bret's. "Here's the technicality."

"Oh boy."

John laughs. "No, I have one. I do."

"You don't have a technicality."

"I do."

"John."

"No, I do."

Hungry for a kiss, Bret wants to grab and hold John's chin closely. Instead, he keeps his attention on the road. "You just don't want to lose, do you?"

"Listen. Here's my point."

"The technicality."

"Yeah, the technicality. Had the boys been wired on this watermelon drink, they'd still be awake now, and I'd win the bet. It was me. I cut 'em off the juice."

Bret squeezes John's finger. An hour into their car ride home, they bet to see when the boys would crash. Clearly, Bret won.

"No deal."

John studies Bret's lips. "Double or nothing."

Bret smirks. "Double or nothing? What did you have in mind?"

With both boys still asleep, they are some thirty minutes from home now. Bret knows the answer to the question he's about to ask, but asks anyway. "Did you give him that Busch beer?"

John feels a wall right before his face.

Bret's voice picks up its edge, the one that says this is serious. "Did you?"

From the quiet, John says, "It's just beer, Bret."

They had visited Greg on their way home from the beach. It was right on the way. Literally, it was right on the way, and Greg had invited them. He said he had something to give, or actually, give back.

Bret tenses. "You just shouldn't have. It was wrong. Lines crossed, the whole thing. Wrong."

They've hit the Nerve, as they call it. Bret continues. "We're going to cash that check."

"You know where that money came from. We are not."

"It's yours. It's ours. And we need it."

John crosses his arms over his chest.

"It's money, John. Just money. It's security for the boys. My salary from the school is *just* enough. And your gym now? Guy, we are just above water."

"No."

"Yes."

They fight now. Angry words, heated words. It's amazing the two in the back sleep through this, but Bret and John have been loud before. Somehow, the boys must be used to it.

When the swearing starts, they stop—as agreed.

Stalemate.

Miles roll along the odometer in silence. Neither yields. Bret doesn't understand why John would give that slime beer. And John wants the money he earned all those years ago to remain out of his sight. Stubborn and both angry, they remain quiet or off-topic until both boys are in bed hours later.

There in the dark, John sits at the small kitchen table eating red seedless grapes. They bought them that afternoon at the farmer's market a mile west of the ocean where they'd spent a few days vacationing. "Bret, no. Just rip the damn check up."

Tired from the drive, Bret is about to head to bed. He turns and sits, though, catty-corner to John. He folds his arms over the table in front of him and settles his chin over his forearm muscles.

John continues. "Just no, Bret. Let it go. Let that go."

"Why?"

"Because that's not me. That guy then…with Louise Amsterdam… he's not me. He's gone. That Greg is all high and proud now, writing off that check for the money he took on that damned birthday of mine… no, it's gotta go."

Bret is silent, and then his green eyes hold a sorrow John so rarely sees.

John, hurt to see his partner upset, shakes his head. "Bret—no, don't do this."

Bret can't speak.

"Just no," John continues. "We're making it. We are. It's just seventeen hundred bucks plus interest." John reaches for his lover's forearm. "Please, stop. Let's just let this go."

Bret stares out in front of him. His focus now is blind. He swallows, but his voice still wobbles. "That you hurt? That this is still here, somehow? Well, that's with me too. You know, we found each other. We did. You met Russ, got into his school…and then with Lyle… those room switches of his…John, we found each other through this, maybe even because of this."

"It's whore money."

"It's money."

"No."

Bret rises. "It's that you're still hurting. It's still there. And you still gave that bastard beer. *Again.* God! Hear this, buddy. You and Greg? What you did? It's still here someplace. Since it's with you, it's with me too." He slaps his chest. "Here. Right here."

"Stop."

Bret frowns. "What? Stop loving you?"

"Bret, that's not what I meant."

"You hurt, I hurt."

"Bret—"

"No, good night. This is just—good night." Bret walks down the narrow hall of their thirteen-hundred-square-foot, three-bedroom home.

John rises and walks the plate he used for the grapes to the sink. Perfectly still, he listens as he breathes. He really listens this time, more so than he's ever done before.

With his eyes closed, he sees the two- by six-inch beams that make up this everyday average ranch home. He sees the wiring, insulation, and the four inches of gravel beneath the concrete patio they always thought they'd replace because, too small, it really is nothing more than a step into their small, boxed-in yard. Without moving from the sink, he sees the boys asleep in their beds down the hall, their Scooby-Doo night-light glowing beside the five-drawer dresser Bret found roadside.

He walks down the hall as if this isn't their house, as if he's never lived here. Everything just seems so different now, so foreign. If he stops right where he is, right beside the boys' hamper, and stares at the ceiling, he thinks he can actually see the stars through the roof that will need new shingles if not this fall, then the following spring.

Bret's right.

He stops at their open bedroom door. Wearing nothing but his new glasses above the waist, Bret has a book propped on his bare, still tight stomach. From the soft cast of the light from the stand on his side of their bed Bret looks so hot, so damn, incredibly hot—not just in muscle but in mind.

And in heart.

And in soul.

And in skin.

John stares at Bret's torso and realizes the strongest men aren't all steel. No, it takes a guy with tough skin to be able to love not just when it's easy, but always.

Bret looks up. "The boys, are they okay?"

"I…I didn't check."

"John?"

John walks to the side where Bret is. "Just hold me."

"Buddy," Bret says into John's shoulder. "I will."

Bret runs his hands down John's strong back, squeezes, and whispers into his soul mate's darkening hair, "I will, John, I will hold you."

John closes his eyes. In the warmth of Bret's arms, he can actually see stars.

About the Author

Will lives in the Adirondack region of New York state. Being barefooted when possible, body surfing in the ocean, and, yes, wrestling are all good things to the author, along with big dogs, starry skies, and laughter. Will is single.

Books Available From Bold Strokes Books

Initiation by Desire by MJ Williamz. Jaded Sue and innocent Tulley find forbidden love and passion within the inhibiting confines of a sorority house filled with nosy sisters. (978-160282-590-1)

Toughskins by William Masswa. John and Bret are two twenty-something athletes who find that love can begin in the most unlikely of places, including a "mom-and-pop shop" wrestling league. (978-1-60282-591-8)

Worth the Risk by Karis Walsh. Investment analyst Jamie Callahan and Grand Prix show jumper Kaitlyn Brown are willing to risk it all in their careers—can they face a greater challenge and take a chance on love? (978-1-60282-587-1)

me@you.com by KE Payne. Is it possible to fall in love with someone you've never met? Imogen Summers thinks so because it's happened to her. (978-1-60282-592-5)

Bloody Claws by Winter Pennington. In the midst of aiding the police, Preternatural Private Investigator Kassandra Lyall finally finds herself at serious odds with Sheila Morris, the local werewolf pack's Alpha female, when Sheila abuses someone Kassandra has sworn to protect. (978-1-60282-588-8)

Awake Unto Me by Kathleen Knowles. In turn of the century San Francisco, two young women fight for love in a world where women are often invisible and passion is the privilege of the powerful. (978-1-60282-589-5)

Franky Gets Real by Mel Bossa. A four-day getaway. Five childhood friends. Five shattering confessions...and a forgotten love unearthed. (978-1-60282-585-7)